The Vengeance of
the Oval Portrait
and Other Stories

The Vengeance of
the Oval Portrait
and Other Stories

by
Gabriel de Lautrec

translated, annotated and introduced by
Brian Stableford

A Black Coat Press Book

ISBN 978-1-61227-009-8. First Printing. May 2011. Published by Black Coat Press, an imprint of Hollywood Comics.com, LLC, P.O. Box 17270, Encino, CA 91416. All rights reserved. Except for review purposes, no part of this book may be reproduced or transmitted in any form or by any means, electronic or mechanical, including photocopying, recording, or by any information storage and retrieval system, without permission in writing from the publisher. The stories and characters depicted in this novel are entirely fictional. Printed in the United States of America.

Table of Contents

Introduction

Gabriel de Lautrec was best known while he was alive as a humorist who contributed to such periodicals as *Le Rire* and *Le Sourire* in the first decades of the 20th century. The most popular humorist of the day, Alphonse Allais, was his friend and mentor, and often referred to him by name in his own humorous articles, many of which appeared regularly in newspapers. Because much humorous writing at that time was marketed for children, Lautrec did a good deal of work of that sort, and published several books for children, including both fiction and non-fiction. That was not, however, his initial ambition; just as most comic actor are reputed to yearn to play Hamlet, Lautrec originally wanted to be an earnest poet and a pillar of the Decadent Movement, which was just hitting its stride when he first arrived in Paris.

The full range of Lautrec's published works is therefore various. He supplemented his early poetry with earnestly erotic and mystical Baudelairean poems in prose, as many Decadent writers did, and soon began to expand those exercises into short stories modeled on Baudelaire's hero, Edgar Allan Poe—whose works were, of course, known in French in Baudelaire's translations. Like Jean Lorrain, Henri de Régnier and Marcel Schwob, all of whom he knew, he soon developed his own distinctive brand of Poesque fantasy, which not only used dreams as a literary device, but attempted to duplicate the inconsequentiality of dreams by means of a kind of "semi-automatic writing." In the most extreme of his fiction in this vein, he used a calculatedly uncontrolled narrative flow to develop prose sequences that are undoubtedly rambling and sometimes quite incoherent, but sometimes have a peculiar dynamic thrust and mesmeric intensity. The comedy in most of his early humorous fantasies is black-edged, often tending toward the kind of *conte cruel* pioneered in the previous gen-

7

eration by the Comte de Villiers de l'Isle-Adam [1] and brought to a slick maturity by Lautrec's contemporary, Maurice Level.

Because the Decadent Movement overlapped to a considerable extent with the Symbolist Movement that replaced it after 1900, partly because the sense of an approaching historical terminus evaporated with the turn of the century, and partly because the latter was not so deliberately perverse a label, Lautrec always employed symbolism in his work, but his interest in the possibility that dreams contained symbolically-disguised meanings gave the technique a more crucial role in his dream-based and dream-simulating works. Partly for that reason, he was one of the Symbolists who became, alongside Alfred Jarry and Guillaume Apollinaire, a significant precursor of Surrealism. Although Jarry and Apollinaire were humorists too, they always retained a much higher reputation than Lautrec, and Lautrec has never been widely cited as a significant precursor of Surrealism, despite the sterling effort he put into such works as "Conte cubiste" (translated herein as "A Cubist Tale").

During his lifetime Lautrec contrived to publish three showcases of his short prose fiction. The first, *Poèmes en prose* (1898), collected his early work in a Baudelairean vein, and his earliest endeavors in surreal humor. The second, *Les Histoires de Tom Joë* [Tales of Tom Joe] (1920) was more heavily biased toward his commercial comedy—the stories that give the collection its title feature a drunken teller of tall tales somewhat reminiscent of Alphonse Allais' Captain Cap—but also included comedies of a more esoteric kind, including "Conte cubiste" and the longest story in the book, "Le château hanté ou la vierge adultère: grand roman passionel et météorologique" (translated herein as "The Haunted Château; or, The Adulterous Virgin: A Great Passionate and Meteorological Romance"), which is reminiscent of Alfred

---

[1] Two collections of Villiers' *contes cruels* are available in Black Coat Press editions as *The Scaffold* (ISBN 9781932983012) and *The Vampire Soul* (ISBN 9781932983029).

Jarry's early exercises in the theater of the absurd in its calculated nonsensicality. The third, *La Vengeance du portrait ovale* (1922), whose entire contents are reproduced here, was evidently intended as a complementary volume to the second, providing a showcase of his fantastic fiction in which humor, where it is present, is of a distinctly blacker stripe.

Les Histoires de Tom Joë reprinted one story from *Poèmes en prose*, "Monsieur House" (translated herein with the same title), while *La Vengeance du portrait ovale* reproduced five: "Le Bocal vert" (tr. as "The Green Jar"); "Conte bleu" (revised as "La Reine amoureuse"; tr. as "The Amorous Queen"); "Le Mur" (tr. as "The Wall); "Le Familial" (tr. as "A Family Matter"); and "Louange de la Lune" (tr. as "Eulogy to the Moon"). In this sampler, I have added a further selection of items from the first and second volumes, in order give the reader a better idea of the full spectrum of the author's work.

Gabriel de Lautrec was born in Béziers on February 21, 1867. His father owned a vineyard but that business was ruined by the *phylloxera* epidemic that devastated French wine-production between 1875 and 1889, and the elder Lautrec went to work in local government as an accountant. Gabriel made his own preparations for a career in teaching, although he had strong literary interests; he initially came to Paris to complete his teach qualifications, and alongside his unsteady literary career—sometimes sporadically—he taught Latin and Greek in various schools.

Lautrec first appeared in Paris in the late 1880s, and immediately started hanging out in *Le Chat Noir* and other literary cafés, making contacts. The fact that Alphonse Allais immediately took him under his wing may well have something to do with the fact that Allais had recently lost his great friend Charles Cros, with whom he had long been accustomed to doing a sort of "comedy double act" in *Le Chat Noir*, much as Cros had once done a double act with Villiers de l'Isle-Adam in Nina de Villard's salon, and Lautrec appears to have become Cros's replacement in improvised performances of that kind.

Although his new friends, and subsequent commentators on his work, were enthusiastic to link Gabriel de Lautrec to the painter Henri de Toulouse-Lautrec, the two men were completely unacquainted, and any family linkage was extremely remote. Lautrec's entitlement to the *particule* in his name arose from his claim to be a Vicomte, but that too might have been a trifle dubious. At any rate, Allais, who was by then the executive editor of the periodical *Le Chat Noir*, made quite a fuss of his new discovery in its pages, where Lautrec's literary career was launched in 1889.

Lautrec also attended the soirées associated with Léon Deschamps' literary periodical *La Plume*, in the basement of the *Soleil d'Or* in the Place St. Michel. Although he did not make any substantial contribution to the periodical, it was there that he met Paul Verlaine, and he became one of the group of young writers who looked after Verlaine in his dying days and maintained a vigil over his corpse. He was subsequently invited to the "Dimanches Gauthiers-Villars" hosted by "Willy" and Colette, where he met a further group of writers, more-or-less completing his acquaintance with the contemporary Parisian literary *monde*.

Lautrec hosted a *salon* of his own in his apartment in the Rue Marceline-Desbordes-Valmore. According to Eric Dussert, who wrote the preface to a 1997 reprint of *La Vengeance du portrait ovale*, his guests not only included Jean Lorrain and Verlaine, but also Oscar Wilde, but the salon does not figure large in the memoirs of any of the writers of the day, and Lautrec always seems to have remained somewhat in the margins of the *monde*, regarded more as a flamboyant character than a man of conspicuous talent. Marcel Schwob, however, helped him land a commission to translate a selection of Mark Twain's stories for an edition published in 1900 by the press associated with the *Mercure de France*, edited by Alfred Vallette, which presumably sold far better than any of his own books.

Although he published, according to his own count, some 200 items in various periodicals, Lautrec never achieved any conspicuous critical or commercial success, and his productions in volume form were a trifle thin. After publishing *Poèmes en prose* in 1898, eight years passed before he published a volume of poetry, *Les Roses noires* [Black Roses] in 1906. After that, he only published translations and 24-page children's books in a series issued by La Lilliput Bibliothèque until *Les Histoires de Tom Joë* appeared in 1920. Although some of those chapbooks can still be found without overmuch difficulty—especially *Le Bon Roi Dagobert* [Good King Dagobert] (1912)—most of his work is extraordinarily hard to locate. Although all three of his prose collections were eventually reprinted, only *Poèmes en prose* remains readily available, especially now that it is available on-line. The other book that he published in 1922, *La Semaine des quatre jeudis* [A Week with Four Thursdays], is so rare that none of the commentators on his work seem to know what it contains (it is probably a novel for children; it was reprinted the following year as a serial in *Gens qui rient*). Although Pierre Versins, in his *Encyclopédie de l'utopie et de la science-fiction* (1972) includes a reference to *Le Serpent de mer* [The Sea Serpent] (1925), he evidently had not read it; again, it is probably a farce for children—it is notable that it bears the same mock-bombastic subtitle as "Le Château hanté ou la vierge adultère."

Versins was undoubtedly correct to observe that Lautrec is of some relevance to the history of French scientific romance, although that aspect of the work reproduced in his three collections is decidedly marginal, mainly because the principal use he makes of futuristic and other quasi-science fictional motifs is in the context of dream stories that are whimsically or surreally fantastic rather than speculative. He did, however, translate M. P. Shiel's *The Purple Cloud* for the periodical *Je Sais Tout*, and the sketchy bibliography compiled by Eric Dussert calls attention to a "petit roman pour enfants" entitled *Le Roi des microbes* [The Microbe King], serialized in *Qui lit rit* in 1905-06. Interestingly, that same bibliography also refers, without giving full details, to a novel for adults entitled *Le Feu sacré* [Sacred Fire], which allegedly appeared in the occult periodical *L'Initiation*, founded by Papus (Gérard Encausse). None of these works is as yet obtainable via *gallica*, the Bibliothèque Nationale's website.

Although Lautrec published a volume of memoirs, *Souvenirs des jours sans souci* [Memories of Carefree Days] (1938), which is quoted by Dussert and by François Caradec, who wrote the preface to a 1989 reprint of *Les Histoires de Tom Joë*, it must be a trifle lacking in detail, since both commentators remain vague about many aspects of his life. Neither mentions Lautrec's first wife, Dora, although Dussert notes that he was married for a second time in 1922, to Marcelle Husson, who was 32 years his junior.

Lautrec retired from teaching seven years after that and moved to Marseilles, presumably in search of a kinder climate, but returned to Paris in direly poor health some years before his death on July 25, 1938. He put himself forward as a candidate for the Académie Française in 1923, unsuccessfully, but he was appointed a Chevalier de la Légion d'honneur in 1936. Dussert suggests, not very plausibly, that he might have been much prouder when his bust was placed in the Salon des Humoristes in 1920.

Most of the items included in this collection speak for themselves without any further comment than the passing remarks already made, but it is worth calling particular attention to one of two items of exceptional interest.

Some of the most unusual stories in *La Vengeance du portrait ovale* are, with one conspicuous exception, the pieces that first appeared in *Poèmes en prose*. It is arguable that the complexity of "Le Mur" and "Le Familial" is more than a trifle awkward, but the author's intention in framing them as narratives was not to clarify or rationalize the dream-based elements on which they are manifestly based, but rather to amplify their quasi-oneiric qualities. "Cauchemar" (tr. as

"Nightmare") is a more extended, and more accomplished, exercise in the same vein, extrapolating the symptoms and side-effects of acrophobia in an interesting fashion by means of dreams-within-dreams. The most extreme of Lautrec's exercises in that hallucinatory vein is, however, "La Terreur polaire" (here translated as "Polar Terror") which first appeared in the prestigious *Mercure de France* in 1904.

Although it is superficially represented as the tale of survivors of a ship trapped in the polar ice, whose descendants build an ill-fated city on the Antarctic continent, "La Terreur polaire" is actually a psychological study, which only begins to make sense if it regarded as a hallucinatory fantasy or a posthumous fantasy taking place entirely, or almost entirely, in "inner space." Nothing that happens in the story, at least once the ship becomes trapped, can possibly be regarded as a record of adventures in the actual Antarctic, the location featured in the story being a place where darkness is eternal rather than seasonal. The story has something in common with Michel Bernanos' surreal castaway fantasy *La Montagne morte de la vie* (1967; tr. as *The Other Side of the Mountain*). Although Lautrec did not translate *The Purple Cloud* until 1911, it is possible that he had first read it before writing "La Terreur polaire;" whether he had or not, there are interesting points of kinship between the two works.

Of the stories imported from the other collections, the one requiring most comment is "Le Symbolisme Latin" (tr. as "Latin Symbolism"), which is not a story at all but a mock-essay, whose labeling as a poem in prose echoes Edgar Allan Poe's labeling of *Eureka* and "The Imp of the Perverse," although its closest kinship is with Poe's tongue-in-cheek essay "The Philosophy of Composition," which offers an obviously-fictitious satirical account of the composition of "The Raven." Poe's flights of fancy cast in mock-non-fictional form are sometimes called "hoaxes," but they are not really intended to fool anyone, and Lautrec's venture into the same exotic territory similarly assumes that the reader is in on the joke from the start. It is included here to illustrate the fact that Lautrec's homage to Poe is more extensive than that offered by most of the America author's other French imitators—although Baudelaire imported a similar sarcastic whimsy into some of his own prose pieces.

The pieces reproduced from *Les Histoires de Tom Joë* are mostly straightforward, but the two items bracketing the selection from that volume, to which attention has already been called, are necessary illustrations of the manner in which Lautrec's interest in dreams and their peculiar semi-coherence eventually led him to the deliberate cultivation of the surreally absurd. Although "Le Château hanté ou la vierge adultère" is the more extended of the two, mocking the clichés of popular melodrama, it is "Conte cubiste" that really attempts to extrapolates the method to its limit, carefully retaining one of the aspects of Decadent style that Baudelaire championed: the deliberate infection of literary prose with ideas drawn from other artistic sources, especially visual art. The story illustrates the fact that Lautrec never lost contact with his Baudelairean roots, even when he was being deliberately silly.

The critics who refused to consider Lautrec as a writer of the first rank, less impressive as a neo-Poesque fantasist than Marcel Schwob or Henri de Régnier, and less significant as a proto-surrealist than Alfred Jarry or Guillaume Apollinaire, were correct in their estimation, but such crude linear comparisons cannot take into account the fact that Lautrec had distinct qualities of his own that are found nowhere else in the spectrum of fantastic literature. Even his most calculatedly conventional stories, written with commercial publication very obviously in mind, have wry twists to them that no other writer would have added in quite the same way, which lend interest even to his most trivial productions, and make him a writer well worth reading and savoring.

The translation of *La Vengeance du portrait ovale* included herein was made from the 1997 reprint issued by L'Esprit des Péninsules in the Collection l'Alambic. The translations of items from *Poèmes en prose* were made from the electronic copy made by Harvard University and available for consultation at archive.org. The translations of items from *Les Histoires de Tom Joë* were made from the 1989 reprint issued by La Bougie du Sapeur.

All these editions contain some obvious typos, and it is not impossible that some of the odd verbal formulations found in the translations arise from misprints; the vast majority, however, are undoubtedly deliberate contrivances on the author's part. A significant part of the effect of these oddities, especially when they involve puns—as they frequently do—has inevitably been lost in translation, although I have tried to improvise English equivalents where possible. In general, I have made little or no attempt to reproduce the persistent peculiarities of Lautrec's punctuation and grammar, except to give a slight flavor of their occasionally-extreme eccentricity.

Brian Stableford

THE VENGEANCE OF THE OVAL PORTRAIT

The Vengeance of the Oval Portrait

The man in question, Don Arias d'Alilaya, lived in a ruined ancestral castle in Estremadura.[2] For 20 years, he had lived alone. A bloody drama that had unfolded during his youth had infected his heart with a ferocious hatred for humanity, and women in particular.

His father, the noble Count Pablo, had ruled his domain like a true king while he was alive. By virtue to feudal customs, he had the right of life and death over his subjects—but all of them, while fearing him, venerated him, for he was as just as he as strong. Having become a widower early in life, he had consoled himself rapidly for the death of Arias' mother. Leading thereafter a dissolute and wandering life, he had confided the child to aged relatives who had lived him and pampered him, in a distant house in another province. The Count came to embrace him between voyages, but his soul was elsewhere.

In the course of a journey through Italy he had fallen madly in love with a charming young dancer. He had abducted her and taken her to his seigniorial residence. The woman was named Juana. She had a bewitching and superhuman charm. After a few months, however, the Count had found the long days that formed preludes to the splendors of the evening monotonous. Satisfied by seeing the divine creature on his return, he soon developed the habit of hunting during the daylight

---

[2] One of the six Medieval provinces of Portugal, and one of Lautrec's favorite locations for exotic stories.

hours, pursuing eagles and vultures over the mountain-sides, expending strenuous physical activity in these exercises.

Alone in the castle, Juana became bored. She soon allowed herself to be seduced by the delicate speeches of the young head groom, who was handsome and eloquent.

One day, on a high plateau, Don Pablo met an old woman who was said to be a witch He asked her if she knew the whereabouts of the eyrie of a black eagle that he had been hunting since morning.

"Why pursue so obstinately a bird that has done you no harm?" she replied "There are other malevolent beasts that you ought to kill first."

Astonished by these enigmatic words, the noble lord pressed her with questions. He offered her all the gold he had on him. She did not want to accept anything or add anything. He returned to the castle, therefore, full of suspicions, much sooner than was customary.

When he had passed through the third defensive wall he perceived the groom fleeing like a thief over the balcony of Juana's apartment. With a superhuman effort, the Count succeeded in controlling himself, but he had the trumpet sounded and ordered that the guilty man be brought before him, without giving him the reason.

"It's the first time," he said to him, "that I shall cross iron with a mere groom. At any rate, this evening, after supper, you will defend yourself to the death in a closed arena. Groom or Count, one of us is surplus here."

Juana knew about the challenge. During the last feast that Don Pablo held in company with his friends, she poured a violent soporific into his brandy-glass, which would only take effect at the time for which the combat was arranged.

The duel with lances took place in the moonlight, in an arena sealed by barricades formed by serried pikes. From the first pass, the astonished Don Pablo felt his hand weakening. He attacked and defended tamely. In a desperate effort, he hurled himself upon his adversary, but the groom's lance, directed by a rapid and sure gesture, cleaved right through the Count's breast.

As he collapsed, the blood gushing from the terrible wound, a trumpet-blast was heard on the drawbridge of the castle, and almost immediately, a young man of proud appearance was seen to appear on the edge of the arena, mounted on a fine black horse. It was Don Arias, who had been armed as a knight the day before and had come to render homage to his liege-lord. He had ridden all night, bloodying the golden spurs that he had hastened to put on.

He leapt into the arena without further enquiry, seeing nothing but his dead father, leapt upon the groom, and buried his sword all the way to the hilt in the other's throat.

When he went into the castle, greeted by universal acclamation, he was informed that his father had a wife that he had never seen before—but she had just fled, terrified, wrapped in a cloak, taking nothing with her but her jewels and the desire to avenge herself against the man who had arrived to kill her happiness.

Count Arias immediately had it proclaimed by his heralds at every crossroads in the domain that all women, no matter what their age or condition, were to leave his lands within three days, under pain of slow death by asphyxiation on the pyre.

They left, and the majority of the men went with them. No one any longer remained in Don Arias' lands but a few old servants whose lugubrious existence had to accord with that of their overlord. Gradually, powerful vegetation invaded the outskirts of the castle, where the young man had shut himself away with two or three domestics, more isolated every day from the rest of the world.

He spent his time in the ancestral dwelling's ancient library reading fabulous romances of the Middle Ages or books of magic. The mystery of these books suited the wild and solitary atmosphere in which he lived. His mind, already shaken by the fatal event, filled with new chimeras every day in the isolation of the castle.

At other times, in his fits of melancholy, he wandered through the corridors and somber galleries. He went through large rooms with walls covered in sumptuous tapestries, which undulated in the wind, leading and appearance of moving reality to the richly-dressed people, the running dogs whose heads were turned, naively folded back, and the falcons borne on wrists, which seemed ready to take flight.

He wanted to remove one of these tapestries to put it in his bedroom. That was an isolated retreat at the end of the great gallery. Imagine his amazement to find behind the hanging, on the wall, a painting representing a woman of marvelous beauty. She was leaning languidly on her elbow in a red velvet armchair. The delicately-sculpted golden frame was oval in form.

Don Arias took the painting and transported it to his bedroom.

Time went by. The lord had fallen madly and unhealthily in love with the lady in the portrait. He had sent his servants on long journeys into all the surrounding regions to try to discover the woman whose image he adored. Their research remained fruitless. Gradually, the conviction took root in his mind that she must have died years ago and that the only reality—a reality that a miracle alone could bring back to life—was that image, the profound eyes of which poured a delicious and mortal enchantment into his own.

His preliminary studies had prepared him for that idea. He imagined that he might succeed in resuscitating the woman he loved desperately, and who was asleep with open eyes in the coffin of the oblong frame. He consulted old grimoires and learned the formulas of incantation. All day and all night, liturgical prayers rose up in the bedroom transformed into a temple, addressed to the idol who smiled ironically and insouciantly, seemingly awaiting the moment when it would please her to emerge from her colored exile.

Finally, one day, weary of waiting and furious at seeing all his efforts had been in vain, he climbed up on a stool with a stiletto in his hand, determined to stab the canvas in order to annihilate the dream that refused to make itself his. He had raised the weapon and was about to strike when, all of a sudden, doubtless solicited by that gesture, more powerful than all the incantations, the image appeared to obey.

The eyes took on a new and savage expression. Don Arias hesitated momentarily, astounded to see his dream realized. But the eyes became animated by a life even more intense. The arms of the portrait detached themselves from the dead, flat surface—and the woman's hand, seizing the dagger, brandished it and plunged it all the way to the hilt in the amorous man's throat.

The unfortunate's incantations had only succeeded in rendering momentary life to the portrait's true soul. And as the cadaver fell at the foot of the painting, the image of Juana, her vengeance satisfied, resumed its funereal immobility.

Sonia's Soul

For Rachilde[3]

It's impossible that I am mad. That will become evident. If I am in my right mind, why am I locked up? I think it's at the instigation of some demon that is pursuing me. We are all prey to larvae and elementary spirits. The physicians know nothing about that, and they laugh ponderously to hide their ignorance when anyone mentions the occult. They're like the priests of the Middle Ages who sprinkled the possessed with holy water. Today, they give cold showers. Scientists have a horror of novelty; it disconcerts and humiliates them.

So, I have been in this little rural house for several days. My cell is tidy. The food is tolerable. I have been given paper and ink. I will be able to work on my great work: *The Objective of the Subjective*. The book is destined to open the doors of the academy to me. Once elected, people will be obliged to admit that I am in my right mind.

Certainly, I have had an adventure. If the physicians had wanted to take the trouble, they would have understood my situation and they would have been able to take account of my condition scientifically. My case is novel, I agree, but, in sum, there's nothing extraordinary about it. It's one of those accidents that only happen very rarely, but which might occur at any time. Humans are bizarre and fragile beings. One moment of thoughtlessness is sufficient. I drank a soul, by mistake. It was Sonia's. With mine, that makes two, if I can count.

---

[3] The principal pseudonym of Marguerite d'Eymery (1860-1953), one of the pillars of the Decadent Movement in the 1890s. She married Alfred Vallette, the editor of the *Mercure de Paris* and became the magazine's leading book-reviewer.

I'll say this very quietly: I'd repeat that thoughtlessness with pleasure. I can't forget the delicate and delightful sensation that I had at the time.

But let's get back to the question. How did it happen? It wasn't planned. It was literature that doomed me. Poets employ an emphatic language; if one takes them at their word, one risks finding oneself in an absurd situation. I wanted to collect that soul on the lips, like a breath. Ridiculous idea! All it took to kill Sonia, and the first imprudence that I committed, in embracing her, was squeezing my hands a little too strongly around her neck. But what does it matter? All the regrets in the world won't change anything. It's necessary to consider the actual situation coolly. I have one soul too many, that's for sure.

Oh, at first it was perfect! I felt like another man. When I went through the streets, it seemed to me that everybody was looking at me with curiosity and admiration. I thought of that character of Edgar Poe's who had lost his breath, and the other one, who had found it.[4] What an implausible story, compared with mine! Besides, taking it seriously, I recall that they were as inconvenienced as one another, the first even more so. That's understandable. Two breaths! It would make one burst. But a soul…a soul isn't something material, in the relative sense of the term. A soul doesn't take up any space. There's nothing less encumbering than a soul. Mine, in any case, I'm sure of it, can't be very uncomfortable. It ought to fit in very snugly with Sonia's soul.

And the latter, since it's no longer anything but a soul, has naturally lost all its malice. It's too distressed. Children, when they're a little bit frightened, hardly ever think of being naughty. And souls, especially women's souls, are children in eternity.

It's necessary to suppose that it's huddled in some corner of my being, and that it's looking out from there with a flickering gaze, liked some sly and timid little beast.

---

[4] Edgar Allan Poe, "Loss of Breath" (1832).

The truth is that her presence doesn't disturb me at all now. The best moments, before, were those when she sat calmly and meekly in a corner of the room, reading beautiful stories while I worked. I wish the situation were different, but one gets used to things. It's nothing at all to have drunk a soul.

It's sufficient to know it, to take account, coldly, of the slightly abnormal situation and act in consequence.

A man who has two souls evidently can't live like everyone else, but it's easy to keep both ridiculous dread and exaggerated pride at a distance.

The important thing is the heart.

I fear, at certain moments, that it might quit its obscure corner and fly towards my heart, and collide with it again.

How is it made, a soul? I don't have the slightest idea.

Sometimes, though, I imagine that it's prowling around my heart, silently, like a mauve bat around a red lantern.

It's mauve! That's what I wanted to know. I'm sure of it now. What a sudden revelation! It's mauve. It's very important to know that.

And what does it see? What does it think? What impression has the change made upon it? Often, in the evening, when she was alive, we discussed the question of life after death. There was no other issue that preoccupied me as much. I remember long conversations in which we whispered in low voices, in the darkness, thinking about phantoms, until our voices were impregnated with terror. I was able to console her then—but now, I'm afraid that she might be afraid.

Then again, if one were sure that things will remain as they are—but I think about that. Suppose that the soul were to die, while lodged in my body. Perhaps there time comes when souls, too, die? After all, we don't know whether souls are mortal or not. Agreed, no one has ever seen one die—but that's not a peremptory proof, since one can't see souls at all.

At any rate, if that happened, I would find myself with the corpse of a soul, which wouldn't take long to putrefy. It would be necessary for me to get rid of it, no matter what the cost. Should I go to a surgeon? He'd look at me suspiciously.

I'd have explanations to make. What good would it do to expose myself to difficulties? Wouldn't it be better to set it free right away? It would have the time to take advantage of that liberty. Then again, perhaps it's suffering, and finds itself constricted in its prison. So far as I know, this perpetual contact might not be pleasant for it.

In the end, it's a question of right.

Has one the right to keep a soul prisoner, profiting, as in the present case, from hazard or circumstance? I'm reasoning like a lawyer, but it's necessary to call things be their name. There has been an undue influence. The fact is undeniable.

It has, all the same, been lucky enough to have fallen upon an honest man. So many others would have no scruples and would keep it—but it's egotistical to want two souls. As if that were possible! Let's see!

One would remain to me. That's quite enough.

My God! I know full well…when one is in love…I could imagine extraordinary things. Two souls making one…just words, follies, at the end of the day. Besides, I didn't love Sonia. What I said just now was literary, for my amusement. I have to get rid of that soul, immediately.

For a moment, I thought of killing it, with one of those long pins that women put in their hats—but I'm afraid I might only wound it, and that it will suffer. Then again, I might not reach my heart.

Besides, why kill it? Isn't that precisely what I want to avoid—a dead heart? Isn't it better for it to live and be happy, if it can? It will go out into the world, as light as a bird, a perfume or a musical note, and when it has found some beautiful form—a flower or a woman—it will take that for its home.

I need to give it a way out. That's easy. The slightest opening would suffice.

There's no point thinking about a revolver. They've taken mine away, on some ridiculous pretext. On reflection, I'm glad about that. In a case like this, a revolver isn't what's needed at all. It would surely be taken by surprise, and the noise would frighten it. It would start fluttering madly around my breast, bumping into the walls, without finding an exit. A dagger is better. Here's exactly what I need—they've left me the slender knife with a narrow blade that I use to cut the pages of books, to liberate the souls of thinkers enclosed therein.

Sonia's soul will fly out through the wound, and I'll keep mine, tranquilly. It has no reason to leave—provided, dear God, that the other doesn't want to persuade it and take it away! But I'm not worried. I know my soul. There's nothing to fear.

I shall set Sonia free.

The Burial of Olasryck

For René Bruneau[5]

The snow had been falling without interruption for months. It covered the countryside with a mantle whose thickness was ever-increasing, and which could not be melted by the wan rays of a Sun that was only perceptible at long intervals, like a vague copper disk hidden behind a livid curtain. The town, already isolated, lost in a valley in the high Himalaya, was now definitively cut off from the rest of the world. Even the wild beasts had fled into the mountains, howling, and there had been no birds in the suffocating air for some time.

Once, a few travelers—bonzes in grey or black woolen bonnets with heavy necklaces of brown-dyed wood around their necks—had arrived at dusk or in the morning light to sound muted appeals on brazen gongs that hung outside the doors on multicolored cords, asking for the road leading to the Temple of Fire. But the last travelers had been buried in the town's white shroud, and their souls were with Brahma.

The temple stood on a hill overlooking the entire town of Olasryck. There were tortuous streets rising up to it from the outskirts, bordered with old wooden houses and shops in which meager objects related to the cult of fire were sold. They were naïve images, metal and wax tablets, and lamps formed like cups. In each of these shops a torch had once burned before an image of the god on the wall, but the torches had been extinguished a long time ago, having struggled in vain against the multitude of white flies that had swirled in the

---

[5] One of the very few references identifiable via Google Books that is not to Bruneau's more famous namesake identifies him as a book-collector with a special interest in Tahiti.

streets at first, then penetrated indoors by mean of the widows and chimneys. Now, the livid sheet had reached the tops of the houses, and snow was piling up in all the extinct hearths.

The event had been as unexpected as it was strange. Perhaps the priests had committed some ritual crime, for, by virtue of the mystery and unusual nature of the cause, it was truly reminiscent of a divine punishment.

On a beautiful summer's day, one of the mountains that terminated the spur of the mountain chain at the foot of which the town extended was suddenly hollowed out at the summit with a terrible din. Without any landslide slipping down the slope, the peak had collapsed, as if drawn toward the center of the Earth by a giant invisible hand. And from the crater thus formed—a phenomenon in contradiction with all natural laws, which was proof of divine intervention—a geyser of snow had been seen to erupt: a column of densely-packed flakes that rose into the blue sky, darkening it with their thickness.

And for month after month, the fantastic eruption had not ceased. The snowflakes fell back *en masse* over all the surrounding territory, gradually burying it as the ash of Vesuvius had buried Pompeii. The cold prevented the snow from melting, and he new ground gradually leveled off.

It was finally decided that the entire population would take refuge in the temple. Emerging from the windows and roofs of the lower town, the unfortunates climbed the slopes, stumbling and sinking into the soft upper layers of the avalanche, and dropping at every step the poor relics of their past life, too hastily stuck into the folds of their cloaks. They had had some brief joy, however, in finding themselves temporarily safe behind the doors of the edifice, where they had accumulated provisions and livestock, and all the lamps burned night and day in the struggle against the cold and dark.

Meanwhile, the snow fell. It piled up higher every day against the walls of crystal forming an immense greenhouse for the numerous galleries in which the inhabitants were camped. The priests had reserved the inner sanctuary, in the middle of which was the altar, for themselves.

On the altar was the idol, encircled with flamboyant light. It was a statue made of some unknown dark red metal, which burned any profane hand that chanced to touch it, like red-hot iron. It was a monstrous statue, similar to the ancient Moloch, which only rejoiced in cruel sacrifices. Every day, a human creature was immolated to it. The face of the god seemed to brighten with a diabolical smile on seeing that liquid fire, blood, flow over the well-washed slabs.

The daily sacrifice seemed increasingly futile, however, as well as the moaning prayers that the heard of frightened incessantly directed toward the vault. There was no sign of an end to the scourge. The presages drawn from the wind and the water indicated the direst of futures. Vainly, at all hours, the candle-flames were interrogated. Instead of rising up like a single vertical sword, they divided into two branches of sinister signification. And it was in vain that, in order to know the secrets of the gods, the priests went to sleep every night with magical leaves of gold under their tongues.

It was finally necessary to have recourse to the great incantation. Already, the transparent walls were bending under the pressure, and the great crystal vault was increasing its curvature as it gradually subsided.

The inhabitants, on their knees, redoubled their supplications. And when evening came, the priests emerged from the sanctuary, in dalmatics with heavy folds, coiffed in blue linen tiaras. They made a ritual tour of the galleries, first from east to west and then from west to east. Then they went to sit down on their chairs of sculpted wood.

Then, amid feverish expectation, thirteen young girls were seen to advance, chose from among the most beautiful. They danced before the mute idol, to awaken its pity. And when they were weary, and an adorable sweat had perfumed the secret of their young flesh like an incense, they all came to stand in line in front of the idol's altar, and servants gave them crowns of flowers. They knelt down on the steps, and the high priest came forward, holding in his hand the large sword of ritual immolations. Resigned and smiling, he cut their throats one after another over the large golden bowls, into which their crimson blood flowed.

All the people ran forward, trampling the suave bodies underfoot, in order to drink the redemptive blood. When the golden bowls had been drained to the last drop, a monstrous intoxication surged from that living beverage—and suddenly, from a thousand mouths, like a supreme and desperate appeal, a frightful clamor made the crystal walls tremble.

Under that formidable pressure, the vault of the temple split, and the thick white layer gradually slid into the interior. Scarcely had the first fragments of snow touched the statue, however, than the entire temple exploded like a powder-keg, burying the priests, the people and the god beneath its debris.

The Spell

For Henri Duvernois[6]

When Marthe got married, I thought that I would go mad with sorrow. I loved her so uniquely that I had never thought of confessing it to her. It seemed to me to be such a natural thing that she would one day be mine. I any case, I would never have supposed that she might marry my friend Pierre, that jovial fellow whose nature was so different from hers. In the evening, in the garden, when I told her my dreams, she listened to me pensively. As soon as she spoke, the mystery of her profound voice oppressed me like a charm. What good was there in pronouncing unnecessary words? Had she not understood me? I didn't even think about Pierre. When the three of us were together, we only had conversations of cheerful banality. But it was Pierre whom she married.

The news reached me in the old family house in which I sometimes like to isolate myself, a few leagues south of Paris. After the initial amazement, I wanted to protest, to claim what I regarded as my right. I wrote to her. I went to see her. She welcomed me absent-mindedly, with an affectionate astonishment, and pronounced the eternal question: "Why didn't you say so?" I had no more to say thereafter. I went to shut myself away, as a dead man seeks his tomb, in the old solitary house, resolved never to see Marthe or anyone else again. And

---

[6] Henri Duvernois (1875-1937) was a prolific journalist, playwright and novelist who developed a considerable reputation as a *conteur* but mostly stayed clear of the supernatural themes favored by Lautrec; a translation of his only significant fantasy novel was published by Black Coat Press as *The Man Who Found Himself*, ISBN 9781935558040.

it was then that, little by little, like a malefactor who slowly forces a door and penetrated with muffled footsteps, the idea gradually insinuated itself into my skull.

When I was a child, I had grim hatreds. An overly rigorous sense of justice made me condemn without appeal all those who had displeased me. My powerlessness exaggerated my fury. In the evening, before going to sleep, I would evoke my enemies, in a setting of despotic power. Slaves would make them kneel down, and when I had reproached them for their crimes, executioners would subject them to slow torture.

It is both a joy and a calamity to retain a puerile soul all one's life. Poets need that perpetual freshness of impression to evoke and express the phantoms of their imagination forcefully, but ordinary men who possess the fatal gift suffer from a perpetual discord between their true soul and experience. They cannot get used to the world that surrounds them. They create another, where they live with the naïve illusion of external command.

Those who devote themselves in solitude to the practice of magic are like that. They imagine that it is sufficient to lock themselves in their rooms, surround themselves with pentacles and say, ardently: *I wish! I wish!* Bizarre encounters have sometimes lent credence to this folly. To be sure, guilty as those practices may be, who among us would not, at decisive moments, have sold his soul to the Devil to obtain what he desperately desires?

I had an entire library of occultism at my disposal, bequeathed by an uncle who was slightly mad. After the initial crisis of despair, idleness and, doubtless, a mysterious impulsion, inspired me to reopen the books that I had often leafed through.

A demon emerging from the pages whispered the accursed advice. My dolor had given way to hatred. As in the times of my childhood, I wanted the person who had taken my happiness dead. Nocturnal visions revealed the enchantment of the myth of Faust—and a few days later, in my solitude, I began the ceremonies of the spell.

I had a photograph of Pierre and a few meager souvenirs, in which, according to magical concepts, his person ought to have left effluvia that would permit me to establish a subtle link between us. I enclosed all the letters of his that I had in a block of wax. I shaped the block of wax into a rough resemblance, sufficient for the evocation.

One moonless night, I took the statuette, hidden in a black veil, to a crossroads in the forest where some wretch had once been hanged. Having bathed it in holy water, which I had stolen from the church, I baptized it in my enemy's name according to the formulae, and made the sign of the cross in reverse.

After that, every evening, for thirteen days—thirteen being the number of love and death—in the remote room where I had deposited the image, I performed the incantations. I cursed him by the seven planets, by the swords and by the wheels. I called down upon him the fury of the gnomes, the sylphs, the undines and the salamanders, in order that all the elements should be conjured. And every time, I slowly plunged a needle into the body of wax, imagining that I was plunging it into the body of flesh—until, on the last day, I traversed the middle of the breast with a gesture of hatred, in order to kill my enemy's heart. Meanwhile, I repeated in a monotonous and obstinate voice: "I want him to die. That is what I want."

I went to bed that evening with the obscure impression that I had just committed a murder. At the same time, bizarrely enough, the very excess of my fury caused me to understand its vanity. As if liberated by the gesture, I began to smile sporadically at what appeared to me, after the fact, to have been childish.

The next day, I burned the block of wax and the letters. A long excursion on horseback dissipated the magical fumes that had confused my brain. Nothing remained to me but the impression of having at least wounded my dolor.

A few days later, I left for Paris, determined to make a new start. I was young. Life still retained a few compensations and joys for me.

On arrival, I found Marthe's letter, which informed me of her husband's death.

In the profound distress into which that unexpected event had thrown her, she had immediately thought of my friendship. I sensed, moreover, more painful astonishment than true sorrow in her words. As I had expected, the marriage could only have been a serious formality for her. She had only experienced the conventional affection that, for many souls—the unfortunate ones!—is the equivalent of love. I searched the letter in vain for a great cry of despair.

The essential thing, however, was the detail of the event. Pierre had died on the evening of the day when I had plunged the needle into the heart of wax. The unfortunate fellow, she told me, had suffered for some time from stabbing pains in his limbs, without any other symptom. The physicians, when summoned, had diagnosed an embolism.

I married Marthe, after a suitable delay, as soon as I was able. It has not been easy for me to make her forget her loss. Have I forgotten him myself? What does it matter? She loves me, and I am happy, in a fashion that I thought impossible, and which still seems so to me, in spite of its reality, however profound that might be. The rest is nothing but chimeras.

If I sometimes feel a slight frisson in thinking about the death that I desired, I reassure myself by telling myself that there is nothing in life but chance and coincidence. The madness of a recluse cannot have any influence over external events.

And if I'm mistaken, if I'm guilty and must one day expiate my sin, I will, at any rate, have gained royally from the exchange. The demons may come and carry me away with their black wings. My eternal memory will make the inferno a paradise.

The Green Jar

After a comfortable dinner, as we were lighting cigars, plunged in profound armchairs, someone pronounced the word "occultism," and our conversation turned toward strange things.

The room was discreetly lit. A warm breeze coming from the neighboring trees caused a widow and some vague drapery to stir. When the first cigar had been smoked a young man leaning back on the cushions gave an exact definition of an astral body; another recounted that he had seen the shade of Éliphas Lévi appear at a séance of initiates. Then the conversation embarked on the perpetuation of human consciousness after death.

A slight frisson ran through the room, and eyes were seen to widen. Someone said: "I had a dream and I'll tell you about it. Perhaps it will interest you."

The second cigar was extinguished, as befits a well-constructed story. Everyone lit up again, and leaned forward to listen.

I've been occupied for twenty years in the patient study of the human soul. I've observed the last convulsions of agonized individuals on cold mornings under grey skies. I've seen invalids die and I've noted all the essential lines that the spasm of death inscribes on faces. I've spent nights examining the disconcerting mystery of human life, holding brains shrunk by alcohol in my hand, beneath a magnifying glass and my weary eyes, and following like a voyager the frightful circumvolutions and furrows along which the sad or luminous demons that are our thoughts follow their routes. But I don't know whether consciousness, the soul of the soul, quits the body or dies with it, nor what happens to us when the shreds of flesh that separate the nudity of our terrified soul's livid eyes from the livid eyes or nothingness come apart.

What I don't know, nobody knows. Who can say whether lamentable secrets are hidden beneath that untearable veil? Our ideas of glory and our vain desire to exist are nothing in comparison to the implacable logic that must regulate the universe. Perhaps the sublime formula, the doctrine of the future life and infinity, before which all poets and believers kneel, perhaps the dogma of the tabernacle, in a logic superior to all our illusions, is only a burst of obscene and grotesque laughter on the part of the absolute.

Lying peacefully in my bed, as tranquil as on days when I ought not to dream, I suddenly found myself transported into what appeared to me to the entrance hall of a pharmacy. I saw the pharmacist and his wife in the rear of the shop, though the communicating door, sitting down to a meal. I'm recounting things exactly as they appeared to me, with the incoherence of the dream, for the sake of absolute veracity. Also at table was the pharmacist's son, and a few friends or relatives, among whom was a domesticated rattlesnake. The presence of that animal did not seem to astonish anyone, except for the schoolmaster, who was not there anyway. For my own part, I would not have wanted to seem unacquainted with the customs of the house, but no one paid any attention to me.

I seemed to be perceived all the details that surrounded me as if through a mist: glass jars and porcelain pots with gilded labels; the pharmacy door and that of the dining-room. I felt a sort of slothfulness impeding my movements; in addition, I felt vague pains in my abdominal region, and I attributed these pains, by some connection I cannot specify, to the effort I was making to reflect. The play of my mental faculties was reduced to an impression of hindrance. I was conscious that my soul, astonished by some modification of my body, lacked the familiar usage of its organs and sensations.

They were finishing dessert; the pharmacist had just read aloud the last article in the *Beacon of the Future*; the question of municipal councilors had been discussed and a little music plated. The rattlesnake had recited a fable. In sum, everyone was greatly amused.

After a rather ridiculous family scene, in which the pharmacist bewailed in Alexandrine verse the death of his aunt, a victim of her zeal in caring for someone gravely ill with cholera, a few people took their leave. Then the pharmacist, advancing into the foreground of the scene—which is to say, toward me—calmly took off his skull-cap revealed a blue-painted cranium on which the maxims of Hippocrates were inscribed in golden letters. At the same time, he exclaimed: "Gentlemen, I'm a pharmacist, and I will never deny pharmacy; I swear it by the anatomical specimens that you see in this jar."

I heard muffled laughter around me, but I leaned vainly in all directions to see the anatomical specimens and the jar. My gestures, In this regard, seemed unusual to me. I thought I could feel my limbs sliding over one another with a viscous motion. At the same time, I breathed in an insipid odor of alcohol.

In view of the strangeness of my sensations, the painful thought suddenly occurred to me that I was doubtless dead, and that nothing remained of my body, destroyed by the universal movement of things, but some part in which my entire soul had taken refuge. In a melancholy fashion, I thought that perhaps it was my skull that had survived me. I was not too unhappy, telling myself that I might possibly be able to recover the subtle calm of yesteryear in some monk's cell.

Then I thought that perhaps it was my hand that had survived me. "Oh! What if my hand alone remains intact, and, living on behalf of my vanished flesh, it is trying to console my soul for the loss of its sad body? That's why I no longer have lips permitting me to recite to the woman I know too well that sonnets that her imperial beauty dictates to me! That why I've seen the light go out in my eyes, of which she is no longer the dearest glory. But perhaps my hand might take the place of the dead lips, and of the extinct eyes. I only need, to console myself, to be able still to trace the tender letters of her name!"

Meanwhile, the pharmacist was telling his guests about a procedure he had witnessed a few days earlier. The subject had died of one of those maladies whose exceedingly rare name evokes profound mutilations and terror-blackened visages. The body had been embalmed, then reduced to ashes, according to the instructions of the deceased. During the embalming, however, the pharmacist had been able to procure the dead man's entrails. Everything else had disappeared.

"You see that green jar in the shop window, next to the door? The guts I mentioned just now have been put in *eau-de-vie*. The spectacle reminds me of the fragility of our nature, and I think, with a certain annoyance, that I shall die one day, even though I'm a pharmacist."

He pointed at the jar. All eyes went to the entrails, and I had the frightful sensation that it was me they were looking at.

At that moment, undoubtedly, my soul, upset by the seal of my hallucinations, must have protruded from the formless folds of that flesh that was imprisoning it, two eyes with a gaze encircled by terror, for one member of the audience remarked:

"The glitter of the liquid is causing bizarre reflections in the jar. One might truly think that those guts were staring at us."

The Story of the Diligence

How can I relate this adventure, and how can anyone believe it? The inhabitants of the New World are hungry for new sensations, and do not recoil from any folly to render their lives more intense. Among all the mysterious stories with which the memory of humankind enriches itself with every passing moment, that of the Lyons Courier[7] had had a particular impact on the child-like minds of my two friends Rex and Jim Corbett, and one day, they decided to re-enact, in the same conditions as before, so far as was possible, at least—the fatal journey.

The secret having been rigorously kept, we found ourselves one evening in a specially-constructed garage on the main road, where the diligence was waiting for us. What a

---

[7] Lautrec expects his readers to recognize this reference to one of the great *causes célèbres* of French legal history. On April 27, 1796 the diligence on which a courier was travelling from Lyons to Paris, in charge of an enormous sum of money in cash and securities destined for the army fighting in Italy, was robbed by bandits south-east of the capital. The courier and the coach's postillion were killed. Several members of the gang were soon rounded up, and among the suspects put on trial was Joseph Lesurques, who had been arrested because of his distinctive blond hair and identified by several eye-witnesses as one of the bandits. After the conviction, one of the actual robbers admitted his own guilt, but swore that Lesurques was innocent, and that he had been mistaken for a man named Dubosc. Lesurques was guillotined anyway, but the guilty party really had been Dubosc (in a blond wig); he, too, was subsequently convicted and guillotined in 1800. The case became the most famous miscarriage of justice of its era, and is referenced incessantly in early French crime fiction—notably that of Paul Féval, who took considerable inspiration from the case in designing the Blackcoats' strategy of framing victims for their crimes.

marvelous evocation! Everything was similar—and it had not been an easy task to bring together all the documents permitting that exact moment of the past to live again. But with money and patience, one can realize prodigies. The carriage and the awning were identical. The box of dispatches was fixed behind the vehicle. There were four horses, harnessed two-by-two according to models carefully studied in the engravings of the time. They carried small silvery bells. The postillion and the coachman, perched on the imperial in authentic costumes, were my two friends, and I was the only passenger. Their wigs were powdered. There were trunks and bales under the awning. What fantastic old trunks, retrieved from fabulous second-hand dealers!

We're pulling away. It was a hundred years ago, to the hour, that the coachman's whip cracked above the vehicle, which shook with a tinkle of bells—and everything is so exactly similar that I don't know whether it's the past that is living again or whether it's us that have been transported magically into the past. The diligence rolls along the road, illuminated by the poor forward lantern. On hills, we get down and push the carriage. My God, how bad it is! The road is stony and there are no springs.

Suddenly, the Moon pierces the clouds, and spreads a wan light over the countryside. One might think we were in a land of phantoms. The trees by the roadside seem to be whispering. We've been rolling for two hours and we can't help being invaded, little by little, by a strange apprehension. In spite of our skepticism, we feel that there's a sort of profanation in trying to revive something that has been dead for such a long time.

Our conversation, cheerful at the outset, becomes awkward, and then dies away. There is silence and solitude. Except, just now, two tramps sleeping on a pile of stones got up painfully as we approached and gazed with amazement at the fantastic vision. In the morning, they'll think that they were dreaming.

Come on, a little courage! A few more kilometers and the first houses of Lieusaint will gaze at us with their red and myopic eyes. What an evocative name: Lieusaint! But no one will murder us—and we regret not having prepared a simulacrum of the most moving episode of the tragedy. It's too late now to finish off this stupid adventure. Finally, here's the last bend, and over there, a dark mass. It's the wood at the edge of the village, which we only have to pass through. A train whistles in the distance.

Suddenly, a gunshot, followed by another fired at closer range. The horses, rearing up, stop dead. And what I see at this moment I shall never forget, if I live to be a hundred.

Two masked men on horseback were standing before us, pistols—not revolvers-in hand. Our friend the postillion, whom the abrupt halt of the vehicle had thrown to the ground, got to his feet, and all three of us were soon out of the vehicle, in front of those masked men. We had no weapons, and I regretted it bitterly. Meanwhile, the men were motionless, a few meters away, leaning over in their stirrups, their pistols aimed at us, seemingly ready to fire.

Jim Corbett, the first to recover from his amazement, bravely took a step forward and spoke: "What do you want with us? We're not travelers bearing treasures. The money that we have in our pockets we'll give you; the sum isn't enormous. But please let us pass. My comrades and I are making a carnival excursion. You only have to look at our costumes."

Having said these swords, our friend returned to us. We emptied into his hand all the money we had on us. The two men remained silent. Jim Corbett unhooked the diligence's lantern and advanced toward one of them. Handing him the money, he said: "Take it, old chap—we have nothing more."

The man leaned down in his stirrups, took the money he was given with an abrupt movement, and threw it down on to the road. The metallic clinking was all that disturbed the silence. Our friend, utterly astonished, raised his lantern toward the men, of whom we had only seen, until then, the vague silhouettes, and he suddenly let out a burst of laughter.

"Look!" he shouted to us.

By the light of the lantern, we distinctly saw the two men on horseback, masked but dressed—just like us—in costumes of the time of the drama. A gleam of light dawned in our minds.

Jim Corbett went on: "The joke's excellent, provided it doesn't go on too long. I'm anxious to know the ingenious friends who have got wind of our adventure and wanted to ensure its counterpart. We lacked brigands. In that respect, it's perfect. If we aren't being robbed, what...?"

The blade of a sword glinted. A blow forcefully landed by the man on the horse caused the lantern to fall, which went out and broke on the road. Then the two men got down and marched toward us.

"No," our friend continued, "that's enough. The farce is becoming dangerous to continue. Name yourselves, and let it be finished. We've had our little fright; you can be satisfied. But I warn you that if you don't unmask immediately, I'll apply a few punches whose marks you'll bear for some time."

The men did not appear to have heard. They headed toward us at a phantasmal pace, took hold of our clothing, tore away our wigs and ripped our lace ruffs, all without saying a word. They seemed possessed of Herculean strength, and we twisted in their hands like wisps of straw. All resistance was futile. They broke the windows of the diligence and set about unhitching the horses. Then one of them climbed on top of the vehicle in three bounds and started throwing the luggage on to the road.

That was too much. While my two friends were trying to stop him, I threw myself on the other one, hands reaching out to strangle him. I gripped him by the neck and squeezed. Horror! His clothing gave way and I felt within my grip a neck as hard as iron, and no thicker than a finger...

With the energy of supreme terror, I seized the phantom's mask and tore it away. And I perceived...a death's-head, which was looking at me with green eyes.

I could do no more. I had no thought but flight. I slipped out of the skeleton's grip. I ran. But as I set off he pronounced two words the whispered in my ear while I ran:

"Lesurques! Dubosc!"

At daybreak I arrived in Lieusaint, disheveled, soaked in sweat, my clothes in tatters. A peasant took me in. After resting and taking a little nourishment, I told him some story or other to explain my accoutrement. Having recovered from panic, I had blushed at my cowardice and the abandonment of my friends. The peasant volunteered to lend me his cart and to go with me. We left, armed with a hunting rifle and a revolver. I remember now—I had told him that I was part of a company of actors and that we had been attacked by thieves.

We arrived at the place where the drama had taken place. There was no longer anything there. The diligence had disappeared. No trace remained of the attack or the fight. The phantoms, my friends, the broken windows, the luggage—everything had vanished as if by magic.

We searched the surroundings, beating the bushes. There was nothing to recall the tragic and horrible scene of the previous night. My companion was very near to taking me for a practical joker, and I began wondering myself whether I might have been dreaming.

But no, I wasn't dreaming. Everything really happened as I saw it—and the fantastic apparition of the bandits who robbed us was nothing but the logical conclusion of the adventure we had tried to reconstitute. No one knows what becomes of the past, and whether it is not still present, ready to revive redoubtably as soon as one summons it with the necessary incantations.

We had been punished, my friends and I—the friends, it is necessary to say, that I never saw again—for having been tempted, by virtue of an unhealthy curiosity, to violate the gates of death. And for my part, I no longer see, haunted though I am by the fear of seeing them reappear, now that we have awakened them from their century-long sleep, the souls of Lesurques and Dubosc.

Number Thirteen

Matters of superstition and childish credulity, said the doctor, when it was his turn to speak, it is easy to resolve *a priori*. But we all have in our lives some story or some adventure in which mystery plays its part, and which leaves us thoughtful. For example, I've always had a sympathy for the number thirteen, which is that of love and death. An entire series of encounters has rendered it dear to me. And I'm convinced that, in one instance, it definitely saved my life.

It was four years ago. I had gone to give a lecture in Brussels. It was the end of winter. The weather was execrable. We disembarked in the city in the middle of a deluge of rain and snow. An icy wind was blowing in gusts. There is no impression more unpleasant than arriving in an unknown city in bad weather. The darkness and cold created a kind of desert around us. I had great difficulty getting to the hotel where I was expected for diner. The lecture was at nine o'clock. Everything went smoothly, but it transpired that the only two people I knew in the city were unable, for various reasons, once the job was done and the compliments had been exchanged, to keep me company.

I found myself alone in front of the hotel. The squalls of rain were getting worse. It was impossible to go anywhere. Strictly speaking, I would have been able to go back an hour later, but I was tired and sulky. I decided to wait until the following day. Perhaps, in the morning, a clear interval would permit me to take a walk through the city. The train wasn't due to leave until one o'clock in the afternoon.

I therefore took refuge, in a very bad mood, in the hotel lounge, where I spent two interminable hours smoking Belgian cigars and reading old numbers of the *Monde Illustré*. Toward midnight, weary of interesting myself in the actualities of the Second Empire, I went to bed, planning to get up early. I was always afraid of missing a train. It is, for me, not an inconvenience but one of the calamities of life. But the night went by peacefully and, waking up at the desired time, I went out to visit the city. The rain had stopped—and I was at the station a full hour before the departure time.

About twenty minutes later, a set of carriages appeared alongside the platform. I sought information. On the affirmative response of station staff, I climbed in and put my suitcase on a rack, along with two or three newspapers on the seat, to reserve the corner. Then I got back down on to the platform. After a few moments, the set of carriages started moving. I was reassured when I learned that it was going into a siding in order to allow the Amsterdam train to arrive.

It was from that moment on that providential error, clandestine and blind illusion took possession of more and submerged me entirely. Haven't you noticed that at certain times, we become suddenly and completely absent from life? An invisible paralysis separates us from the environment. We no longer think, or think differently. We lost the exact notion of reality and the sense of adaptation. The cruelest memories are those in which this unconsciousness arrives unexpectedly in the middle of an amorous adventure. I have—we all have—the keen vision, at a distance, of a moment when one only has to extend one's arms or lips to pluck the most delightful of flowers. What temporary blindness prevents us from seeing, at that moment? Later, sometimes an hour, sometimes years afterwards, one suddenly realizes it, and curses it furiously. For a man smitten with a woman, the memory of those joys offered, but stupidly neglected, is a remorse unique in life.

But the ironic divinity sometimes changes into a benevolent demon. That's what happened to me that day. I watched the Amsterdam train come along the empty track and draw up alongside the platform. And, suddenly convinced that I was not going to Amsterdam, but to Paris, I remained in complete tranquility, repeating to myself mechanically, in order to be persuaded, that it was necessary to wait for that train to disappear, to make way for the one that I needed to take.

I listened, as if petrified, to the departure signals; I saw the doors closed; I looked at the clock, merely astonished that the train was leaving exactly on the hour, at the same time as mine. And it was only at the moment when the carriages moved off, drawing slowly away from me, that I had the sudden, blinding intuition, that it was not one that was heading for Amsterdam, but the one that had come from Amsterdam and was going to Paris, having picked up on the way, on another track, the set of carriages formed in Brussels, in which I had left my suitcase. I had that sudden vision, just at the moment when it was too late.

I shall pass over what followed: the desperate perspective of the whole mortal afternoon, until the evening train. It was one of those stupid frustrations that cause nervous individuals to think, momentarily, that life is not worth living. When I was a little more resigned, I sent a telegram to friends who were due to meet the train, and another to the stationmaster at the frontier, asking him to collect my suitcase from the carriage during the halt and to keep it until I passed through that evening. Then I trailed miserably from café to café, drinking insipid commonplace beer, crossing streets in the squalls of rain and snow that were gaining fury again. The time passed, with its sinister slowness. I eventually found myself back on the platform and took the train, this time with no hitches.

On arriving at the frontier I hurried to the stationmaster's office. That functionary greeted me with an embarrassed expression. He had, indeed, received my dispatch and had searched for my suitcase when the train went through, but without result. In addition, a singular accident, which had caused a man's death, had occasioned a certain disturbance for several hours.

On the very train that I had missed, when it arrived at the frontier, a passenger had been found collapsed in his seat, his torso pierced all the way through by a frightful wound. The cadaver had been transported to the mortuary and the carriage detached, in which the traveler's luggage had been carefully left in place. Although he had been found alone in his compartment, research carried out on the track had permitted the tragic scene to be reconstituted. A large branch, broken off by the storm from a tree alongside the track and leaning over it, must have come through the open window in the carriage door and struck the passenger full in the chest, with all the velocity of the train.

I had a sort of presentiment—and anyway, I had to recover my suitcase. On my insistence, I was allowed to visit the fatal carriage. We climbed up—and I perceived my suitcase in the rack where I had placed it myself. Beside it were other items of luggage. But below the suitcase, where I would have been sitting if I hadn't missed the train, exactly in the middle of the padding, was a large bloodstain.

My fearful gaze moved up again, and I saw, above the back of the seat, the seat-number that I hadn't noticed the first time.

It was, naturally, number thirteen.

The Amorous Queen

For Dora[8]

In a legendary country, far away beyond the sea, lived an old king and a young queen, in the midst of the adulation of their courtiers. There were adventures there like those in fairy tales. The lords addressed their declarations to the ladies on a daily basis, and the ladies took care to put on pink make-up so that no one could see them blush. The people, naturally, were overwhelmed by taxes, but thought that they were very happy, because they were used to it. Anyway, the trees in the Royal Park were several hundred years old and the hall of the palace were ornamented with profound mirrors, perfect for the multiplication of the floral patterned dresses worn by the queen and the ladies of the court.

After the queen and the king, the most important person in the aforementioned court was the king's jester, to whom an immemorial right granted a seat on the Council of Ministers, where he began to speak immediately when his august master fell silent. His name was Tripetus,[9] and he claimed decent, by the distaff line, from one of the most ancient aristocratic families in the land. The monarch liked him a great deal, and boasted of his wisdom in all matters. The ladies of the court could do no less than follow such a noble example, and all day

---

[8] The author's first wife. He married again in the year that *La Vengeance du portrait ovale* was published, but I cannot find any information as to what had become of Dora.

[9] In the version of this story contained in *Poèmes en prose*, "Conte bleu," the jester's name is Mangetout. The reason for the change remains mysterious.

long, a swarm of pretty women swirled around the jester, passionately delighted by his impertinent conceit.

Tripetus spent his time making up puns and puzzles, which he subsequently recopied in beautiful characters in a red notebook, with Indian ink. When he was not working, or listening disdainfully to the declarations of ladies, he slept or smoked his pipe. He was an intellectual. One ran into him in the kitchens, sniffing the perfume of dishes and saucepans like a food critic. Master chefs in large white pointed hats passed by gravely. In the window-bays there were purring cats sitting on scullion's knees, and hundred-year-old women, entirely clad in black with mildewed skin, with the red blaze of the fire on their faces....

Tripetus, in his half-red, half-green costume, which made him resemble a parakeet, arrived slyly beside tables, cut thick slices of bread and dipped them in the soup. He had put on a lot of weight, and his short stature caused his fat belly to stand out. When politics shut down, the jester's gluttony alimented the newspapers with jokes—always the same—at which the idiotic people always laughed heartily.

One day, however, when the trees in the great park were shedding melancholy leaves in the crazy autumn wind, the aforementioned young queen leaned over her balcony in the direction of the forest, letting her blonde hair stream downwards, just as Tripetus went by. He was going to the forest to gather dry leaves for his pipe. The jester was very miserly, and had come, in the wake of a ministerial crisis, to pad out a two-sou packet of tobacco.

The lady was very pretty, but Tripetus did not see her, and as such great beauty demanded that a heart should be captivated, it was the queen's. It was the forest's fault, although perhaps it is also necessary to blame her feminine nervous system. Besides, there were in the person of the jester all sorts of extenuating circumstances for the queen not having previously perceived his beauty.

As soon as the queen was in love, she quit the golden balcony and went back into her boudoir, where she set about thinking very sadly. Sitting on her sculpted chair, on cushions of old silk, she made a few very beautiful and exceedingly weary gestures, and then headed for the mirror and the rice-powder. Convention satisfied, she sent for her maids of honor and went to look for the king. The halberdiers stood aside in the calm of the galleries and carpets, and in the doorways she brushed past, plaintive pages in white satin costumes burst into tears.

When she had made her request, in the most polite terms she could find, the king said: "Madame, it displeases our very courteous power to forbid you, being the queen, any whim or sensuality, no matter how sumptuous it might be—all the more so if it's simply a matter of my jester—but I have no wish to come down in the world in too brutal a fashion, and I require that the chosen one should render himself worthy, to the extent that is possible, of the great honor reserved for him by you. His education is very poor, his qualifications deplorable. From now on, I shall provide him with the best teachers. When he has become a veritable man of the world and a great savant, you can, without losing prestige, offer your imagination the violins and amorous feast that it desires."

The king's orders were immediately carried out. The queen could only comply. The best teachers were chosen. Tripetus learned fencing, Latin, gymnastics, Japanese and the piano. The director of protocol came every morning to show him how to display reverence and dictate to him the pretty speeches that he had to learn by heart. After that, to complete his education, he was sent to study rhetoric for a year at Louis-le-Grand.[10]

Then something curious happened. Tripetus, who concealed a beautiful soul beneath his coarse exterior, gradually acquired a taste for study. He became a serious man, a lover of logic and the rigorous sciences. As the queen, unknown to the

---

[10] The Lycée Louis-le-Grand is Paris is reputed to be one of the most demanding French secondary schools. Its alumni include Voltaire, the Marquis de Sade and Victor Hugo.

king, sent him a great deal of money, he bought books and philosophical instruments. In the meantime, it seemed that his original ugliness had disappeared. The books had made him pale; he had cut his hair and no longer made puns. So, when he had to return, cries of admiration rose up throughout the kingdom.

Coaches with large plumes emerged from the royal stables and turned majestically into the court of honor to go in search of him. All along the avenue whose paving-stones were outlined in grass, the people, dressed in their Sunday best, waved their hoods and extended their hands when the halberdiers opened the gala procession. Tripetus scarcely took the time to put on his court costume, and went to find the queen. During his absence, naturally, he had fallen in love.

He made her a very fine speech.

"This is no longer Tripetus," said the queen. "This man talks too well. He looks like a poet, with his pale face." Turning toward him, she said, sadly: "I'm unable to love you."

During Tripetus' absence, a new stable boy had been taken on at the palace. He was extremely stupid, but very robust. He was the one who accompanied the queen when she went riding in the forest.

As soon as the king saw Tripetus and heard about the queen's reply, he went to find her. He was very angry. "Madame," he said, "A queen must keep her promises. You have perjured yourself; therefore, you must die."

The people were immediately summoned, by a trumpet-blast, to the terrace of the royal palace. A scaffold was set up, draped in black velvet, around which torches in the hands of sad pages reddened the night, and the queen's head was cut off with a golden axe.

The executioner was very awkward. Never, in human memory, had a capital punishment taken place in the country. The newspapers took advantage of it to launch a violent attack on the government. The executioner's duties ceased, from that day on, to be a sinecure. What a fine opportunity to demand their suppression on the grounds that they were unnecessary!

Tripetus missed the queen terribly. His conduct, on the day of the funeral, was above reproach. He continually raised a fine lace handkerchief to his eyes, and pronounced a few very tactful words over the grave.

Then he handed in his resignation as jester, not wanting to remain in a city that had such sad memories for him. He went to reside in a neighboring country, where he began writing his memoirs. He lived in a comfortable old house with old oak furniture and antique porcelain on the walls. In a large room whose windows overlooked a large garden, Tripetus smoked a long Dutch pipe, and sighed as he gazed at a portrait of the queen set above the fireplace, which the king had kindly given him as a souvenir.

Nightmare

For Henri de Régnier[11]

The day went by slowly. Heavy clouds passed over the narrow street, darkening it at intervals, and the windows that Tiburce could see opposite his own were more mysterious than ever. He was familiar with the indefinable attraction of windows, those enigmatic lights open on the existence of the thousands of phantoms who respire around us.

What a haunting, to imagine all those animate forms moving around, all the way to the horizon, behind doors, walls and streets, with cries and gestures intersecting, calling out to one another, replying to one another, making the vast Earth into a supple mantle of humanity! And every one of those forms has its interior and intimate life, like ours but also different. An almost guilty curiosity directs the eyes of an observer toward the details of interiors perceived in the vicinity. The other life marks itself out in various arrangements. The corner of an item of furniture, a painting on a wall, a lamp on a table, all have stories to tell. The vague souls of objects retain the memory of presences and frictions. A silhouette passes through the bay of a window, or behind the closed pane. Slight concerns and preoccupations reveal themselves, sometimes ridiculous, sometimes suggestive of emotion, sometimes avowing that profound resignation that is the consciousness of objects, animals and the majority of human be-

---

[11] Henri de Régnier (1864-1936) was a regular at *Le Chat Noir*, where Lautrec presumably met him, and he became a leading light of the Symbolist Movement. He produced two collections of fantastic short stories somewhat akin to Lautrec's, *La Canne de jaspe* (1897) and *Histoires incertaines* (1919).

ings. Some, just like all the rest, after a few oscillations, remain motionless in the same place, and are never astonished. The succession of the minutes is, for them, an ordinary game.

Tiburce's mind, wandering, crossed the street and rose up as far as the balconies of the upper floors. In his imagination, he clung on to the narrow margins of balustrades, afraid of falling, with a real sensation of effort, and then of fingers losing their grip, of his body plunging to the pitiless pavement. Then, suddenly, breathing deeply, he found himself sitting in the low-ceilinged room, at ground level, with flat earth beneath his feet.

All the familiar objects, contemporaries of and witnesses to his bizarre life, seemed to be congratulating him for having escaped the danger.

It was a sensation analogous to that which one experiences in a dream, when one thinks one is falling from a height. In the dream, however, one always wakes up before hitting the ground, because, if the illusion went as far as that, the cerebral shock would be such that one would surely die. Many sudden inexplicable deaths during sleep are doubtless caused by mortal dreams that are not interrupted.

As a child, Tiburce had supposed that the uniform Earth did not extend limitlessly, and that one would arrive, somewhere, at the edge of the world. The concept if an immense globe, whose center was *down* and its entire circumference *up* did not enter his head, any more than it occurs to any being who is naïve, either by virtue of age of lack of culture. Cosmologies must still exist corresponding to that state of mind. Savage humans believe that the world is a vast round surface bounded by a circular ocean or the void. That is the science of Homer. Why not? We smile at these primitive concepts, but either progress is only a vain word—and which of our scientists would accept that hypothesis?—or they have to admit that, one day, their explanation of the universe, such as they understand it today, will seem as ingenuous and false as that of Ptolemy or the Hindus. Genuine discoveries inevitable transform other verities into errors and infantilize them. All forms disappear in their turn.

But this is the present form. In space, there is neither up nor down. Otherwise, what a fall at the edge of the world! We would be like Victor Hugo's Satan, eternally falling from the sky.[12] On the contrary, for anyone who knows the laws of attraction, is it not amusing to imagine, an undeniable fact, that the approach of a more voluminous star, emerging from the depths of the abyss at our zenith, might overturn natural laws, and the Earth, without having moved, might suddenly find itself *up*, with its streets upside-down and its roofs hanging down.

There are people who are carried away at birth by a fairy—perhaps wicked, but whose smile is persuasive—to be imprisoned in a palace of enchantments. What a mortal rose is thought! And what torments those whom its perfume intoxicates undergo! Their sentimentality, like their reflection, is exasperated by excessively numerous and overly various impacts. That astonishment of life, like a new wine, lasts for many years, sometimes a lifetime. And their intelligence is nothing but a flickering flame shielded from the wind in the hollow of the hand, which does not prevent them from bumping into a wall every three paces.

For there is no durable route. Every idea that one follows to its end arrives at absurdity and annihilation. Happy are the philosophers who suppose that problems are resolved by the declaration that there are no problems! Happier still are those who blithely accept antinomies with a light heart, and rejoice in the fact that one can affirm the opposite of everything—which proves that truths are numerous—and work tirelessly to

---

[12] This image is appropriated from Hugo's unfinished epic *La Fin de Satan*, begun in 1854. with which he became disenchanted after an excerpt was rejected by his publisher in 1857; he added more text at intervals, but probably thought that it had been superseded by *La Légende des siècles*; the existing text was published posthumously in 1888. Because Satan's fall is endless, the role of humankind's tempter is taken in the poem by Lilith.

construct the temple of their ignorance, sustained by columns that are alternately black and white, taking great hope from that diversity of color for the solidity of the edifice! Even happier, finally, are those who renounce inventing theories, and accommodate themselves to live in some appearance of truth that the crowd passes from hand to hand, like false coins whose circulation is hurried. It is necessary to accept life without interrogating it, and avoiding thought with jealous concern. Besides, what evidence is there that thought is not a disease of matter—like a pearl, in spite of its beauty?

Life can only subsist by grace of insouciance. It's a sort of conspiracy. The human race is like a traveler marching alongside a gulf into which he is forbidden to direct his eyes, on pain of being attracted by the depths. No more can he raise his gaze toward the starry sky above his head, for the slightest false step would be fatal. Pascal lived in that terror, equally anguished on the side of a bridge over the Seine and the brink of mathematical infinity. Thoughts, like gestures, refuse to lean over the edge of the top of the tower.

No one was more vulnerable to vertigo than Tiburce. It is one of those impressions to whose experience everyone is susceptible on occasion, like fear, but with a very different intensity. Some people cannot look down at the ground from a distance of a few meters without suffering it. Others climb up on scaffolding, or go to plant flags on the spires of cathedral, with perfect tranquility. The mere thought of such a height terrorized him. For a long time he had conjectured, with laudable modesty, that this infirmity was no more than a sign of an inaptitude for sublime ideas. His general dispositions were strongly down-to-earth. But he reflected one day that a slater working on a church steeple might have low ideas. Such reasoning reassured him. For him, it was an unmerited torture to lean out of a window. Just as one experiences an imperious desire to scratch an itchy wound, he leaned over, breathlessly, clinging to the railings, defying the formidable summons— without, however, ever forgetting, even once, mechanically to verify the solidity of the balcony of any apartment whatsoever.

The idea haunted him, if he chanced to sleep in an upstairs apartment, of waking up after a fit of somnambulism—no matter how improbable—lying in the street with his skull fractured, just conscious enough to know that he was doomed.

Curiously enough, that anxiety never tormented him in dreams. The association of ideas takes place mechanically there, without the control of reason. One skims over impressions, in perpetual flux. That vagabondage explains why the preoccupations of the day do not necessarily return during the night. The mind is weary of them, and does not persist. This is so true that it is sometimes sufficient, to expel a redoubtable image from slumber, to think about it before going to sleep. One might even suppose that the sensations which present themselves are complementary to those of the day. In the same way, when one studies a red disk for some time, it is a green circle that one sees when one closes one's eyes. Heavy people sometimes dream that they have wings. Tiburce's imagination, weary of vertigo, found an opposite torture in the nocturnal shadows. His nightmares involved believing himself to be buried alive in a grave. He was familiar with the futile effort of trying to lift a stone solidly positioned by a gravedigger's hands, and the terror of picturing the blue sky, the open air and birds singing to the Sun, from which one is separated for all eternity by the heavy black Earth. But space only tormented him in his hours of lucidity.

His everyday ideas reflected this preoccupation. The influence such visions had on his judgments and actions cannot be overestimated. A particular dread, which one cannot admit for fear of ridicule, can sometimes turn our existence in a definitive direction. Every one of us has one of these insignificant traits, of great importance to him alone, in his character. Tiburce did not hate traveling, but he usually stuck to the seaside. Mountains overwhelmed him with their mass if he stayed at their feet, and, on the other hand, he obviously dreaded climbing their slopes, with his procession of phantoms, even to inscribe his name, with patriotic pride, at the summit of

Gauri Sankar.[13] He would never go up in a balloon or an aeroplane. What madness to launch oneself on the conquest of the air! Humans are made to live on the ground and maintain the contact that gives them strength, like Antaeus. They will never be the equal of the birds, any more than deep-sea divers or transitory scuba-divers are really fish.

Literature and art furnish fuel for similar opinions. The Tarpeian Rock and the gulf into which the Spartans threw deformed infants were celebrated in his memory. He hung breathlessly with the archpriest[14] from the tower of Notre Dame, and saw the convulsed visage, the fingernails scraping the stone, the feet of the cadaver-to-be pulled down by an invisible and implacable force.

Is it not permissible to suppose, however, that a fall from a great height ought not to have the tragic horror that one apprehends therein? Everything that is exaggerated thins out or fades away. In all mortal things there is a semblance of death, which is only a shadow. Have not travelers, returned from some accident on a mountainside, recounted that they experienced an indefinable voluptuousness in feeling themselves floating in space? There is surely a mysterious appeal in the attraction that is the source of vertigo.

At any rate, that manner of dying has something seductive about it, as well as the familiar horror. There is a grandiosity in launching oneself majestically into eternity. The emperor Heliogabalus, a priest of the Sun, had a tower constructed with a base paved with precious stones, for the purpose of a pompous suicide. This supposes, in that Caesar, a conception of life and death that was scarcely banal, which ought to elevate him to the rank of hero. Everyone knows how an artless soldiery prevented him from realizing his dream by massacring him ignominiously, but one can imagine that the

---

[13] Gauri Sankar, a mountain in the Himalayas, was still unclimbed when Lautrec wrote this story, and remained so for many years thereafter.

[14] Claude Frollo, in Victor Hugo's *Notre-Dame de Paris*.

gems and enamels, cleverly arranged in a mosaic, might have depicted in advance the traces of actual blood with which they were to be splattered.

It is the most elegant death, the prompt return to the earth from which humans have emerged. But the moderns have forsaken the ancient gesture. Tradition has done away with it. Such forgetfulness can only be explained by the ever-increasing ignorance of propriety and natural law. No one knows any longer how to make an exit. Suicides from the tops of towers displease the people down below. Scarcely once a year does some unfortunate conservationist leap from the top of the Arc de Triomphe—and the purity of the act is always spoiled by some sort of patriotic memory. Provincial notaries climb the steps thinking about Napoleon and salute their last sunrise like that of Waterloo. All men of taste experience embarrassment in the face of that circumstance—a slight but painful sense of the ridiculous.

For it is necessary not to profane rites. The fear of the abyss, and the fatal desire to fall into it, surely have a profound origin. The law of attraction governs the entire realm of matter. The corresponding phenomenon in the spiritual world is love. It is the most mysterious and the most universal of all laws.

The same reasoning lends an appearance of justice to the custom of burying the dead. The pyre is only a simulacrum. Smoke does not escape gravity. Barbaric and deprived of logic are the tribes in which cadavers are exposed in the branches of trees or near the nests of vultures. It is true that in future the branches will be transformed into humus and that the vultures will cherish the ditch after their death, but burial respects the return more promptly, and allows readier comprehension of the unimportance of the individual. Humans return to the earth, as the waves, having briefly surged forth, fall back into the oceans. And the whole is Nirvana.

After a day of wandering metaphysical pathways, Tiburce went to bed, with the hope of following his visions o the extreme. Besides, it was only in sleep that he felt that he was in full possession of his imaginative faculty. Night is favorable to the appearance of astral forms, the advent of messengers send by the Beyond. It would also favor the blooming of unusual flowers. Certain of seeing interesting things, he enveloped his head in the white woolen fabric propitious to evocations.

Jupiter's priests wore woolen bonnets, subsequently reduced a plume of the same substance, which no longer had a symbolic meaning, although people symbolically put their cloaks over their heads to devote themselves to meditation. Jupiter's priests conserved the sacred fire in his house. Tiburce knew that the sacred fire was shielded by a veil, and that thought, too, is a fragile flame that needs to be protected, and prevented from dispersal by any wind. Besides, the most recent scientific discoveries permit the brain to be seen as a real source of energy, which is manifest externally, in certain conditions, in phenomena of light and heat.

He had a dream.

In the aftermath of some fall, or some departure from life, his soul and body found themselves in the inferior land—which is to say, the caverns that the vulgar populate with gnomes, guardians of subterranean treasures. It might be that the heavens—or, at least, what we mean by that name, the goal of our aspirations—are, in reality, below us. That hypothesis would favor the adoration of fire, since the nearest fire, that which might naturally be our guide toward the distant, is situated by geologists in the center of our globe, of which it is the heart. One might also consider successive humankinds, living one on top of one another, becoming more perfect as they occupy inner circles, in an opposite fashion of Dante's Inferno, the diminution of the spheres as they approach the material annihilation of the nucleus being no obstacle to their existence. One admits that it is at the summit—the place where the lines vanish—that a pyramid, for example, has its full reality.

At what depth the region lay to which the sleeper found himself transported, he was never able to ascertain, having had neither the sensation of departure nor of travelling. Or perhaps he had forgotten the passage from exterior life to that one. Already, though, the space had become, in one sense, excessively limited. That habitable world was all breadth, like the galleries that miners hollow out in coal, whose height is measured by that of a man. But roads, in places, headed toward distant dwellings, forming crushed crossroads. Here and there, on the walls, metal lamps were fixed, whose indistinct light illuminated a few meters of the road. And from black cavities in the walls, whose darker patches could be vaguely made out, murmurous speech emerged, as if the people of that realm were hidden in houses or feat of a dubious daylight. Those houses had to be like tombs, and the life led therein, bleak and dismal as it undoubtedly is beneath the sunlit surface, that of the interred dead.

At any rate, the dreamer experienced, as soon as he took his first steps, a singular impression of deliverance and security. His diurnal dreads were abolished, and the emotion that he felt, having arrived in this unusual situation, had nothing in common with his habitual haunting. Immured in a catacomb vaster and more definitive than the hypogea of Egypt, he might be apprehensive of everything, but he no longer had any fear of falling, having the ground above him. And the protective earth surrounded him solidly—except that sometimes, raising his head in certain passages, he was surprised and disturbed, as if by an inverse vertigo. Large gaping openings, as if carved by blows of a pick-axe or produced by an explosive charge, appeared in the ceiling of the gallery. Given their irregular form, one might have thought of them as abandoned inverted quarries. They plunged upwards through the black rock for several meters, but had no exits, and one sensed all the thickness of the ground weighing down upon them.

A funereal bird, flying toward that illusion of space, fell back after three wingbeats, having touched the depths of the hollow. They were doubtless the remains and marks of puerile attempts to reach the Beyond, empty monuments to Icaruses who had tried in vain to flee. The sole remaining results of these efforts were the heaps of debris on the floor of these passages, needlessly obstructing the route.

But the road became easier as he became accustomed to it. It possessed an insensible slope, and he understood that, instead of a regular circumference, the discovered land must follow a spiral toward the nucleus. The law of progress was verified in this world as in others. Those descended from the exterior experienced a greater lightness at every step, the slow and continual realization of equilibrium, and ought to walk toward the declining horizon as towards a deliverance from imperious gravity. Always getting closer, they were circling their ideal. What did it matter if the road became narrower with distance and they had to bow their heads to cross the threshold of mystery? They would soon stand up again, in the unreal country, with their freedom from the weighty laws of the exterior world complete.

His attention was attracted as he went by lights other than those of lamps, moving around in the depths of the darkness. One might have taken them for hand-held torches. The inhabitants of the subterranean region were doubtless running away, alarmed by his approach, as people would be at the sight of a celestial monster descended to our world. No more noises could be heard behind the walls, save for that of hushed breathing. The audacity of the explorer did not go so far as to lean his head or extend his arm through the black openings of the windows. What shadowy hand might have reached out to seize his own?

But he went on, insensible to the threat of such an adventure—or, rather, so profoundly lunged in an ocean of fear that all his senses were submerged by it. At crossroads, he perceived altars hollowed out in the walls, around which more lamps burned. His curiosity was solicited by the form of the idols, but the cavities were sealed by close-knit grilles, and the depths of the retreats seemed too distant for anyone to be able to make out what was there. His eyes were barely caressed by a vague glint of gold on the folds of some vestment. He did not know, and never found out subsequently, what Hecate these infernal people worshipped.

He was undoubtedly going through a city. Other familiar images denounced the presence of a human race. Partly burned logs, beside a boundary-marker, revealed a recent fire. Besides, sad coronets of flowers posed on silent thresholds allowed the supposition of a lugubrious celebration, or perhaps marked the door of some tomb within the tomb.

And there was the sensation of walking more rapidly at every step. The slope had increased and the ground was falling away—without, however, giving any other impression than that of still being equally safe.

But the silence was disturbed. The traveler perceived a sort of murmur issuing from a distant gallery. He cocked an ear. Was he about to hear the voices and know the language of the dead at last? The noise gradually increased. A cry went up, which became several. The darkness was tinted with a diffuse light. And as the road opened into another, broader one, the seer, recoiling instinctively, barely had time to take refuge in a shadowy corner. A crowd was moving past him, so close that he could have touched their garments. By the light of a hundred torches, uttering moans, a disorderly troop of lugubrious men and women, the inhabitants of the black region, went by.

There were all those that a fatal attraction, or some intolerable despair, had precipitated into death. There were all those who had fallen from houses, towers, tall trees or the tops of sea-cliffs. Old men and children, supported on crutches, let their twisted limbs hang down. With a sinister pride, the heroes of the air went by, vain Titans rejected by the heavens. Wretches with broken spines, folded in two, had the ridiculous attitude of disjointed puppets. There were all those who, wandering through the countryside on moonless nights, had not seen the black holes open before their feet and had suddenly stepped into the void. Heads were swathed in bandages through which blood had oozed in large stains—for it is on the head that the unfortunate fall, and a man summoned by the

63

abyss turns over to touch the earth in accordance with his center of gravity.

As the funeral procession unwound, terrified faces were visible in the light of the flickering torches. Thin and convulsive lips retained the heroism of the supreme resolution. Sad mothers passed by, their hair sparse, clutching tatters of bruised flesh to their hearts: they children with whom they had leapt from the top of the walls on the day that a city was captured, after having hidden them, to conceal the sight of death from them, in the folds of their cloaks. And all the madmen, all the inventors, all the Icaruses, vain challengers of vertigo, went along the corridor toward the objective toward which they had launches their first prodigious leaps. And the fearful canticle that rose up from the crowd was compounded out of every single scream, howl of joy or wail of distress uttered by each of them as they fell.

The sleeper uttered a cry of anguish himself, then— which woke him up, and whose prolongation he heard in the darkness, even after having emerged from the tragic shadows of sleep. The vibrant sensation perpetuated itself. He heaved an ample and profound sigh, and found himself back in his bed, seeing once more amid the vague flowers of the tapestry, in the glimmer of the night-light, arms and crippled bodies, heads burst open like ripe pomegranates. Then his fever calmed down. An immense lassitude overwhelmed him—and gradually, he fell back into unconsciousness, and the dream.

It was a different vision.

It seemed to him that he was sitting in the middle of a high-ceilinged room, whose walls were as white as chalk. There was no trace of any other furniture than the chair he was occupying. As the light penetrated broadly through an opening in the wall in front of him, he conjectured that he was on the uppermost floor. It had to be a house similar to those one finds in the centers of populous cities, with a stone ledge running along the façade, and window-panes in the wall that rose up, mansard-fashion, toward the roof And the winter months had surely come, for the light that designed a pale square on the

64

floor was descending from the cold Moon. In spite of the silence and the solitude, the seer knew that, all around him, other lives were hidden behind the facades, in the shadow of bleak chimneys, near balconies with iron bars.

How long had he been there, and for what purpose? He did not know, as one does not know, in dreams, the most logical things, and does not even wonder. But his heart was heavy and his soul was tormented by an indefinable anxiety. The distant corners of the room were lost in obscurity; all the tragic and future interest of the situation was concentrated in the middle, in the square of light in which the chair was set. And on the other side of the narrow street, separated from him by the abyss, he saw a window in the house opposite that appeared to be the mirror image of the one placed in front of him.

Suddenly, the window opposite opened, and a form appeared. It was a woman dressed in black. The folds of her dress descended harmoniously to the floor. She must have been beautiful, but the charm of her face had vanished. Nothing was legible in her features but an expression of slight anxiety and solemn resolution. Her lips moved, as if to pronounce a few mysterious formulae in a low voice. She stood up straight on the façade, her eyes raised and lost, her feet level with the window. Then she opened her arms crucifix-fashion, leaned forward in a regular curve, and let herself fall.

The seer started in alarm and, reproaching himself for his nonchalant stupor, ran to the door and downstairs. Never had steps seemed so numerous. He had the impression of passing an infinite number of floors. Finally, he was on the tiles of the ground floor, but could not get out. The corridor was crowded with all the inhabitants of the house, who had already come down, and the threshold as obstructed by a pack of curiosity-seekers, who had the same somber and ecstatic expression. Exclamations and satisfied sighs were audible on all sides. The sound of ringing bells was audible in the distance, which might as easily have been a festival carillon as a knell. It was permissible to conjecture, judging by the conversations, that a noble and ritual act had just been accomplished.

The witness of this strange scene finally succeeded in pushing his way through the groups, and when the crowd had dispersed somewhat, the view of the street revealed forms in pious attitudes, all heading in the same direction. They seemed to be following a cortege whose prayers could still be heard, borne by gusts of wind, and the torches of which were snaking away into the darkness. A few meters away, veiled women, tearing off their veils, were collecting the blood from a large pool that was reddening the ground, with respectful gestures.

And the sleeper finally woke completely, upset by the images that had been set before his eyes.

He searched for a logical connection between the two scenes that had appeared. Was not the second, by virtue of a mysterious inversion, the prelude and antecedent of the other? That woman had adored vertigo, and had doubtless already joined the lugubrious procession of the interior world. She was marching, as her shade, toward the gravity-less center.

And the idea came to him of a future religion, with simple and terrible ceremonies. Science has followed religion. Why not suppose, on the contrary, a religion born from science? Has the theory of universal attraction not beauty enough to be deified, while waiting for a new progress of human thought to overturn the theory and find another formula for the universe? In the meantime, might it not count its martyrs and its fanatics? And doubtless, one day, women will be seen, adorned for sacrifice, precipitated by the hands of priests, from the height of temples and towers, toward the subterranean Moloch.

Is not death divine, and is it not the only way to go toward God? It is from death that life is born, in a perpetual exchange. The bloodstream and a flame are tireless in their movement. The creative power destroys forms and renews them; it separates in order to reunite. It is necessary to draw away from the heart of the world incessantly, in order to return thereto.

Sunlight came into the room, dispersing nocturnal fears. Tiburce remained laying there, his head on his pillow. A ray of light fell upon a red wall-hanging facing the bed, and brought out the color. He remembered the lugubrious procession and the pool of blood in front of the house of death.

And he knew that life is red.

Fragment of a Tale of the Future

It was one of those visions that it is necessary to write down as soon as one emerges from a dream, at the risk of being unable to recover, on re-reading the story, anything but unintelligible babble.

Certain phrases, in sleep, seem admirable and definitive. We are in haste to recover our entire consciousness in order to note down those absolute expressions—but as we emerge on to the surface of the sea of dreams, into the atmosphere of normality, the phrase with such a clear and beautiful meaning is transformed, without any of its syllables changing, into a sequence of incoherent words whose ensemble is nothing but absurdity. It remains to know at which moment we are right. But past misfortune ought not to deflect us from that concern, for it is not always thus, in particular when it is a matter of a dream of some importance. Dreams were prophetic in Antiquity. They still are today. Once the harvest is in, one still has to separate and throw away the weeds. In the net that the fisherman brings up from the depths of mysterious abysses, in the midst of algae and debris, shines a beautiful fish with golden scales.

My mind was subject at that moment to the influence of some reading. On the previous days, I had plunged with ardor and conviction into the study of paleontology. I have always had a penchant for that science; it is poetic. There is nothing certain and positive in it; it is an ingenious creation.

It seems that, in my sleep, I ought to have reviewed herds of plesiosaurs grazing in the shades of giant ferns, or a prehistoric man armed with a heavy club battling a cave-bear—but it was the opposite phenomenon that was manifest. My imagination, doubtless to rest from its repeated voyages into the past, transported me into the future.

I found myself living in the midst of a distant human-kind, in an era that it is impossible to specify. An indefinable presentiment, however, informed me that the epoch in question could not be less distant from ours than a thousand times a thousand years. It was one of those absurd notions that one perceives in dreams, and which one accepts without thinking of disputing them.

I gave no more thought to wondering how I had been introduced into that strange new world. It happened without any usual or familiar delay, and I doubtless passed days, months, years among those future humans.

The houses where they spent their lives did not appear to me much different from those of the present day. I only noticed an exclusive predominance of curved lines; one searched in vain to find a corner. Those with walls were rounded. According to what I was able to understand of scientific principles, all geometry stemmed from the circle, the ellipse and analogous figures. It was absolutely impossible, in the course of my conversations with the scientists, to give them the slightest idea of the triangle. Still less was I understood when I tried to propose the religious formula of the same concept, with the initial point, the father, from which one can only trace one line to arrive at the opposite point, the unique son, and the last, which one can attain by departing from either one: the third element of the trinity—which, in our apostolic symbol, proceeds from the father and the son. For they had no longer had any idea of religion. I could only make them understand the term in the etymological sense, that of bondage, and very imperfectly at that. One single word, already archaic, represented all analogous concepts in their language: chain, constraint, hindrance, shackle, narrow-mindedness. Their vocabulary, from certain points of view, was very restricted.

Even the gestures of these people had something circular about them. Their manners were courteous and their speech unctuous. The animal is hidden infinitely better in them than in us. In addition, they speak very little. The long habit of living enables them to understand one another by implication.

69

The form of their bodies is little different from the ancient—or, rather, it is the same form perfected. The eyes, nose and mouth, ideal in their design, are disposed as they are today. There is only one detail, albeit a very important one, in the ensemble of the face that is in absolute contradiction to the present arrangement. To get some idea of it, imagine, for example the mouth in the place where our eyes are, or something similar. It's forbidden for me to say more. A sentiment analogous, in its imperious character, to what we presently call modesty, although it is completely different, absolutely prohibits making the slightest allusion to that physical disposition. And I would be too afraid, if I broke the sacred silence, of finding myself once again in the midst of that future humankind in a dream, and being subject to the horrors of the most terrible death, in expiation of the unforgivable sin.

However, I appeared, in spite of my rapid adaptation, to be something of a foreigner, and a foreigner of distinction. There was no celebration that was not put on for me. I was present at numerous ceremonial dinners. In this respect I fear that my description my description lacks originality, but our dreams, even the strangest, borrow their elements from terrestrial experience, and I must have remembered the attempts made in our day to reduce nourishment to its minimum volume. Scientists have thought that the substantial elements might be isolated and presented in a chemical form. Nitrogen, carbon, hydrogen are assimilable other than in cumbersome compounds.

The progress still has not been realized in our day that will permit a month's rations for a campaigning army to be carried in a small box. The problem is complicated by the fact that it is insufficient to nourish the body, but still necessary to furnish a mass sufficient to the muscular and other work of the digestive organs, until the organs have been modified by adaptation in the desired direction. It is not astonishing, however, that in my dream I saw meals served on minuscule saucers, in which the most redoubtable appetite was satisfied by a pill the size of a small pea.

Snobbery, moreover, had not lost all its influence. Certain guests, to give proof of refined habits, affected to nourish themselves on ridiculously small pills. I saw some of them searching their plates for invisible aliments with the tip of a needle, under a microscope. The interest afforded to them seemed to me to be analogous to the esteem in which we hold expert gourmets.

It is now necessary that I say something about the manner in which these people were breathing. On my appearance among them, it seemed to me that I was waking up with the sensation of an inexpressible malaise. I opened my eyes and found myself lying on the edge of a sidewalk. A circle of curious individuals surrounded me, while one man with a serious expression leaned toward me and held under my nose a translucent blue tablet whose strong odor reanimated me. When I had recovered my senses, he urged me, by means of gestures, to keep the tablet under my nose. I found out later that it was solidified air, and that it was breathed by emanation.

For a long time, in fact, all—or almost all—of the oxygen had disappeared from the air. We complain that, in our cities, air and space are in short supply, and that it is almost necessary to pay to breathe, as we do to eat. But here, that was not a joke; air was purchased, literally. It was impossible for me to find out whether that suppression of oxygen was caused by human action or a natural phenomenon. I saw the blue-tinted translucent tablets that were on sale in shops, but I did not have the leisure to ascertain whether they came from factories or mines. Perhaps industrialists had monopolized the fluid, and had condensed it by means of powerful machines. Perhaps the transformation had been produced spontaneously, in consequence of the passage of time, and the compacted air, taking refuge in the bosom of the Earth, had slowly solidified, as primitive vegetables did to form coal. I could not resolve the problem, or did not pay attention to it.

Evidently, in such conditions, one would not expect to breathe several times a minute, as we do without even noticing. Whales breathe at long intervals, however, and they are

71

animals with lungs like us. A slow education—an adaptation, to put it more accurately—had led these humans to use air as we deal with food. Their bodies were accommodated to the necessity. From time to time, one saw people take out their tablets and take several deep breaths. I think, too, that the air in question, composed of almost pure oxygen, was more vivifying, and that it was less necessary to multiply aspirations.

The usage of air having become similar to that of food, one bought the tablets as one bought bread. There were shops in the street. The price of air varied according to supply and demand. If it rose too high, the people rebelled. Fat men with ruddy faces were breathing beautiful blue tablets insolently, with full noses and full mouths, while poor devils were wearing themselves out on a meager debris of dirty and dusty air that they had picked up in the gutter, or pausing beside passers-by and timidly asking for alms. Some of them had not breathed for three days.

As the vivifying atmosphere had been suppressed, another had replaced it, and that simple transposition had permitted the problem of aerial navigation to be solved. An exceedingly dense layer of neutral gas extended upwards for hundreds of miles and encircled the globe. Scientists had long ago found a formula for its unlimited manufacture. With medium-sized wings, people flew effortlessly. From the first day, after a brief apprenticeship, I had the impression not of flying but of swimming, but without any dread of being submerged. Soon, I no longer had any anxiety, and was able to deliver myself entirely to the joy of floating freely above the imperious ground, which had once retained me with its leaden hands.

That joy was superhuman. It is only in dreams that we have the illusion of flying, and yet, very often, that flight is nothing but an undulatory skimming, a few meters above the ground. With one bound, though, as one jumps a stream, I launched myself over monuments and hills, far from the abruptly vanished ground. I no longer felt the weight of my body. Certain intoxications, it's said—that of ether, for example—procure that sensation of deliverance, but here I was plunged into the ether.

And how light life, in its entirety, had become! People no longer set off on journeys in heavy earthbound machines, but flew. No more roads, no more rails and customs posts, but svelte apparitions gliding through space with as little fear of collision as the stars in the sky. In terms of movement, it was the conquest of the third dimension.

On fine nights, one saw lovers taking flight together, to the top of a tower or a hill, their wings blanching in the moonlight. Sometimes, two light forms, carried away by their intoxication, would rose so high into the air that they never came down again.

The wings were taken from a particular kind of bird that was bred for that purpose. It was a strongly-built species with large vigorous wings, doubtless obtained by cross-breeding. When they were fully grown, their wings were amputated for adaptation to the human body. Children were taught to fly, as they were taught to walk. All of them received wings when they were strong enough.

In addition, by virtue of hereditary adaptation, their arms had gradually acquired a prodigious force and development. It was hoped that children would one day be born with wings.

For a long time, people had been aware of the superiority of birds relative to us, of which we can only have an incomplete knowledge at present. Their dwelling is the upper sphere, and those we see only form a minority. We have no right to judge their totality by the rare individuals that descend as far as us, any more than fish can form an idea of what we might be on the basis of divers and the drowned. Their race is more perfect than ours, for it is more evolved. They are unacquainted with heavy labor and the deformity of pregnancy. They are borne from a solitary egg, like the world in ancient cosmogonies.

The conquest of the air has not been without difficulties. I was told about the terrible wars to which that rivalry had given rise. But our species had triumphed over others once more. As the breathable air disappeared, plumed cadavers covered the ground in greater numbers, to the extent that nothing any longer remained of turtle-doves and vultures, nor of forms never previously observed that were seen to descend successively from the more-or-less distant heights at which their lungs exploded. Apocalyptic monsters spiraled down to land at the feet of terrified crowds. One day, there were no longer any but the single species retained for the use of its wings, the choice of which had been determined by its robust form.

These things were told to me while I floated voluptuously above that strange world. A city unrolled beneath my eyes. I saw terraces from which wings were fleeing. I had passed over the white terraces when I perceived some sort of broad, deep ditch between high walls, near the city gates. There were black masses in the depths of the ditch, agitating in vain leaps, as if permanently crippled. Among them, in the dust and ordure, lay fragments of air over which the creatures were fighting voraciously.

And I recognized, with an anguish and a sudden pity, by their amputated stumps, the mutilated bodies of the birds from whom human wings were borrowed...

The Wall

For Albert Lenoir[15]

From all memory, that humankind had sheltered itself under tents, as under an external vestment. They were afraid of the infinity that surrounded them, and wanted to hide from its eyes. Their initial dwellings were made of fragile canvas which the desert sand, arriving from the depths of the horizon, passed over untiringly. The shepherds of the origin had planted in the ground the curved staffs with which, while on the move, they directed their herds; their cloaks, placed over that naïve frame and falling to either side, formed the walls behind which they sheltered the mystery of their lives. The wind that penetrated through the oblique cracks caused the fire set in the center, on two black stones, to flare up. The family grouped around it, and created itself.

Humans already, when they had found shelter, they regretted the sight of leaves and clouds, and the animals that had once lived with them they saw hasten toward the mountains or the variegated plain. To distract themselves, they decorated the interior of their abode with strewn green branches. The feathers of birds and skins of beasts were extended over the walls. When, later, art was born, the deception of objects was imitated by painters. The most sumptuous tapestry evoked the faint memory, effaced from the wall, of the tree-branches that had been scattered in indeterminate times inside human dwellings to perpetuate for the eyes, indoors, the landscape beyond. And the same symbolism was realized in the monuments whose construction was made possible by the science of later ages. Humankind had multiplied. Encounters of genius had

---

[15] Albert Lenoir (1801-1891) was a famous architect.

75

presented future ideas to the gazes of sages. The soul of humankind had grown with the dwellings of humankind. From one side of the globe to the other, thoughts and sensations flow on wings of fire. A vast city was born of scattered cities. There was no more open country, and the proud mountains had bowed down, but a universal city, crossing the torrents and the deserts, slowly sowed its columns and palaces over the planet.

The walls of those palaces loomed up within the city, and glistened in the grandiose exterior, as if silently slumbering. In the immutable sky, they followed horizontal lines that clouds of the same light whiteness continued as they pass by, in slowly metamorphosing vaults. People sitting on terraces, modeled on the form of those spirals, talked about the future. There were priests at the crossroads, with thorny staffs in their hands and tortuous jewels round their necks, who sang psalms when anyone passed by. Their black patches were picturesque at the feet of the wall. Springs ran between two walls, and another was visible in a subterranean passage, with peaks whose reflection in the water was tremulous. And that whiteness, which, seen from afar, gave the city the grandiose appearance of a gigantic battlefield where armies of dead gods had left their ivory bones, was covered on the inside by paintings in the latest hues—the spectrum of the colors continues beyond violet and beyond red. There really was, on the edge of their dwellings, a kind a duplicate of their real life, less profound but more vain, which they loved for its silence and its durability.

Those who, in ancient times, retained the childhood which, in the hearts of some, even in old age, never dies, lived almost from then on the mute life of images that never breathed. One saw adolescents smitten with a painted muse, and poets celebrate rhythmically, with new chords, chimeras whose name, not even an image, was traced on the fronts of sanctuaries. Who can say where death ends or life begins? If He who made all things created beings with a conscience—or, at least, believing in the possession of a conscience as fugitive as a flash of color or the echo of a sound, why would he refuse it to creatures more imperfect than human beings? Is not life similar to the ruby liquor that everyone carries in his cupped hands, a single drop of which, falling on the ground, is sufficient to bring forth a flower of life? The awkward figure that we draw on the paper takes on a personality. It has a soul, as tenuous as the form is imperfect, whose sensations are rare. But a masterpiece is already breathing. Such an image of a saint, with her hands upraised, is thinking about the lost paradise. She has only one single gesture, her thought is eternal and simple; it is an existence without depth, but endowed with a profound charm. Have we not, for hours on end, during those nights scarcely blurred by the nightlight, with staring eyes, contemplated the banal flowers of tapestries, in which the demon of images made us see fantastic and implausible forms apparently emerging from the wall? And the stone monsters that project from towers in ogives, like the laughter of the monument, do you think that they do not have souls, by dint of being contemplated, from the street-corners, by the crowds that raise their heads on Sundays and holidays toward the bell-tower? But they have no thought of anything but the rain, the Sun and the wind, and no visions but those of birds passing through the air in front of them, uttering shrill cries. Every word pronounced and every line drawn has a soul that follows them, like fearful shadows following the golden staff along the edge of the black Erebus.[16] Life is everywhere; everyone sows forms and sounds in space. And when a man has gone mad for having dreamed too much of his work, it is because his soul has abandoned him in order to animate the work he has created. An unfaithful mistress, vaingloriously delighted with the beautiful château that the king has built for her, abandons the man who loves her to imprison herself in its golden gates.

Nothing dies. The infinite circulates through finite things And that people had had the divine sense to multiply the forms

---

[16] The reference is to an episode in the *Odyssey* where Teiresias carries a golden staff while serving as a guide in the Underworld.

of existence around itself. In its dwellings, beside paintings in which mounted armored warriors rose up in forceful colors, light frescoes were to be seen reminiscent of virgins in transparent tunics. Expanses of lifeless gold covered the space between two doorways with porphyry columns; the mat gold was interrupted by pale heads, hands bearing theorbos. Processions of dancers wound along the halls. In temples, bare and divine, the objects of worship were represented on the walls. The only real thing, in the middle of the sanctuary, was a cup of some unknown metal, on a heavy ebony table.

Those temples were numerous, and marble columns bordered them, having around them, at human height, liters of black cloth on which the symbols of immortality were inscribed in silver lines. Between the columns passed the silent movement of the people. Mouths pronounced magic words. At the back of the temple was a wall, extending from the ground to the vault and from one wing to the other. It loomed up in the distance like some vast empty page.

The religion of the people was similar to that wall. They dared not find there the face of a limited god. The painters who evoked the adored image, with a pious brush, on the backs of decorated choir-stalls, were deceived many times over! Their illuminated idols had not lasted. Every thousand years, someone came, and his hand, steeped in errant streams, wiped the image from the wall. But the same traveler, in the same place, established the face of another god.

Many of these temples were on the shore of the sea, and yet surrounded by gardens with living hedges where the mysteries had to be performed. On evenings when the leaves were agitated and marvelous insomniac nights, sighs and sobs were heard. Priestesses with lamps passed along distant pathways. Servants went in great haste to find harps and flutes carved in the docile black wood. The wind carried the odor of myrrh toward the sea, like a light homage. The sea was out there, a broad breath: the monotonous sea, over which the low clouds erected vain monuments.

On the side opposite the sea, the city extended. It went toward the great curved line and climbed the mountains, putting clusters of humankind on the flanks. A crowd gesticulated in the streets; raised arms were seen and a few cries heard. Windows opened on the supple air. The silence of that superhuman city made a clamor in infinity, and stray birds fell, dead of fright, when their wings merely brushed the iron doors with heavy knockers. The open country where they had been able to fly free, amid the murmur of leaves, was disappearing by the day. The Earth, that living being, felt itself being gradually devoured by a marble leprosy. And the isolated dwellings were markers placed along the road pointing to the horizon; thus, the first houses, in the country, in the approaches to our cities, advance sparsely to meet the traveler, to give him a good welcome, before the crowd of serried roofs.

They arrived at the edge of the world, beyond which there was no more land before the fall into the void. And the sky appeared from top to bottom. Life and humankind had reached their final limit. Guided by the human folly that is to enclose oneself incessantly and search childishly on the canvas of the narrow tent for the reflection of the immensity, instead of reaching out with widespread arms toward that very immensity, they had the vain idea of building the ultimate enclosing wall on the edge of the abyss, where some divine child might, in the course of some idle stroll, trace his name awkwardly with a stump of charcoal. That wall would summarize the effort. It was like the obscure barrier that the men of times past had imagined on the horizon of space, when they had not yet discovered that space is infinite. Blocks of stone and iron were brought. A powerful will lifted up the heavy loads. In olden times, the energy of magicians was manifest in musical speech; a single gesture made everything move. Beneath the Sun and the shivering rain, slaves bent their weary backs. Generations disappeared, exhausted like the tribes of the Hebrews. And the wall was harmoniously reminiscent of the monuments of ancient Egypt. Humankind, emerged from the cradle by virtue of a divination, had placed the pyramids in the center of the known world. Now, in the dusk, an immense wall followed the curvature of the horizon, distanced from the center according to the rite of the ripples made by a stone thrown into water.

The Sun rose behind the wall, and all day long its sad eye wandered successively over the city. In the evening, it sank toward the sea, where its red globe was deformed, a torch dropped from a hand and stamped out on the ground. The sharp gables of the dwellings still retained a gilding of light at their summit. Down below, in the inextricable streets, the crowd was already moving in darkness. At that tragic moment before nightfall, the entire city was silhouetted in infernal lines on the posthumous whiteness of the wall. Then, the people who had lifted up the marble blocks with their hands and their breathless breasts, and had arranged them toward the firmament, reassembled on the edge of the city and began to moan. Their convulsive hands veiled their eyes. Regret, that bleak god, was born in their hearts. Confronted by the lofty work, they had just remembered the little wall of dry stones that a Galilean goat could jump over, covered in vines and ivy, which had once enclosed the domain of their puerile happiness.

On the highest platform was a chapel consecrated to Herostratus.[17] The priests who succeeded one another, as in all ages, before the fire—the lamp of the Catholic church or the Latin torch of the vestals—received prayers, incense and gold from the hands of the crowd, wandering on worn-out knees. The only arched window in the smooth walls of the temple was an open red eye. People spent their days lying on platforms, in varied attitudes, voicing the same anxiety. They had taken cloaks, and the women, at dawn, did not forget their

---

[17] Herostratus burned down a temple of Artemis, claiming that he did so in order to immortalize his name. His judges attempted to frustrate his ambition by forbidding further mention of his name, but it leaked into histories anyway. He thus became a symbolic figurehead of the cult of celebrity: someone famous for doing something stupid and wicked in order to become famous.

puerile cares in front of a mirror, until the day when one of them thought she could make out, like the advent of space, a slight shadow on her mirror. What grim and vagabond god had tarnished it with his breathing mouth? The priests revived the hot coals beneath the myrrh. When the crepuscular mantle fell, all the people got to their feet with a slightly weary final effort. But suddenly, from incalculable depths, like another great white page, an unreal wall loomed up in the clouds.

Vain were the measured cries of the priests, vain the supplications of the amazed crowd. After the vision, nothing else happened—just the grey smoke of bowls of perfume and pyres passing, unsuspected, over the empty screen. The pale enigma lasted until daybreak. Toward dawn, it faded away, and the people, their hearts henceforth alone forever, slowly made their way back to the city. Human sadness respired. Mystery, once more, had had faithfully kept the promise previously made, and the future god remained future. For one could not accept, if not with smiles, in the midst of universal doubt, the tale of an adolescent lost in the crowd, troubled by the memory of the beautiful legends with which, instead of coarse stories, the light sleep of infants was lulled. He claimed to have perceived on the wall, in the interval of a musical note, the form of a motionless female in a veil with numerous folds, who bore on her veil, on the forehead, the well-know seal of eternity.

The Three Companions

For Georges Geiger[18]

They were three poor partisans who were coming back from the Spanish wars—in the year one thousand and some, to be precise. They had lost the main body of the army, one day when they had been delayed in a tavern in Estremadura, and had never found it again. And since then, they had been travelling in easy stages, without a sou, living by plunder, and very poorly at that. By night they bedded down in the woods when they did not have the good fortune to find hospitality in some peasant's dwelling—but that latter stroke of luck was rare, for the country had been ruined by the war, and the government was dragging its feet in order to pay indemnities and replace the clepsydras, or water-clocks, which the enemy, following its age-old habit, had carried off as it left. Also, the land-owners looked at men-at-arms with a bleak and mistrustful eye.

So, the three poor devils, who were four with the one that they had in their purse, wandered in a melancholy fashion along the roads of Spain, with miserable armor on their backs, which no longer comprised anything but a few threads and a dented helmet on the head. And they sighed, their belies empty, as they thought about the rich land of Flanders, of which they were natives. Thanks to their godfathers, who had a literary bent, they were named Amador, Mathurin and Gaetan.

---

[18] Georges Geiger was a friend of Lautrec's who had some small reputation as a humorous writer; he might or might not have been the same person as a similarly-named physician from Ulm who published several medical treatises in the early decades of the 20th century.

One evening, when the day had been more painful than usual, twenty-four hours of hunger having followed twenty-four hours of hunger, the worthy fellows, exhausted, found themselves on the edge of a wood in the mot desolate and sinister landscape that they had ever encountered. There were no other habitations in view but a miserable hut made of branches and mud, hidden among the trees. What a sudden joy there was, however, in seeing that the hut was surmounted by a chimney, and that smoke was escaping from that chimney! *There's no smoke without fire*, our three companions said to themselves, rendered subtle by starvation. *And fire sometimes accompanies a saucepan hiding some sort of precious stew.* When one is truly hungry, there is no better roast.

Just as the famished bellies, devoid of ears, were already opening wide eyes on a hypothetical feast, however, the door of the hut also opened abruptly, and out of it, howling and gesticulating, came a abominable old crone with wisps of grey hair escaping untidily from a dirty headscarf. Raising her arms to the heavens, she cried: "My cat! My cat! Oh, poor Beelzebub!"

Our three companions were surprised by this sudden apparition, and they took a step backwards. Ugly as the old lady was, however, she belonged to the fair sex, and our worthy Flemings were gallant—especially as they could see a fireplace through the open door, with a cooking-pot on the fire, in which something was simmering. The old lady's panic permitted them to suppose that it was not cat stew.

Mathurin raised his eyes heavenwards in a gesture of supplicant piety—and he perceived a black form moving in the branches of a tree. There were two gleams in the middle of the form that had to be eyes. Mathurin did not hesitate. He ran to the tree and climbed into the branches. Taking advantage of the animal's surprise—it had believed itself to be safe—he slipped into his coat pocket, made a rapid descent, and presented himself before the crone, to whom he held out the cat with a courteous gesture.

"Thank you, young man," she said. "Wait there! It shall not be said that you have done me a service for nothing."

She disappeared into the hut, without even inviting the three companions to come in. However, they saw her rummaging in the bottom of an old wardrobe, fm which a rat fled. She finally reappeared on the threshold, and handed the three objects she had in her hands to the young men.

"Take this," she said to Mathurin.

It was a napkin made of cotton—calico, as department-stores call it—which had nothing extraordinary about it. Mathurin had seen similar ones, before the war, selling for six francs eighty-five a dozen.

He accepted the napkin thoughtfully.

When it was the turn of the other two others, Amador received a brass ring, which was certainly not gold, and Gaetan an old copper coin, probably no longer legal tender, and certainly very rusty.

"Thank you again," squeaked the crone.

And, while the three young men considered these strange gifts, stupidly, she bounded back to her hovel, with a cackle that resembled the sound of a badly-greased well-chain. Once past the threshold, she closed the door, which she bolted behind her solidly.

Amador, Gaetan and Mathurin were immobilized by amazement. Recovering their senses, they raced to the door and hammered on it forcefully. What good were those ridiculous objects to them? What they wanted was supper. In fact, in spite of the hour, they would have been content with a good breakfast. It was in vain that they knocked, however, first with their fists and then with their feet. No one answered. And the door held firm. It was a solid door, primarily designed for closing.

There was nothing to do but go away, and go without supper that night, as they had the night before. Swearing a mortal oath to give them courage, the three companions drew away from the inhospitable hovel. Mechanically putting the crone's ironic gifts in their pockets, they followed the first path they came to, and were fortunate to find a cave whose floor was carpeted with dry grass. Gaetan took an old morsel of bread out of his satchel, so hard that he had been hesitating for a fortnight over eating it. He cut it into three with two blows of his sword, and, to help it go down, sprinkled it sadly with the water they had in their gourds. When the lugubrious meal was concluded, they lay down on the dry grass, went to sleep as best they could, and dreamed all night of bloody meat, fresh bread with a golden crust sprinkled with white flour, and wines of the most renowned vintages.

The song of a skylark heralded the day. Our three companions shook themselves, yawned and sat up on their makeshift bed, with bewildered expressions. A moment later they were standing up, thinking about the problem of breakfast. It is a terrible thing to lack food every day, even when there is no bell to advertise meal times.

"Ah!" said Mathurin, "I'd far rather have a dinner without a napkin than a napkin without a dinner!"

As he said these words, he took the napkin the old crone had given him out of his pocket, with a scornful gesture, and threw it on the ground, where it spread itself out, very squarely.

"If only," the brave soldier continued, extremely exasperated, "there were a nice roasted turkey-hen on that napkin! I feel so hungry that I could eat it all myself."

Surprise!

Scarcely had he pronounced these words, than there appeared on the napkin, from who knew what devil's kitchen, a fine porcelain plate, and on that plate a superb turkey-hen, cooked and browned to a turn, with large bumps on the skin whose black transparency permitted the supposition that the animal must have died of an indigestion of whole truffles.

"No!" said Mathurin, dumbfounded.

"Yes!" replied Amador, reaching out to touch the turkey-hen and assure himself that it was not a phantom. The result of the experiment was entirely satisfactory.

"There's nothing lacking," sighed Gaetan, "but bread and a few bottles of wine."

The turkey-hen was surrounded by four bottles, whose glass let generous reflections through, and four crisp loaves of the best pre-war bread extended like walls between the four bottle-towers to complete the sturdy fortress. A wasted effort—an hour later, the structure was entirely dismantled, the enemy's skeleton lying in the dungeons of stomachs and the empty towers strewn on the ground.

His face illuminated and joyful, Mathurin had jealously folded up the napkin and hidden it in his bosom. Amador, flat on his belly, was searching the dry grass for his brass ring, which he had dropped, while Gaetan was juggling his old coin and addressing the most pressing exhortations thereto. Then he rubbed it, as he had heard rumor of Aladdin's lamp—but still with no result. In the end, war-weary, putting off his experiments until later, he picked up his old leather purse and carefully deposited the coin therein, in solitude.

Meanwhile, a cry of joy was heard. "I've found it! I've found it, and I'll never be separated from it again...."

Gaetan and Mathurin turned in the direction from which the voice had come, searching for Amador with their eyes.

Amador had vanished.

"Why are you looking at me with those stupid expressions?" the voice continued. "Look, here it is, the ring. What's so special about it?"

Amador had just appeared before them, as if suddenly sprung from the ground. He showed them the brass ring that he had just removed from his finger.

It was necessary to yield to the evidence. The ring made its wearer invisible. Another marvelous discovery. Meanwhile, only Gaetan remained miserable in his corner. What if his old coin did not have the same virtue as the napkin and the ring? As he got up, in a melancholy fashion, he uttered an exclamation.

"Lord, how heavy I am!" He put his hand in his pocket and took out his purse awkwardly. He opened it. It was full of gold pieces bearing the effigy of the king of Estremadura.

Then there was a royal celebration. Our companions were the masters of the world. They began by dividing up the contents of the purse, carefully leaving the old copper coin at the bottom. It filled up again, without any apparent effort. Then, before embarking on the conquest of the universe, they spread out the napkin in the middle of the cave and had themselves served with a feast compared with which the famous wedding of Gamache[19] was nothing but a timid essay in slow death by starvation.

They woke up three days later, their heads very heavy, totally devoid of memories—but their first gesture was to seek out the three talismans. The coin was in its place, and the ring too. As for the napkin, it had been firmly kept in place by the sleeper's feet.

The only inconvenience was that Amador, in a last spark of reason, had put the ring on his finger, and did not think to take it off again; his comrades were stumbling over him, or stepping on his feet in the most impudent fashion.

But they were the first, and doubtless the last, since they were the only ones there, to laugh at these slight inconveniences. Everything was set in order again once Amador, confused by his dazed condition, had taken the ring off his finger, and the three companions had drunk long draughts from a nearby stream.

A few weeks later, no one in the King of Estremadura's capital was talking about anything but the three mysterious individuals who had arrived in the city a short while before, whose deeds and activities were occupying public opinion uninterruptedly.

---

[19] The wedding in question is an episode in Cervantes' *Don Quixote*, whose legendary status was further augmented in France by a famous painting of the scene by Henri-Charles Baron, first exhibited in 1849.

First of all, an individual named Mathurin had presented himself at the palace one evening and had applied for the job of head chef, rendered vacant by the death of its previous holder, who had succumbed to an indigestion of roasted anchovies. Mathurin, accepted on trial, had quickly made himself indispensable. The king had a hearty appetite and the queen, Dora, did not disdain nice morsels. The new cook possessed an entire intuitive science. There was no dish so complicated that he could not immediately find a perfectly-realized recipe. The king, although a sober man, had three indigestions a day, so incapable was he of resisting Mathurin's temptations.

There was only one bizarre detail, which formed a part of the mystery that we mentioned just now. Mathurin left the task of preparing vulgar dishes to his assistant cooks, but when it was a matter of one of the more exotic dishes, of which he alone knew the secret, once a large fire had been lit, he shut himself away in the kitchen and forbade anyone, on the most severe penalties, to enter it. That was only a pretext, however; as soon as Mathurin was alone he laid out he napkin and the dish immediately presented itself on demand.

This bizarrerie seemed natural in a man of genius. The king was very fond of Mathurin, and would have appointed him prime minister if he had not feared distracting him from more important occupations. In the meantime, he gave him a salary superior to what all the ministers of the court earned in total. The President of the Council, who was known as Tiger because of his moustache, spent his time conspiring fruitlessly against Mathurin. He possessed the monarch's heart, but Mathurin was the master of his stomach.

Meanwhile, Amador and Gaetan had also made progress since leaving the witch's hut. Amador had gained the confidence of the king, to whom he had made the offer of taking responsibility for the most secret missions, and fulfilling them to general satisfaction, that of the king in particular. He was placed at the head of the espionage service, and worked marvels there. The prince was fully informed of all the intrigues being woven in his own court and neighboring courts. He did not know, of course, about the magic power of the ring, and had all the more admiration or Amador's talents. He had assured him of the most brilliant situation, and always treated him with assurances of the most distinguished consideration.

The most important person in the court, however, was not the king; it was Queen Dora. Beautiful, intelligent and ambitious, her hair curled every morning with little iron tongs, she could make her husband do anything she wished, for his character was weak and he recognized the superiority of his wife—with whom he was, moreover, very much in love. And if the queen appreciated Mathurin's fine cuisine, she attached more real value to the services that Amador could provide. She had been quick to conclude a sort of treaty of alliance with him, all the more so because, from the very first day, he had fallen in love with her. The lady had had a rather pensive air for some time, which rendered her ten or twelve time prettier. As the people of Estremadura believed in witchcraft, a legend was established to explain the queen's shadowed and contented eyes; it was whispered that she was visited at night by an incubus, a sort of invisible demon that she could only know by means of its embraces—and the respectful esteem in which she was held was increased by it.

The truth was that one evening, Amador had taken advantage of the ring to introduce himself into the queen's bedroom. On feeling him next to her, in the bed, she had initially utterly a faint cry of alarm, than had turned precipitately to the button on her bedhead, to light the resin torches. But she had seen nothing, and her emotion had been such that she had abandoned herself, stupefied by the mystery, to the reality of which, in spite of the negative testimony of her eyes, she was convinced—penetratively, let us say.

In any case, it did not lack charm, for so virtuous a woman, and the sighs that she uttered attracted anxious chambermaids who thought that she was ill. They looked furtively though a crack in a door, then retired discreetly, laughing up their sleeves, even though they were in their nightgowns, but reassured.

From the reports they gave him, in the morning, the palace astrologer concluded that the queen had received the nocturnal visit of an invisible god, or a demon, and that the heir to the throne would be a superman, as the German philosophers of the present day put it. Not being absolutely sure, however, he did not want to say anything to the lady's august spouse, in order not to cause him any false joy.

As if the city had not had enough subjects for gossip, a noble lord had been seen to arrive in the capital at the same time as Amador and Mathurin, whose magnificent appearance had immediately seduced everyone, and who was none other than Gaetan. Without bothering to conquer the royal favor, which he would be able to purchase whenever he wanted, he had bought the most beautiful palace in the city with coins of full weight that rang true. He had furnished it sumptuously and had immediately thrown splendid parties. The entire court and city were pressed around him, for he had a generous hand and willingly tended to the great lords' needs. Everyone praised his fine demeanor.

There were a few lacunae in his education, and his table manners were not perfect—he was not afraid to pick his teeth with his knife and ate salad with his spoon—but the fare was exquisite and the liveried lackeys impeccable, pouring the best wines in the entire kingdom and its surrounding lands into glasses profusely. So, Gaetan's vulgarities were deemed to be delightful eccentricities, and all the women were very taken with him.

Naturally, he was received at Court, and there was no cajolery that the king and queen did not lavish upon him. The queen welcomed him into intimacy, and soon acquired the habit of taking him with her on her excursions through the city—and the brave Gaetan, dazed with pride, threw handfuls of gold coins to the crowds that cheered her. The queen's popularity was affected, and that of the king, without the latter, who was the most modern prince of his dynasty, being in the least offended by it. Thus, one of our companions became the joy of the queen's nights, and the other of her days.

This charming life continued for several months, but grim destiny was lying in wait. The queen had realized, gradually, that there was something strange about the three individuals' existence. The mystery of Amador had been unveiled some time before. Having read a certain amount of literature, it had been sufficient for the queen, one day—or rather, one night—to feel the ring on her invisible lover's finger, for her immediately to ask whether it was the instrument of his power of invisibility. The admission had been extracted from him amid voluptuous sighs, and henceforth, they had taken it in turns to wear the ring. Their amour had undergone a renewal in consequence.

Dora had suspected, since then, that the other two companions must also be in possession of some talisman—and she swore to combine, for her personal profit, all their respective advantages. With Maturin, it was child's play. Commanding him to secrecy on pain of death, she had the castle architect bore a hole in the kitchen ceiling, and from the room above she watched the operation of the napkin. It would be an insult to ladies who read to admit for a single instant that they might suppose that it required more than twenty-four hours for the queen to steal the precious piece of cloth.

It will similarly be no surprise that the very next day was the king's birthday, and that the lady took a malign pleasure in summoning Mathurin to her presence and demanding of him, for that celebration, the mot sumptuous and complicated of feasts. The poor devil, utterly stunned—for he had just become aware of the theft, without suspecting the culprit—could only bow very deeply, murmuring something unintelligible. For the rest of the day, he devoted himself to fruitless research; then, assured of his misfortune, he left the palace secretly, never to return.

With Gaetan it was easier still. The next day, the queen invited him to accompany her to church. At the exit, there were the usual dispensations to all the hurrying beggars. Gaetan dipped into his purse, which was progressively refilled, taking care to leave the old copper coin at the bottom—to which it was, in any case, solidly attached—until the moment when the queen seemed to become impatient with the lamentations of an old man who was shouting more loudly than the rest. She snatched the purse from Gaetan's hands and threw it to the unfortunate, who caught it in mid-air and immediately disappeared. Gaetan was so stunned that he dared not say anything

As soon as he arrived at the palace, he summoned the most eminent policemen, promising fabulous rewards to whoever brought him the purse, but the old man stationed by the queen had acted diligently, and had already received a royal reward—naturally—in exchange for the purse.

There remained Amador. Knowledge of his secret singularly favored Queen Dora's projects. On the other hand, the fancy she had taken to him, which lent a greater attraction to the mystery, was worth less henceforth that possession of the ring, from which she expected to obtain the most precious advantages. So, one day when he was merely paying her a visit, and fully dressed, she took the ring playfully, then threw it into the back of a wardrobe, the door of which she swiftly locked, in front of the poor devil, whose stupor knew no bounds when the queen started uttering screams of distress and crying rape.

Chamberlains and valets came running. Amador, proven guilty of having made an attempt on the queen's virtue, was miraculously able to flee. It was arranged that he would not be too strenuously sought, and explanations were avoided. The king, however, immediately issued an edict by which Amador and his companions, denounced as accomplices, were banished from the realm, and all their wealth was confiscated. Then he embraced the queen, who was still all a-tremble, and had a *Te Deum* sung in the cathedral.

A few hours later, three poor devils at the end of their tether were making their way miserably along the roads of Estremadura. Coiffed in badly-dented helmets, and clad in breastplates held together by pieces of string and nappy-pins, they were heading vaguely in the direction of France, where recruiting-sergeants had told them that enrolments were being taken for the war against the Huns. Meanwhile, in alternating stanzas, like ancient rhapsodies, they were cursing the perfidy of womankind, the eternal subject of meditations ever new to the other half of the human race.

The Warning

The Reverend P. W. Morrow emerged from the church where he had just celebrated the divine service. A fine drizzle was falling. It was typical London weather, grey and sullen. Umbrellas were moving back and forth in the street. The sidewalks were glistening.

The clergyman hesitated at the top of the steps, frustrated, holding out his hand toward the raindrops in a mechanical interrogative gesture. His hesitation was interrupted, however, for, at the same moment, a carriage drew up in front of the steps. The door opened. A lady got down and rapidly climbed up to toward the man of God. Her voice was breathless.

"I'm glad to have got here in time," she said. "Come right away, I beg you. It's for a gentleman who's about to die. He's extremely worried about the state of his soul, and wants to see you as soon as possible."

The lady was unknown to Reverend Morrow. She was still young, and appeared to belong to the best society, but her clothes were slightly old-fashioned, and her fixed gaze had something distant about it. The clergyman could only concede. He followed the lady and climbed into the carriage with her. The coachman flicked the horses, and they drew away.

The unexpected traveler expected to obtain some clarification during the journey. He was only able learn that the sick man's name was Sir Edward Burrton, and that he had heard mention of the incumbent from friends who had represented him as a man of remarkable knowledge and piety.

Sir Edward Burton's name did not bring any light into the obscurity, but the lady did not seem to be in any mood to say more. Her fingers drummed the carriage window feverishly. Her anxious gaze sought to perceive the approach of the destination. Emerging from the familiar neighborhood, the carriage went along streets that P. W. Morrow could not recall every having traversed before, although he knew where he was. Finally, after about half an hour, the carriage stopped in front of the door of a private house. The lady, increasingly nervous, urged her companion to get down without delay, so he leapt out of the vehicle and rang the doorbell. A lackey appeared, and he asked to see Sir Edward Burton without delay.

"I've just learned," he added, "that he's gravely ill and that he wishes to see me."

The valet struck an astonished pose and replied that his master was perfectly well.

"But this lady..." said Reverend P. W Morrow, turning round.

The lady and the carriage had disappeared, as if by magic.

"Well, I'm not dreaming, though," he continued, as soon as he had recovered slightly from his amazement. "That lady came to find me; I had just come out on to the steps of the church. We climbed into the carriage, and I accompanied her here. When I rang the doorbell, the carriage was there behind me. What's happened, then? It's impossible that you didn't see it..."

The lackey seemed to be wondering whether he was dealing with a practical joker or a madman. The venerable and sincere appearance of his interlocutor left him perplexed—but the door of the house was still open. A man appeared on the threshold. It was Sir Edward Burton.

"What is it?" he said.

The clergyman explained to him as best he could what had happened. He gave a description of the lady, whom he had not thought to look at attentively.

"I don't know anyone among my present relatives who corresponds to that description," said he master, after a moment's thought. "But it doesn't matter. Since you've come this far, would you do me the honor of coming in, and excuse me for having left you outside for so long?"

As soon as they were installed in the drawing-room, Sir Edward Burton reflected: "It's very strange that you should find yourself here at this moment—far stranger than you can imagine. Your visit anticipates a desire that I would not have been long in expressing. I returned a short while ago from India, where I spent several years, and although I'm in very good health at the moment...I don't know whether it's the influence of the climate to which I'm now subject, but I have vague anxieties that I can't quite define. It's as if I were menaced by some danger as imminent as it is unknown. I'm conscious of having always lived as an honest man, thanks to the instruction of an admirable mother, lost too soon, whose memory I guard piously. But every man, in apprehension of the future life, judges himself severely, and one can't take too many precautions. I'm haunted by the idea of making my complete peace with God. If my apprehensions are vain, they will not have been futile, wherever they come from. In this disposition, I have talked, since my return, with a few religious friends, and I've asked them, having lost sight somewhat of the metropolitan clergy during my long sojourn out there, to point me in the direction of a spiritual physician. They fell into accord over your name, and I was about to seek you out when you arrived."

The reverend bowed. His host told him the names of the friends who had given his name, and P. W. Morrow recognized them.

"Let's leave aside, if you will," added Sir Edward Burton, "the mysterious manner in which you came here. We'll examine the material problem on another occasion. We can admit, for the moment, and with every chance of being right, that it was God who sent you to me."

The reverend then put himself at his host's disposal. They conversed seriously for more than an hour, and the man of God only left after having restored calm to that troubled soul. Wanting to perfect his work, he made an appointment to meet Sir Edward Burton again the following morning.

Sir Edward Burton did not come to the meeting. The clergyman was vaguely anxious, given the strange circumstances of the previous evening's visit, but he was retained by various obligations and could not satisfy his legitimate impatience. He sought in vain to reassure himself, in the meantime, telling himself that it was only a fortuitous delay or that a perfectly excusable negligence on the part of his penitent merely proved that he had fully recovered his self-composure. All the reasons that he invented could not satisfy him, though, and in the evening, as soon as he was free, obedient to an imperious appeal, he went to Sir Edward Burton's house.

The same valet came to open the door, in tears, and informed him that his master had died the night before, and hour after they had parted.

Profoundly moved by this sudden death, and particularly amazed by the alarming coincidence, which seemed bewildering, the reverend asked to be taken to the dead man in order to render him one last homage and say a final prayer. As they were going through a drawing-room on the way to the mortuary chamber, however, he suddenly started. Seizing the valet's hand, he pointed, with a fearful gesture, at the portrait of a woman on the wall.

"Who is that lady?" he stammered, in a voice strangled by emotion.

"Sir Edward Burton's mother," the valet replied. "He had a veritable adoration for her. It's now fifteen years since she died. My master never got over it."

Reverend P. W. Morrow had recognized the lady. It was the one who had come to fetch him.

The Red Diamond

This happened a long time ago, in the land of Maghada, which was ruled by a powerful rajah named Nehmi. By virtue of his wealth he had triumphed over all the princes of the fabulous Orient. His palace was marble and cedar-wood, with golden ceilings and porphyry columns. Caskets of rare wood were heaped up in the sumptuous halls, edged with jewels and precious stones. There were diamonds as big as pheasants' eggs. For ten years, he had been able to let pearls stream between his fingers, whose nails were painted red, without exhausting the pile that he had. He also possessed tapestries embroidered in gold, silver and silk, and others whose somber verdure perpetuated the placid mysteries of the forest on his walls.

His armies were powerful and well-equipped. The elephants and the horses, whose number he did not know, had thousands of servants and lived in a marble palace with troughs made of Lebanese wood. A host of slaves moved through the courtyards, gardens, halls and vestibules. Some carried golden urns on their heads.

There were houris from all the countries in the world, the beauty of which they represented, having arrived swaying on the backs of camels, to whom he would throw the handkerchief of his whim in the evening, after the feasting and the music. But the most beautiful of all, and the best-loved, was his wife, the Maharani. By virtue of her grace, she resembled the most subtle of lotus flowers, and the gaze of her eyes was enchanting and troubling, like the Moon over the woods by night.

She was of the bluest blood—so blue that, by comparison, that of a sapphire seemed pale. The origin of her glorious family was lost in the night of time. Her royal lineage was so ancient that the parchments on which the names and titles of her ancestors were inscribed, laid end to end, would have traversed the peninsula from Mount Davalghiri to Cape Comorin. But others said that she was even more illustriously born, and that one night, her mother had received the visit of Indra, the god of the sky.

Now, for the queen's birthday, wanting to celebrate his love, the maharajah chose the most beautiful jewel of his treasure. It was a diamond that had the perfect form of a dove's egg, the dove being consecrated to the goddess born of the foam of the sea, but its water was so limpid that the whole sky seemed to be reflected therein. And when he gave her that gift, he asked her to swear, on the head of their young son, never to be separated from it—for there has always been a religion of jewels: a vague obscure religion of gleaming stones and their occult influence on human destiny. The loss of the diamond would surely lead to the loss of the woman who no longer had it.

In the same palace lived a brother of the maharajah named Kali. He was an unscrupulous, scheming prince, who was mortally jealous of his brother and the latter's wife, although, of necessity, he had to put on an amiable, or at least indifferent, face. He had not forgiven his brother for being loved and having acquired a position that he would have been very glad to have for himself. Everything that his inferior position evoked exasperated him. He had coveted the marvelous diamond, among others, for many years without daring to ask for it. He had always hoped that his brother might divine his desire, for he never ceased to make allusion to it, praising the diamond's beauty every time he saw it, and sighing that the person to whom the prince, in his munificence, might make a gift of it, would be very happy. But he made the great mistake of not asking openly for what he coveted; one never gets anything by means of sighs and allusions. Perhaps the maharajah would have been embarrassed to respond negatively to a request to a frankly-expressed request, but he could not and did not understand—and without a doubt, he would rather give pleasure to his wife than his brother, since it was to her that he gave the diamond.

So, there came a night when the spirit of evil, weary of keeping silent, whispered in the ear of Prince Kali—and he prince got up from his sumptuous bed, taking care not to wake his servants. He slipped into the darkness, through the odorous gardens and along the marble veranda, until he arrived at the place where the maharani slept.

He crept toward her like a panther slyly approaching its prey, and when he was close to his victim in the darkness he stopped, listening to the light, calm breath that the young woman's lips exhaled. Momentarily, he hesitated, perhaps touched by the beauty he divined beside him without seeing it. Perhaps he was also thinking of his brother's wrath, if the guilty party were discovered—but cupidity was the stronger. He reached out his hands, groping for the princess's neck, in order to unfasten the necklace from which the marvelous diamond was suspended.

His hands were trembling in the darkness, however. His gestures were awkward and he became impatient. As he tugged abruptly, the maharani woke up.

She uttered an exclamation of sudden terror on feeling a black hand upon her. The wretch was terrified; the cry might wake someone. If anyone came, he was lost. He saw himself suddenly surrounded by servants bearing torches—and in that imminent apprehension, with an unconscious and feverish movement, without thinking, he seized his dagger and plunged it to the hilt in his victim's delicate breast. There was a slight sigh, a few convulsive movements on the thick carpet of the room, then silence and immobility.

There had been no movement in the palace: no sound, no light. The murderer stayed there momentarily, listening; then, reassured by the mortuary tranquility that reigned around him, he seized the diamond and tore it away with an abrupt gesture, scattering the rare pearls of the necklace around the room. Without any regret for his victim, he hastened with a light and prudent step toward the palace gates.

A fast horse, fully saddled, was attached to the grille. He mounted rapidly, after having hidden the precious jewel in his bosom, and rode away at top speed.

All night and all day he rode, only stopping when the horse fell dead of exhaustion. Then he sat at the foot of a tree, in the dying light of dusk, took the fruit of his crime from his clothing and contemplated it with tremulous admiration. Then he shuddered.

On the clear beauty of the diamond there was a large bloodstain—the royal blood of the maharani.

Kali rubbed the precious stone vigorously with a silk handkerchief. The handkerchief was stained red, but the stain did not disappear.

Slightly alarmed, he went to the nearby river, dipped the diamond in the water, and rubbed and scraped it, carefully and patiently. The bloodstain was still there. Sometimes it disappeared, only to reappear more intensely on the other side. The wretch became desperate. What profit had he obtained from his crime, except for having bloody and bright remorse with him forever?

He sought the shelter of a cave, and lay down on a bed of dry leaves, where he ended up going to sleep, worn out by fatigue. But his sleep was heavy, haunted by frightful nightmares. In his dreams he saw the god Shiva, the destroyer with the cruel gaze. Frenzied women twisted at his feet, their hearts pierced by daggers with crystal hilts. Cascading streams of diamonds fell from Shiva's hands, over which an infernal light emerging from the divine eyes caused ardent red reflections to pass.

Kali awoke at dawn, with the vague hope, in the softness of the cool morning, that the reality of the previous day might vanish with the nightmare of the night. But he saw the stone and the stain again, and it seemed to him that it had become larger. All of the following day, weary and desperate, he ran through the countryside, stopping at springs and wells to dip the fatal stone therein. But days and nights went by, and the stain did not disappear. Every day, on the contrary, it increased in breadth and intensity. A splendid red leprosy devoured the diamond.

He went to sanctuaries, implored the divinities; he tried conjurations and incantations—in vain. The diamond did not recover its purity. He became terrified then, and despaired. The stone the color of fire, which he had hidden in his bosom, was now burning him to the utmost depths of his heart.

A pious Brahmin whom he met and consulted, without telling him the whole story, advised him, as a last resource, to undertake a pilgrimage to the sources of the Ganges and the Brahmaputra, where the sanctuaries of the gods were, beyond the plains and the clouds, near the summits of the Himalayas. So he went northwards, and walked so far that his feet bled, and reached the sources.

With many fervent prayers, he steeped the stone in the sacred waters day and night for a week. At the end of the week, the diamond had become entirely red—the red of blood. No stone like it had ever been seen. It shone with a magical glare, and all the splendor of the crime was in its fires.

Then the wretch lay down on the brink of the springs, on the bare ground; his eyes closed, and night fell, with swirls of snow that made him a white shroud.

In the morning, the priests found his body. He was still holding the ruby in his clenched fingers. The priests took the new stone and, with appropriate incantations, embedded it in the forehead of Shiva, the god of death.

The Vestal

It was an obscure redoubt, with walls of unpolished stone, a sort of sad, low-ceilinged cell. Damp oozed from the walls and ceiling. A lamp in the form of a bird gave a feeble light. On the edge of the niche, near the lamp, a morsel of coarse bread was visible, and on the floor of compacted earth beneath it, a jug. There were steps rising from the floor toward the ceiling. A women was sitting, motionless, on the bottom step, her head swathed in veils like the statuettes of mourners.

The woman was named Julia Fausta. Belonging to one of the oldest and richest families in Rome, she had been conse-crated since childhood to the cult of Vesta, the austere god-dess. She marched in the processions before the venerable statue.

One day, when she was passing through the city, she had come across the cortege of a condemned man who was being taken to his execution. In accordance with the privilege granted to the Vestals by law, the encounter saved the man. He was the son of a senator, sentenced to death for having con-spired against the security of the State. His name was Caius Spurius. His youth and audacity were admired.

Julia Fausta was as beautiful as the statue of Beauty, and the distant inaccessibility in she was maintained by her vows rendered her more desirable. Caius conceived a wild passion for the woman that had saved his life.

The young woman shared that love. She struggled in vain to keep intact that chastity that she had been forced to avow one day, as an ignorant child. Cupid is the first of the gods, and all the others vanish at his approach like fearful phantoms. One evening, the vestal fled by means of the hidden door of the sanctuary. She met Caius. In a villa hidden in the depths of the Roman countryside, they tasted brief but unfor-gettable joys. Then lictors armed with fascia surrounded the villa. The young people were taken back to Rome, amid the ignominy of a howling crowd. Justice was pitiless. For having allowed the sacred flame to be extinguished in her soul, Julia was interred alive in the crypt that would be her tomb. She had bread and water for a day or two, and the lamp, whose brightness—the image of life—would go out after a few hours.

Oh, it was not that she regretted expiating her crime, if it was a crime, but only that the black face of Destiny had not, at least, appeared later. The gods were cruel to have become jealous of her happiness in love so quickly. What right did anyone have to forbid her to live as other women did? Why had her life been bound forever, at an age when she was still too young to know what life was? Was it necessary that a grim law should separate her from the rest of humankind, to make her, a frail child, similar to those ephemeral insects which die of their first embrace?

Julia Fausta got to her feet. How many hours she had been enclosed in that subterranean prison she did not know— but the lamplight was beginning to pale. The young woman knew that there as a heavy stone above her head, then a thick layer of earth, and beyond that, separated from her forever, the open air, the blue sky and the delicate perfume of flowers. Perhaps, by digging with her feeble hands, patiently, in the black soil underfoot, she might find the roots of trees whose foliage spreads out majestically up there. Oh, to know that life was there, present, and to find, forever, the other side of life!

Suddenly, a slight noise made her shudder. Then she became still. The sound continued, regularly, and more emphatically. It was as if someone were digging in the soil heaped up over the cavity. The young woman remained nailed to the spot, listening with her heart.

A hard object collided with the stone. Then a crack of light designed a straight line. And the trap was lifted, pulled by vigorous hands, letting through a flood of light, air and life.

A form cast a shadow from the top of the steps, and a man came down. It was Caius.

"You!" cried the bewildered young woman. "It's you! Oh, praised be the gods, who did not want me to die before seeing you again! What am I saying, *to die*? We're going to live. This funeral cellar will be the veritable cradle of our love."

Caius was now beside her, and he shook his head sadly. Other shadows appeared at the entrance. Man descended into the crypt. There was a centurion accompanied by two legionnaires. The slender shadows of lances carried by other soldiers outside were visible on the steps.

The centurion spoke, in a clear, trenchant voice.

"Caius Spurius, the Senate had absolved you of your first crime, but it was not able, without injustice, to pardon you for having betrayed the faith of the Vestals and soiled one who served the goddess of the hearth. It grants you the death that is your due. By a residuum of pity, it has permitted you to wait for it beside the one who was your accomplice. Caius Spurius, thank the clemency of the Roman Senate, the master of peoples and kings."

Julia Fausta was plunged into a stupor. Caius, with his back against the wall, seemed a hunted beast, ready to launch himself in a desperate effort—but the centurion went back up the steps impassively, followed by the two legionnaires, and disappeared. The sound of the stone moving was heard, and a black shadow extended. Then Caius leapt toward the steps. He tried to reach the light through the diminished passage. Brutal hands shoved him back, and the funereal stone fell once again.

The smoky lamp, reanimated by the air from outside, lit the lugubrious scene. Caius lay down at the foot of the steps. Julia Fausta stood beside him, sobbing.

Eventually, she touched his shoulder gently.

"Oh, my Caius," she said, "what does it matter if we are separated from humankind for eternity? Are the two of us not together? Death leaves us a few hours. We can encapsulate in those brief moments an entire loving existence."

But the man had got up. His eyes wandered slowly, and his gaze made a tour of the cell. Julia knelt in front of him, extending her hands in a gesture of adoration.

"Bitch!" he cried. "Immodest bitch, who saved me once only to make me die more horribly! Get away from me! Back! I hate you. Cursed among all days be the day when your mother conceived you!"

While blaspheming, he perceived the morsel of bread deposited in the niche next to the lamp, and the jug of water on the ground. He seized the jug, lifted it up, and drank in long, savage draughts. Then he advanced to grab the piece of bread.

The instinct of self-preservation awoke in the young woman. Love suddenly foundered. There was no longer any presence but that of two starving beasts. She too extended her hand.

There was a rapid encounter; a brutal gesture by the man. The lamp, knocked over, fell to the ground. There was darkness—and in that darkness, the anguished cry of the woman was heard, as she was seized around the neck by two brutal hands. The cry died away into a croak, and finished in a sigh.

A delicate cadaver fell on the compacted earth. And the man remained alone in the darkness, with, to prolong his torture, the bread, the water in the jug—and the flesh.

In the Next World...

For Georges Vésier[20]

The first time that I visited Doctor Crooker, I was primarily attracted by the reputation of his scientific work. His name was one of those that had seduced me a long time ago, to the point of making me ardently desire to know the man as well as the scientist. It would be inexact to claim that normal curiosity was not mixed with another, slightly anxious, such as those inspired whom one suspects of being in relation to a mysterious beyond. I knew that the physicist in him was combined with a redoubtable mathematician—one of those who, by virtue of a poetic and magical intuition, believed the abstractions of number to be realizable in the material domain, having read Pythagoras, whom everyone interprets as he pleases.

Dr. Crooker's ideas went much further than the formulae one finds in books. His theories regarding the fourth dimension were not only theories. He believed not only in the possibility, but also in the existence of a world based on other geometrical axioms than those of the world in whose midst we live. I had the vague sensation that the unknown universe in question, evoked by a visionary in its sudden reality, would be a terrifying thing for minds possessed of the usual concepts.

Needless to say, I was led to return, attracted by interest in what the doctor had to say, by the redoubtable novelty of his remarks, and especially by the presence of a feminine form whose ideal perfection all geometrical description would have tried in vain to define. She moved around him like a blonde fairy around a black magician. From the first day onwards, her

---

[20] Another of Lautrec's less famous friends; he was an engineer.

smile suddenly became for me an inescapable spell. I knew that she was Dr. Crooker's niece, and that her name was Kate. She was the orphan of an Irish mother, and her uncle had taken her in. She undoubtedly represented all that that strange man could feel of human affection, and it appeared to me that she had also taken an affectionate interest, insofar as her feminine mentality permitted, in his work. But the brightness of her eyes was like the emerald green ocean from whose shores she had come, and merely by virtue of gazing at her golden hair, I had all the honey of Hymettus[21] in my heart.

My scientific qualifications were sufficient for me to be able to render the old man a few commonplace services. I was able to become indispensable without revealing the prodigious interest that surpassed all other considerations so far as I was concerned—and a day came when I moved into Dr. Crooker's house. We were alone, the three of us, with a deaf, almost mute, maidservant and a very old gardener.

It is a vast and ancient dwelling in the suburbs of the city, only connected to the rest of the world by walls and deserted alleyways. Side-doors once opened in the walls on to now-abandoned gardens; they have been sealed by dust and branches, and moss carpets their fractured doorsteps. The house is preceded by an avenue of linden trees. Its melancholy and flat façade has a northern exposure. A large clock on the ground floor chimes the hours implacably through the stairwell and the gloomy corridors. We live a secluded existence, which has nothing monotonous about it for me, illuminated by love and fear. Kate smiles when I speak to her, and without her saying anything to me, I know that her smile is for me. Emerging from unforgettable conversations, I go into the doctor's study with anguished apprehension.

The furniture is austere. Two large windows without curtains pour a white light of infinite bareness and sadness. Large

---

[21] Hymettus was a mountain ridge near Athens celebrated in Classical literature for the quality of the honey produced there.

blackboards cover the walls, and on those blackboards chalk lines intersect and interlace, some of which are familiar to me but of which the others, by their novelty, pose a challenge to my not-inconsiderable knowledge. In the place that is reserved for me, I find the day's work: equations to solve; diagrams to draw—work whose details I understand in a limited sense, but which is connected to a vast general plan whose totality escapes me. I am like a technician whom a great engineer allows to fashion a few isolated components, whose eventual juxtaposition and ultimate objective is known to him alone.

I almost never find myself alone in the study. It seems that the doctor experiences a reluctance to leave me in intimate association with his work unless he is present. That reserve has aggravated my curiosity since the very first day, and the impossibility of satisfying that curiosity renders my existence more bizarre and more painful as time passes. I would already have fled, were it not for the golden chain that retains me in this abode. I have the impression that a more anguishing mystery is unfolding by the hour. Prey to an increasing exasperation, which has gradually killed my discretion, I have reached the point of picking up torn pieces of paper that are sometimes strewn on the carpet. It's rare that I can decipher a word or a formula in these strictly personal indications, in which he almost always uses notations who alphabet in unfamiliar to me.

For once, however, he has been obliged to emerge from the unexpected in order to run into the garden, where something untoward has just occurred. A fragment of paper, irregularly severed, as if torn off in a moment of impatience, was on the table. Twenty lines of tormented script remained. I've picked it up. He'll think that he has thrown it away, or that it has blown out of the window, which was open just then. I shall read it this evening, in my room, behind closed doors.

I hastened to find myself alone. The day has gone by. The doctor, on coming back on his study, made no allusion to the disappearance of the paper. We dined silently, all three of us, served by the dead maidservant. Then Kate went to bed. I've come up to my room.

I've bolted the door, discreetly. I've moved a few books in order that the doctor, whose room is next door, should not suspect my impatience. Now I'm sitting next to the lamp, reading:

...material, but having only two dimensions, length and breadth. If they exist, only the faces would be visible to us, since they have no thickness. They would escape us in one direction. We can have some idea of them by comparison with mirror-images, in which the body had three dimensions for sight, but only two for touch.

On the other side of our world are beings with four-dimensions: length, breadth, thickness and a fourth, which extends an unknown direction. Perhaps, reasoning by analogy, we can say that two-dimensional beings are represented by surfaces, but are limited by the elements borrowed from the first dimension, lines. Three-dimensional beings, solids, which have length, breadth and thickness, are limited by two-dimensional surfaces. In the same way, four-dimensional beings must be limited by solids. And thus, in consequence...the world in which these beings move, even those closest to us, must infinitely surpass the coarseness of ours. It's the place of a worse fall, the terrible world inhabited by...

The manuscript was torn there.

For some time, he has remained locked in his study all day long and almost all night. I am no longer permitted to enter. If he comes out, even if it's only for five minutes he takes the key with him. A few furtive appearances, at meal times, permit me to observe the ravages of his obsession. His eyes are haggard. His lips move incessantly, only to produce incoherent words at rare intervals. In vain, Kate begs him to think of his heath. He shrugs his shoulders or looks at her with an alarming expression. The poor girl is ominously depressed when we're alone. I've suggested that we go away together, quitting this house where I have the impression that some strangely deadly web is being woven. She refuses. She doesn't want to abandon her uncle. She loves me, though. I know that now. Her heart is mine—but her soul is in the fourth dimension.

Every day, I observe the progress of the doctor's madness fervently. He has evidently set off in pursuit of some horrible chimera. Exiled from the room where he works, I sometimes go as far as the door, dreading some misfortune. Most of the time, I can hear him moving about feverishly. He paces back and forth, with hurried strides, or stops in front of a blackboard, which he covers in chalk with rapid strokes. At other times, he talks to himself, incoherently. I've noted a few words and phrases that recur, like bewildered moans, in his monologues: *unknowable...so close and yet so far....the forbidden country...*

At other times, he seems prey to some grim conflict with an invisible enemy. His voice becomes hoarse. He exerts himself, doubtless cursing the terrifying phantoms of his imagination—and sometimes, rarely, he utters a cry of triumph, which frightens me more than anything else.

The other day I stood for an hour with my ear stuck to the door, without hearing the slightest sound. I was afraid. I didn't dare knock; I went into the garden. With the aid of a ladder, I succeeded in raising my head to the level of the window. I saw...

He was sprawled in an armchair, breathless, his eyes lost in sinister contemplation. On the blackboard in front of him there were geometric figures, evoking faces such as the Gorgon never saw in her most frightful nightmares.

Now I have to describe the infernal denouement. The unspeakable scene is before my eyes, never to be forgotten. I'm writing these notes in pencil, without knowing whether I'll be able to read them, so much is my hand shaking.

This evening, he didn't even make a furtive appearance at dinner. We went to bed very anxious. I dropped off anyway, but my sleep was troubled by lugubrious visions and cries of terror; I couldn't tell whether they were imaginary or real, until one clamor, more terrifying than all the rest, woke me up.

I realized that I was no longer dreaming. The anguished scream continued, expressing all human distress. I leapt out of bed and looked at my watch. It was after midnight. I dressed in haste and rushed precipitately out of my room, to find Kate on the landing, candle in hand, paler than her night-gown.

Without pronouncing a single word, we went downstairs. The racket was terrible. We arrived at the study door, which I broke down with a blow of my fist. The room was illuminated by all the torches in the house, and in the middle, Dr. Crooker, howling and gesticulating, seemed to be fighting invisible demons.

We remained nailed to the threshold. The howls and gesticulations increased in intensity. A monstrous dolor was legible in the poor fellow's face. He didn't see us. At one moment, tough, he reached out a threatening hand—and then....

Then, we suddenly saw the arm disappear, as if cut off at the shoulder. Fear paralyzed me. Kate fell down in a faint.

It was the turn of the other arm, then the head, as if cut off by some shadowy executioner—and the body disappeared one fragment after another, sliced up by an invisible blade following geometric sections. But the howls became more intense as the human body was annihilated, gradually penetrating into the world of the fourth dimension, which devoured it—until, amid the clamor in which all the hounds of hell seemed to be baying, there was no longer anything there but a few drops of blood on the floor of the room.

A Macabre Wager

As to stories about students, Doctor Selkof said, pensively, I could tell you more than one. I've frequented various European schools, and found myself in company with young people of all nationalities. But the crazy adventures that are most readily invoked are much the same everywhere. It's the necessary seasoning of banal drinking sessions. There are traditions of facile gaiety, which the differences between countries modify very slightly. I prefer to recall a story of another sort, the tragic vision of which still haunts me today. It has no other merit than its authenticity, and its very complicity causes it to remain more vivid in my memory.

I was in Prague at that time—and I'm talking about thirty years ago. All those who were then my temporary contemporaries have died or dispersed into the wide world. One thinks with melancholy of the various existences one has lived in different places. I kept myself to myself in those days, having always been something of a savage, only keeping company with a small number of my study companions, who came from all parts of Europe and naturally formed groups according to the affinities of their origin. Among those I saw most often, however, was a Pole whose doubtless bizarre and complicated family name I've forgotten, and whom we had acquired the habit of designating by his forename, Nathaniel. Research carried out in common brought us together, and when we came out of the lecture-theater I appreciated his easy-going and meaty conversation, which was not confined to technical matters.

He was a simple and jovial fellow, in perfect mental health, totally inaccessible to ideas that were macabre or simply disquieting. In literature, he gladly affiliated himself to the

113

school of Boileau,[22] and shrugged his shoulders politely when I talked to him about some abstract theories of life and death that that I had extracted from what Edgar Poe calls, so expressively, "the foam of German metaphysics."

I think there might be a destiny that amuses itself with the contrast of suddenly causing the phantom of a great horror suddenly to appear to calm and ingenuous eyes. In the wake of what conversation—or, perhaps, what exceptional libations— did we get the idea of that stupid wager? I don't know. But Nathaniel, with a fine insouciance and a mocking smile, immediately took the bet. He willingly admitted to never having experienced what we call fear—which, for him, was only a word.

"Fear of what?" he asked. "A sane man may find himself in the presence of danger but has only, from then on, to confront it courageously. As for nurse's tales and other nonsense, it's better, since we're reasonable men, not to talk about them."

To convince us, moreover, he gladly agreed to lock himself in the dissection room that night, where the cadaver of a young woman was on the wooden table, having been brought in that very morning, and to drive a dozen nails into the edge of the table with a hammer, as the amphitheater clock sounded the twelve strokes of midnight.

To ensure a rigorous execution of the program, three of us, including me, decided to install ourselves in the vestibule behind the amphitheater door. Nathaniel had gone into the room at eleven o'clock. Naturally, we were counting on the enervation of the wait to modify our comrade's placid disposition, and we had carefully refrained from telling him that we would be on watch behind the door.

---

[22] Nicolas Boileau-Despréaux (1636-1711), who harshly criticized any departure from nature and reason in literary works, disapproving of the fantastic, except in the context of moralizing fables like those of his friend Jean de La Fontaine.

So far as I was concerned, I confess, I would not have been displeased to see him emerge from the hall after a few minutes, declaring that the affair was ridiculous and that he refused to lend himself to the grotesque game any longer. He did not seem in the least affected by the lugubrious appearance of the hall, which was feebly illuminated by a candle placed on the table with the hammer and the nails. When we left him installed in a comfortable armchair, in the process of stuffing his pipe, we were certainly more disturbed than he was.

Having closed the door and made a show of leaving, we sat down silently on the top step of the staircase and waited, beginning to curse our ingenious idea internally. We dared not say a word, which would have revealed our presence. The time dragged by lamentably. The darkness did not permit us to check the time on our watches, and we were doubtless in the process of wondering whether the entire night had not run lugubriously by when, all of a sudden, in the blackness of our impressions, the clock in the amphitheatre, breaking the absolute silence, began to chime.

It was a deliverance. We breathed out. The second stroke followed, then the third, hastening implacably—each one doubled, as by a echo, by a curt and urgent hammer-blow.

All went well; the twelfth stroke sounded. Finally, silence....

Then, to our mortal amazement, a sharp and bewildering sound—the thirteenth—cut through the darkness. It was not the clock, though. It was the cry of a human mouth: a solemn, unique cry, a desperate appeal before eternal silence.

With one bound, we threw open the door and were in the hall. The candle was burning with a red flame, and the obscure play of the light picked out—was it an illusion?—a smile of sad irony on the face of the original cadaver. But Nathaniel was lying in the ground at the foot of the table, in a desperate effort to flee, now motionless.

It was definitely death that, at the supreme moment, had reached out to him with its fearful hand. And we saw that he was pinned to the torture table, tragically and grotesquely, by the flap of his jacket, unto which, unconsciously, maddened by haste and the darkness, he had driven the last nail.

The Evocation

Madame Isabelle Moreau had been a happy woman since she had made the acquaintance of Henri Vautier a few weeks earlier. Married without love some ten years before, she had not even had for the man whose name she bore the sympathy to which esteem and habit can give rise. He had remained so indifferent to her that she had not thought that he could have experienced any other sentiment for her than those he inspired in her, and she had never wondered whether the reserved attitude that he had adopted in her regard was natural or dictated by a fierce jealousy.

She carried out the duties that the conjugal association imposed upon her. All day long she devoted herself to the concerns of the important dressmaking business of which her husband was the director, but she looked forward to the moment when dinner time would come and then, when the meal was over, he would go out two or three times a week to his club, from which he only returned at midnight or, more often, one o'clock in the morning.

These excursions did not take place according to a regular timetable, but almost every time, with the complicity of a blindly devoted maidservant, who stayed up waiting for her mistress, Madame Moreau escaped after her husband's departure to meet her lover, Henri Vautier, who lived in a neighboring street. The maidservant, Marguerite, and Isabelle agreed on the pretext that would be given to her husband if he returned unexpectedly—a pretext that could evidently only be used once, although they were tranquil, since the occasion had not yet arisen.

Meanwhile, the lover, uncertain as to which day would be free, waited in every evening. And every evening he went to bed at eleven o'clock, the hour when his lover left him to dream about her, whether she had come or not. He too was happy. He did not even have that bitterness which comes from the thought of the husband, when one can picture him, for he had never seen him—and Isabelle, for her part, was perfectly sure that Monsieur Moreau did not even know Henri Vautier's name.

She could not, however, avoid certain obligations, and that very day, in the afternoon, her husband had reminded her about a dinner invitation for that evening, which she had completely forgotten. It was in the home of old friends, the Hussons, whom they saw on a regular basis. It was impossible to get out of it, especially so late, for Monsieur Husson had also invited the son of one of his associates, Jacques Carmellin, in order to introduce him to the Moreaus, whose business he was due to join. Isabelle was terribly annoyed. She had not seen Henri for a week. She thought briefly about sending a warning via Marguerite, but that would have been an imprudent step. Besides, her lover was not specifically expecting her that evening rather than any other. She consoled herself somewhat in thinking about the joy that they would both have the following day.

They had just left the dining-room. The coffee was served in the drawing-room. Madame Husson brought a small occasional table, on which there was a box of cigars and an ash-tray.

During the meal, the conversation had touched on spiritualism.

"Here's an occasional table," remarked young Carmellin, "that would be marvelously appropriate for the evocation of spirits. Do you believe in table-turning, Madame?" The question was addressed to Isabelle.

"My God, Monsieur, I don't know. I've heard people talk about extraordinary things. Others, on the contrary, shrug their shoulders when anyone mentions communicating with the spirits by that means. If I had an opinion, I'd incline toward the negative, but I repeat, I really don't know."

"We could try to find out," said Monsieur Husson. "Shall we join forces to evoke the soul of a dead person?" He turned to his wife to add: "What do you think, my dear?"

"I think I'd be very frightened, if something actually happened."

"Bah! The drawing-room is well-lit, and women are only afraid of the dark."

"For my part," Isabelle affirmed, "even if I were a little frightened, I'd be very curious to take part in such an experiment."

"And what's your opinion, my dear Moreau?"

"It might be very interesting. Especially if…but no…it's absurd. Ah! In any case, I'll gladly take part in the experiment."

The table was cleared. The five individuals arranged themselves around it, and put their hands on the table.

"So," said young Carmellin, "we're going to evoke the soul of a dead person. It's a god thing we can't summon that of a living individual. That would be a very disagreeable surprise for him…"

"Come on, come on," said Moreau, a trifle feverishly, "no more talking. A moment of silent meditation seems indispensable to create the right atmosphere."

The ten hands were placed flat on the table, the extreme fingers touching. There was a silence.

Moreau, seemingly absorbed, fixed his eyes on the center of the table. His host leaned toward him. "It seems necessary to me to know which soul we're evoking. I don't know— someone that we've known well. A friend whose loss we regret…"

Moreau seemed to reflect, then said: "Certainly, but perhaps it's better to seek information first, to find out whether there might also be a spirit present in the table. Spirit, if you're here, would you like to manifest your presence? We're waiting."

A few minutes went by, in sight anguish. Then the table slowly rose up on two of its feet.

"Spirit, you're here," said Moreau, in a firm voice. "Would you permit us to speak to you, and are you disposed to answer our questions? We'll agree on one knock for yes, two knocks for no. For the rest, I'll recite the alphabet, and the table will tap its raised foot when I pronounce the necessary letter. Is that agreed?"

The foot that was in mid-air set itself deftly on the floor and lifted up again.

"Perfect. We thank you for accepting. Would you do us the favor of telling us your name?"

Two raps of the table.

"No? Would it be permissible for me to insist?"

Two more raps, more forceful.

"That's a definite no. I'm disappointed. Can you, at least, give us a few indications about the place where you are at present, on the…"

Moreau's speech was abruptly interrupted by two more raps, even more energetic.

"We're sorry. Would you consent, in that case, to put us in communication with another spirit? Can you do that And make it come here?"

One rap.

"Wait. I'd like to evoke the spirit of a man I knew well, and who would undoubtedly have interesting things to reveal to me."

At that moment, the drawing-room clock chimed midnight. There was a pause, during which the chimes measured out the time. Isabelle thought sadly that her friend, weary of waiting, had gone to bed and must be asleep.

Her husband continued: "Would you, then, fetch the soul for me…?"

Isabelle looked up fearfully, as if agitated by an obscure and terrible presentiment.

"The soul of our friend Vautier—Henri Vautier. Do you hear?"

The table rapped once.

"You can make it come here? Whatever the conditions in which it finds itself might be? Can you do that?"

The summoner's voice was bland and unemphatic. The witnesses followed the conversation, slightly anxious. Isabelle fought to avoid fainting. She had almost cried out: "But that's impossible. He's not dead." She had stopped herself in time, but what a fright! Did her husband know, then? Strangely enough, he had not glanced in her direction.

And how—by what terrible mystery—could a living being be evoked? The idea did not even occur to her that she was the victim of a misconception and that there was another Henri Vautier, that one dead. She knew only too well, on looking at her husband's face, that it was hers that was meant.

The table rapped once. The summoner's voice seemed to take on a sinister inflection.

"So, dear spirit, since you can, do it. We're waiting for Henri's soul…"

Henri—he had said Henri, as she did when she thought of him. What redoubtable familiarity! She summoned up all her strength, but she would rather have been in the void. Her hands were trembling convulsively on the table. Her husband appeared to have noticed it.

"Please, my dear. I understand that all this might seem a trifle disturbing, but we're not running any risk, and it's so interesting. Those around this table are in no danger. Besides, nothing prevents you from treating it as a game. Come on—a little calm!"

"Evidently," young Carmellin agreed. "Besides, we're not doing any harm. The spirits are free, it seems to me, to answer us or not…"

The Hussons' curiosity was keenly overexcited.

"We'll soon see," said the lady, "whether your poor friend will answer the summons."

"Shh! We'll undoubtedly need patience. That's the hazard. One never knows where souls are. Perhaps there's some special difficulty in the present instance. Let's wait…"

Silence fell around the table.

A quarter of an hour went by. Madame Moreau had had time to recover her composure.

Suddenly, the table rose up on one side. Or, rather, one might have thought that it was trying to rise up. There were brief little jumps, uneven, as if spasmodic. Then it fell back.

The voice of the summoner was heard, stern and imperious this time. "Spirit! Are you there? Answer!"

A series of rapid taps. Then immobility...

Suddenly, the witnesses shivered. On the drawing-room piano, three meters away, a note had just resonated: a deep, lugubrious note.

They all looked at one another, alarmed, ready to flee.

"It's nothing, it's nothing," said Moreau. "Sit down and let's resume."

Other notes sounded, slow and monotonous. One might have thought that it was a death-knell. Then there was silence. A few moments were required to calm the general emotion.

Moreau spoke. Perhaps it was only a collective auditory hallucination. Such cases occurred frequently. It was necessary not to be frightened, at the precise moment when interesting manifestations were surely about to be produced.

But Madame Moreau's face was as white as a shroud.

Then the table rose up on one foot several times, with precipitate raps. One might have taken it for a mute making impotent gestures.

"Wait. I'll begin the alphabet. Calm down, my friends, calm down. Would you care to tell me your name? Knock on the letter. A, B, C..."

The table remained immobile until the he had almost reached the end of the alphabet. As the letters were pronounced, Madame Moreau's eyes widened with fright.

"S, T, U," her husband continued, "V..."

The table rapped once.

"Ah! Perfect. Is it you, Vautier—Henri Vautier?"

Another tap, then disordered movements.

"Wait! Why are you getting agitated like this? Let's see, you're dead now. Now, are you suffering?"

One rap.

"Are you really suffering?"

Three energetic raps.

The summoner explained, in a cold and learned manner: "One rap means *yes*, two raps *no*, but three, ordinarily, signifies an emphatic *yes*. The soul we're evoking must be suffering a great deal." Then he addressed the table again. "That's understood. You're still in pain, by virtue of having quit your body, no matter how long it is since you found yourself in that state. Perhaps something happened to you that you weren't expecting?"

The foot rose up, and, as the table fell back, made a cracking noise that sounded like a groan.

"Well then, I'd like to do something for you. We have no intention of tormenting you. Are you there?"

One faint rap.

"You ought not to think about getting your body back. It's lost to you. Souls, once emerged, never re-enter their bodies. Their presence cannot prevent the work of decomposition, which is regular, fatal and definitive. That would be an indiscretion. This is what you should do. Listen to me, please. You must go to Egypt. Souls travel rapidly. When you get there, go to the pyramids. Beside them is the sphinx, its feet buried in the sand. Stop in front of it, in the sunlight. And I give you permission to spend all eternity imploring it to tell you the secret of life and death."

The table rose up, as if in bewilderment, leaning toward Madame Moreau, who had stood up, rigid, her eyes staring hypnotically.

The table leaned over further, then lost its equilibrium and fell at the poor woman's feet. There, it no longer budged.

Monsieur Husson looked at Madame Moreau, who was in great distress, and could not help protesting, timidly: "Perhaps it's wrong to carry out such experiments on the dead."

"It would be a terrible thing," said Carmellin, if one could, in the same conditions, evoke the souls of the living."

Alice's Story

For Joseph Hémard[23]

In those days, the maidservants in inns had a miserable time. It was necessary for them to get up before it was light, as soon as the cock crowed. Otherwise, the old shrew came to wake them with thrusts of the broom. In winter, they emerged from the bed shivering and leapt on to the cold stone floor with bare feet. They sang *The King's Daughter* in timid voices, in order to imagine themselves thus, but they had to get down to the ground floor quickly. All day long they worked, serving soldiers and peasants, washing jugs, drawing beer and lighting pipes. In the evening, they cleaning the crockery in a dark corner, which the inn's guests huddled around the fire, eating chestnuts and telling ghost stories.

After having toiled from one St. Sylvester's Day[24] to the next they received three écus a year and a pair of Candlemas sabots.

Little Alice was a servant in an inn in a village lost in the middle of the woods. The houses were scattered along the main road that cut through the forest. The bell-tower of the church mingled with the crowns of tall oak trees, and when the wind blew hard it seemed to sway like them, but in an opposite direction. It was also covered in moss, like them. There were crows that flew around and through the bell-tower, cawing raucously. In winter, there were some that settled in the

---

[23] Joseph Hémard (1880-1961) was a prolific illustrator; he illustrated Lautrec's *La Semaine des quatre jeudis* [A Week with Four Thursdays], which appeared in the same year as *La Vengeance du portrait ovale*.

[24] New Year's Eve.

middle of the road, and the falling snow put white patches on the black crows.

No one knew who Alice's parents were. She was as more of an orphan than anyone has ever been. Sometimes, when the Sun threw its gold coins on the ground through the foliage of the trees, she thought that she might perhaps be the abandoned child of some great lord who had gone to fight a distant war, and that she would be a princess one day.

In the meantime, though, she sent her life in a big kitchen with a low ceiling; then she was summoned to the main room by fists thumping loudly on the tables and she ran out carrying large jugs of beer, always fearing as she went that she might spill the foam.

In the afternoon, when the laborers were in the fields and the carters were no longer passing by, she was sent out with a basket to gather mushroom in the forest, where she learned to sing with the birds—and she went there all alone, under the trees, very far, to places where no one else ever went. In fact, people dared not go through the middle of the forest, because of the wolves.

Alice was not afraid of wolves, however, because she had never read the story of Little Red Riding-Hood—and she was sure, in the heart of the forest, of not encountering the miller, who ran after her to throw her under his mill-wheel, or the beadle with the long wig, who threatened her with his stick, or the village children, who threw stones at her as she went by.

The days passed in succession, however, for time marches on whether one is happy or not. The year was approaching its end, and people were preparing to celebrate the death and rebirth of the Sun, as they have since the beginning of the world, without ever doubting it. That year, Christmas fell on a Sunday. All through the preceding week, the villagers made great preparations. Floors and walls were washed with plenty of water and brasses rubbed energetically. The men had themselves shaved a week in advance and bought beautiful red cravats from hawkers.

Three months earlier they had begun fattening the geese in order to eat them on the day of the festival, and people both large and small were preparing to put their sabots in the hearth. The geese had been brought together in a flock; each of them bore the name of its owner around its neck, and poor Alice, lent out by the inn, took them to graze on the common.

The animals, which did not know the maidservant, were very naughty for the first few days, seeking all the time to escape, going up the slopes to either side of the road and escaping into the forest. The child chased the fugitives, getting out of breath, and when she finally caught them the geese pecked her hands. Gradually, however, by dint of patience, she ended up establishing herself as their mistress and getting them to love her. They could now be seen marching very meekly, with a heavy and awkward waddling gait. Alice had had the good idea of attaching them together with long ribbons, and they no longer went astray, as docile as sleep. Their guardian loved them now, with all her heart. She counted the days sadly, thinking that the unfortunates would soon be killed and eaten.

But the geese had no suspicion of that, and they stuck out their necks with an innocent curiosity in the direction of death. Why, after all, had they got such long necks, if not for someone to cut through them?

Thus Alice consoled herself.

Finally, the day arrived. The previous evening, all the geese had been gathered together in the main hall of the schoolhouse. They were to be sacrificed the next morning. In a last gesture of affection, Alice had removed the calendar bearing the fatal date from the wall. There were still maps on the panels and textbooks in the cupboards. There was little sign, though, that the geese wanted to profit from their last day—or, rather, their last night—by perfecting their education, somewhat neglected until then. Alice had wept when she left them, and they had all embraced her with their beaks. She knew full well that, at the celebratory feast, no one would give her even a morsel of her friends, with chestnuts. She would not have

126

had the heart to eat it anyway. She went to bed very sadly, therefore, in the attic whose skylight fortunately overlooked the forest.

The poor child did not even have the resource of putting her sabots in the hearth, like all the other people in the village, for the room had no fireplace, or even a stove. It was only warm there in summer.

Alice wept a little, went to sleep, and had the most beautiful dreams in the world.

The night went by, as usual, in the most profound darkness. Then daybreak came. People woke up, rubbed their eyes, got dressed and went downstairs to devote themselves to their usual tasks, with the hope of a good dinner. Suddenly, however, cries of surprise and disappointment emerged from every house in the village.

All the fireplaces were empty. Instead of being full of joyous gifts, the sabots than had been placed in the hearth had disappeared.

The schoolmaster, also stupefied before his empty fireplace, ran downstairs quickly, vaguely anxious. He went as far as the schoolroom where, the evening before, the geese had been lodged. The room was totally deserted; there was no longer even a single goose.

It was a very sad festival. For all the inhabitants of the village, the day was spent barefoot on the main road and the forest pathways, searching for the fugitives, but nothing was found and the question was raised: had the sabots carried off the geese, or the geese the sabots?

As was only to be expected, suspicion fell on the maid-servant. She was accused of having got up in the night, hidden the sabots and stolen the geese.

She did not think of defending herself—and anyway, what could she have said? It was necessary to punish someone. She was expelled from the region, shamefully, and after the official ceremony, the village crier, in the middle of a circle of gossips in the square, forbade her ever to return.

127

So there she was, alone on the road, not knowing where to go.

Fortunately, the moonlight was brought and the violets were perfuming the edges of the road.

Poor Alice was hungry. She picked violets and ate them. Then she set off again. At first, the landscape was familiar, but she soon found herself in the heart of the forest, which the road traversed from end to end, and as very afraid, for they were trees she had never seen.

She walked on regardless, until her feet were hurting by virtue of fatigue. She walked for much longer than she had ever walked before. Surely, she thought, as she went on all through the night, I'll arrive somewhere in the morning.

The Moon set. There was a diffuse light on the other side of the sky. Dawn came, and the bright mist in the willows, and there was still the road, with no village on the horizon. And even when she reached another village, would she not encounter people just as hard-hearted there, and would she not be condemned to carry jugs of beer or tend the village geese throughout her young eternity?

The poor girl, exhausted and discouraged, sat down on the roadside, at the foot of a mossy tress, and fell gradually half-asleep, in spite of the cold.

Slowly, softly, a vague noise becomes audible. Alice stirs in her semi-slumber. She is dreaming. She hears a murmur in the difference, which becomes more distinct and emphatic. It's as if someone were riding through cotton wool. There! It's the cortege of the Prince Charming who is coming, from the land of dreams, to marry the young shepherdess. A shepherdess and an inn-servant, when they are pretty, are the same thing. Alice wakes up, little by little. The rumor grows louder. No more doubt. There are the gilded carriages, with lackeys hanging on behind, upright, clinging to leather straps, and, comfortably ensconced on the front seat, a chubby and pot-bellied coachman.

Alice suddenly opened her eyes—and there, on the road she has travelled, was a distant cloud of dust, and a great tu-

mult, coming toward her. One might have taken it for the
hoofbeats of a troop of horsemen.[25] Abruptly turning her head,
Alice perceived all the geese, joyfully flying after her with
unequal wings. At the end of a long ribbon tied around its
neck, each of them was dragging a sabot—all of which made
an infernal racket as they bounced over the dusty ground.

They were all the sabots of the village, which the worthy
animals had stolen. They were full to the brim with various
objects, which were rebounding and falling to the ground.
There were flowers and toys, fans for damsels, garters and
ribbons, and pipes and tobacco for the old folk.

The little girl was surrounded, in the midst of a deafening
tumult. Her friends made a great fuss of her. Then two geese,
the fattest, approached haltingly, holding a vast sabot in their
beaks. It belonged to Anatole, the old beadle, who was also
the gravedigger. Before Alice' marveling eyes, all the geese
made sacrifices, plucking out a few feathers, and the young
girl sat down a queen on a feather bed in the middle of the
huge sabot.

With the former ribbons, all her fiends harnessed themselves to this improvised chariot, and the cortege, taking off,
brushed the treetops and disappeared over the horizon. It went
all the way to the Moon, which is not as far away as people
think, where the people gave the company the friendliest of
welcomes. In a nearby village, Alice was easily able to sell the
objects contained in the sabots—the majority of which were
great novelties—for a tidy sum. The snuff-boxes, in particular,
were a great success, and the pipes and tobacco, which the
local people were seeing for the first time; it was from that
exact day onwards that pipes were smoked on the Moon.

Alice lived very happily, and only kept the geese thereafter to amuse herself. With the provision that she had, she was
able to change her sabots every day. The ones she kept for

---

[25] There is a punning reference to *sabots* here that cannot be translated—the word is used in French to refer to metal horseshoes as well
as clogs worn by humans.

Sundays had long points, and the rims of the openings were decorated with blue plush.

A Family Matter

Old Hop Jones, the founder of the famous mercantile enterprise at the sign of the Black Diamond, who was familiarly known as "Uncle Jones," had been dead for some time. His old establishment on the quay would not have recognized him. It had once watched him come and go, from its affectionate windows, in his afternoon routine, year after year, small and plump, his wig on sideways, his jacket worn at the elbows by the friction of the tall desk, tapping the flagstones of the quay lightly with his cane. One day, however, without any apparent pretext, there had been a crowd of black coats and top hats outside the open door, in mourning: relatives and friends, with appropriate expressions, had energetically shaken the hands of nearer relatives, representatives of the communal grief. Eyes had been raised to the ceiling, and lips curled into the arc of a circle, in warranted amazement.

From that day on, people had acquired the habit, on the steps, of considering the actions of old Hop Jones as if they had been affected by such commercial depreciation that they had been reduced to zero. Life had continued, with other faces and other canes tapping the sidewalks, and the old gentleman had become, in the eyes of his entourage, a mere supposition of the past. Even his old suit, hung up somewhere in the house in the most obscure wardrobe, no longer remembered his rounded shoulders.

But there was a son of Hop Jones sitting in front of the cash-box and the big ledger, in the same attitude as the elder one. There was a son of Hop Jones, pen at his ear, rebuking the packers in the dispatch-room. There was a son of Hop Jones, fat and solemn, his chin laden with ruddy side-whiskers, rounded out in a large armchair in front of an oak table on the first floor of the house. He was the most important Hop Jones. Within range of his hand were acoustic tubes and

131

telephone apparatus. At the far end of each one, far away or close and hand, were other Hop Joneses—grandsons, cousins or nephews, some sitting in armchairs, others standing up in front of some transmission apparatus, listening, with varied expressions and movements, to the words of the most important.

That individual himself, in the midst of his calculations, was distracted and irritated at regular intervals by the sounds of a piano on which the same notes were played, invariably, for ten hours a day, by slender fingers that must belong to some demoiselle Hop Jones, gaunt and gauche, ripe for marriage. Is it necessary to add that, in the provincial branches, Hop Jones brothers-in-law were putting weighty letters into the post on a daily bases, bearing that same name in their addresses, while one encountered other Hop Joneses, younger and more distantly-related, on the platforms of railway stations, travelling on behalf of the business, and moving at a light and rhythmic step, suitcase in hand, along avenues of beautiful and rather solitary plane-trees, toward the melancholy of little towns that cool down, and close down as rapidly, at dusk? Old Hop Jones was dead, but Old Hop Jones' descendants were more numerous than the pages of the big ledger, or those of Receipts and Outgoings, and the house was rich enough to deem the death of the ancestor to be a simple matter of profit and loss.

A few years after the events whose supposition is permitted by the preceding lines, the entire Jones family came together in a vast glazed hall, lit from above. Not one of those who bore the illustrious name had failed to respond to the invitation. There was an imposing crowd of Hop Joneses there, young and old, all the ladies well-dressed and the men in suits. Second-class return tickets had been solicited in unusual quantities on the preceding days. For those who lived in the house on the waterfront, the journey had been easier.

A few of the ladies, in response to a coquettish impulse that the continuation of this story will doubtless excuse, were wearing all their diamonds. They were, naturally, the oldest and the ones with the lowest necklines. There were smiles there as old and as vainly charming as the sparkling stones and gold, and shoulders were drooping. A few young women, all Hop Joneses, made a pleasant contrast with massive towers of corkscrew-curls and false headbands; and hired women with powerful bosoms, bearing in their arms the latest offspring of the family, clad in white bibs and ridiculous outfits. All the costumes and silks were sparkling at the back of the hall. At the opposite extreme stood a strange object on which all eyes and attention seemed to be fixed. It was a tall and delicate item of furniture posed on a tripod. A green serge curtain suspended from the ceiling, rising or falling, impeded access to it.

One day, one of the younger Hop Joneses had revealed to other family members a few ideas that seemed strange and new, but persuasive, the result of which was the presence of all these people at the gathering. The event had just been completed. All the Hop Joneses, in succession, had sat down in the tall armchair; the important individual on the first floor had made the springs of the egalitarian chair creak under his finery, and the young woman with the long fingers had give up her piano-stool for him. Widowed aunts had uttered faint cries. Meanwhile, the necromancer, whose existence was a sin against the Sun, lifted up the heavy drapery for each one in turn, and the same glassy gaze had appeared every time, round and jealous. That implacable and mocking gaze seemed, within the interval of a lightning-flash, to fix itself furtively on every face; one might have though it the eye of a formidable stranger, seeking to recognize forms and shadows that resembled him as they passed by and passed on.

Now they were waiting. A certain vulgar anguish oppressed their hearts, and falsely calm words enunciated conventional banalities.

"What advantage will not stem," said the head of provincial branch, a second-cousin, "from vulgarizing this procedure! I think few discoveries justify the fine name of the age of enlightenment better than this one. If we adopt a philosophical viewpoint, it's a fine example of synthesis: taking the images of several individuals, united by blood ties, and combining all those images into one, representing the *trading name* of all the rest, if I might put it thus."[26]

The individual who was speaking was thin, with long grey and white side-whiskers; the shape of his mouth was suggestive of indulgent bonhomie, and his mannerisms were full of self-confidence.

"Oh," said another, much younger, junior relative, "the real advantage is the economy of the procedure."

There was laughter, and a few chairs stirred; then everyone fell silent.

The necromancer had just come in. He was holding a modestly-sized piece of card in his hands, and was looking attentively at the individual represented in the image.

The eyes of the audience turned toward him. Curiosity led them to contemplate the features of the face, and a vague anxiety in their souls made them apprehensive. Did that unique face, resulting from the combination of theirs, that imaginary individual, resemble anyone? What mystery was more disturbing than that of the consciousness and the soul represented and imperiously necessitated by that gaze, too lively never to have lived.

The necromancer held the image out to them. An exclamation of amazement and anguish escaped their throats. It was Old Hop Jones's own face that was smiling at them.

Before the air vibrated by their clamors of alarm had calmed down, however, the door of the room opened wide, and on the threshold, in the midst of gestures of recoil and hands veiling faces, appeared Old Hop Jones himself, with his cane and his wig, in flesh and bone...

After the fainting-fits, everyone hurried forward. The old man was pressed against waistcoats and the shop-fronts of

---

[26] This wordplay, fundamental to the story, does not translate as well as it might; the phrase I have rendered here, in its usual conventional sense, as "trading name" is *raison sociale*, which obviously carries more plangent echoes of general and wide-ranging relationship than its English equivalent.

dresses. Everyone wanted to shake his hand. He let them so do, with a slightly sad smile, and then asked about his familiar windows and quayside. No allusion was made to his absence; even the slightest would have been in bad taste.

All ceremonies concluded, heading for home, on the cushions of the carriage, Uncle Jones, shaken by the jolts, abandoned himself with an inclination of his old-fashioned head to visions of monuments and trees, cut off by the rim of the window, sudden scenes that he recognized by virtue of having encountered them by day, in the rain or bleak sunlight.

A great celebration was held. The entrepreneur of funerals and marriages, the lighter of nocturnal lamps, from his shop with the black hoarding, summoned the same suits and the same finery as before, to the same rendezvous—but they came waving open letters of invitation. A joyful family occasion was announced. Carriages rolled noiselessly along the riverbank all evening. There were apparitions of bright cravats and flowers in hair. Men armed with torches bowed before ladies with their skirts gathered in their hands, moving lightly toward the door open to beautiful luminous vestibules. There was a certain amount of embarrassment at first. Then, with the uncle, sitting in an armchair by the fire, in bright candlelight, the party got going. Monologues took flight.

Uncle Hop Jones recovered his place at the family table. The old round-shouldered coat remained in the dusty wardrobe; a new suit was inaugurated to celebrate the joyous occasion, and when the numerous but unique image, the cause of the prodigy, was hung on the wall of the study, the ancestor sat opposite, and the provincial offices regulated their dispatches.

As the days passed, however, and external events became more similar every day, a slow and dull disturbance penetrated the house. The novelty of the phenomenon, unperceived in the surge of first impressions, appeared to rested eyes. The revenant had resumed his afternoon walks in the sunshine, but in the street, the sound of his voice was strange, and a confused thought arose in everyone's mind, that he ought not to linger at dusk, not for his own sake but that of frightened others. Something had returned that should not have returned. As soon as the curfew sounded and the family meal was ready, the ancestor went back inside, where his servants, under the puerile pretexts of possible assistance and cares, crouched behind the doors, keeping track of his respiration. Fear imprisoned everyone.

The ancestor had, however, never been more similar to himself in the time of his first existence. The ancient gestures rediscovered, when he passed in front of a mirror, prey to vague doubts, reassured him as to the mystery of his tenebrous identity. But it was that identity itself which frightened him in its turn. There was, in his fashion of leaning on his elbows and sitting down, an element of *déjà vu*. Exterior scenes suggested other images to him of which he knew nothing, except that they had existed. That movement of lifting his hand to his forehead at times when his mind was thoughtful was not new. Sometimes, in the dark, a thought whose form he could not distinguish, but which he sensed all the more real and present for it, came to die on the frontier of his life. It came from somewhere immeasurably more distant than his anterior existence. One might have thought it a chimera, luminous in the dark, with green-golden wings, fleeing an inexhaustible frisson through vanished worlds, the last of which was unfolding in his present surroundings.

At the same time, the old man felt a new soul emerging within his own, composed of all those distributed around him. He recognized himself in some gesture or some play of expression observed in one of the Hop Joneses, and at other times, by contrast, paused thoughtfully as he noticed in himself, in the blink of an eye, some attitude that drew his memory imperiously to some cousin or other. It seemed that his consciousness, a vain and obsolete thing, was obliged to borrow, in order to dream, the shreds of the lives of more present consciousnesses, his descendants, as, in the ancient folktale, the empty heads of the dead drink the blood of victims before answering.

All these mysterious images moved within a singularly vulgar frame, for one thought moves through a thousand different ones, all true. The ridiculous and sulky old man was depressing for the house. Why was he not still in the shadows, which his time to enter had come? Quarrels broke out. His place had been taken, with respect to the smallest quotidian details; that finally became obvious. These were verities of observation and not of reasoning. Besides, it seemed that the man, having lived more than once, had more than one bitterness in his heart; he complained. The belated fear that he inspired was not a sufficient pretext for respect, and the commercial honesty of the Hop Joneses had got the upper hand again. By what right had he come back, demanding his part in a game from which a superior will had excluded him the first time around? His wealth had been shared out. He lived on in his descendants. To claim, beyond that, some personal existence, seemed to be a kind of blameworthy plurality that ought not to be encouraged.

It did not take long for Uncle Hop Jones to become odious to everyone. The old man, bending under that reprobation and the burden of two existences, slowly made his way toward the route from which his steps had strayed, to some cypress-planted crossroads, and while his gestures were designed more rarely and more uncertainly, hasty and ardent joys awaited his funereal immobility.

It was on an evening similar to the one that had seen him reappear. All the upsetting things that inspire fear of oblivion, remedies and souvenirs, had been brought into the room. The entire family was assembled around his death-bed; candles had been lit all over the room to illuminate everything, for it seemed that the most frightening visitor was about to enter the room. One candle was placed on Uncle Hop Jones's bed-head, whitening the old man's face.

As the moment drew nigh, a greater serenity became legible in his features. Calm had repossessed his soul at the approach of a familiar country, and, as the wind agitated the treetops, and came through the window open on the distant darkness to caress the old man's hands, it really seemed to be a breath from beyond.

Uncle Hop Jones smiled, as did the demoiselle at the piano; the wind blew more strongly through the windows, and all the candles went out, except for the one at the head of the dead man's bed.

Monsieur Ciboire, Innkeeper

Monsieur Ciboire[27] was an innkeeper in the Rue Saint-Jacques, at the sign of the Crowned Ox. He was, moreover, when he got up that morning, in a very bad temper. All night, the sleep of his legitimate spouse had been disturbed. Her husband had moaned, turned over and over like a fish on a hot stove, causing the virtuous mattress to groan in chorus with his plaints, and launched the unmade bedclothes across the room at hazard. Madame Ciboire was distressed; her husband was going mad.

The profession of innkeeper has, among other inconveniences, one more serious than the rest. It is necessary to lend an ear to clients and their sometimes-perverse theories, and it was the memory of conversations with the regulars of the Crowned Ox that was tormenting Monsieur Ciboire.

People in cafes have been known to take a malign pleasure in making an idiot of the lady enthroned at the counter in the midst of precisely-calculated and sugar cubes placed one atop another, in much the same fashion as the stones making up the pyramids were measured by the geometers of Egypt and set in place by the Hebrews. They talk to her about absurd things, which bring a smile to her lips, and her torturers track the progress of madness in her troubled brain on a daily basis. The same thing was happening to Monsieur Ciboire, and for days his dreams had been troubled by nightmares.

Among the inn's regulars there were painters who spent their time like the majority of young painters, wearing strange

---

[27] *Ciboire* is the French form of the Latin *ciborium*, whose original literal reference was to a kind of seed-pod, but was appropriated into the terminology of the church to refer to a canopy over an altar or, more commonly, a goblet with a lid in which communion wafers are kept.

clothes and emitting superannuated paradoxes. One of them, named Brancowich, who had been smoking his pipe at the second table on he left for ten years, while waiting until he could get a place at the Institut's manger, had chosen the innkeeper as a victim. Had he not undertaken to demonstrate one evening last week, with supporting evidence and indubitable philosophical citations, that color did not exist?

To tell the truth, the existence of certain painters is an energetic and continuous protest against the reality of colors—but Monsieur Ciboire's innocent soul had never raised the slightest doubt about the existence of colors. Monsieur Ciboire's fine blue eyes had never regarded the various hues of everyday objects as anything but luminous verities. Monsieur Ciboire did not understand philosophical theories at all. He would never, like Descartes, have shut himself up in an earthenware stove in order to attain, ten years later, the sublime discovery that what exists, exists, and that what doesn't exist, doesn't. If anyone had told our innkeeper about such procedures, he would have shrugged his shoulders while looking sympathetically at the little earthenware stove on which he warmed water for shaving in the morning, and would not have hesitated to consider any man who proposed using a similar object for philosophical experiments as a madman. Monsieur Ciboire's logic did not admit such compromises.

Thus, his mind was singularly disturbed every time he found himself in the presence of a correctly-presented paradox.

Monsieur Ciboire got out of bed slowly and regretfully. Madame Ciboire, who was sensitive to cold, swathed herself in the bedclothes and flattened her nose against the wall—firmly decided, a superficial observer would have thought—to contemplate the flowers on the wallpaper at the closest possible range until death. A sonorous snoring, which rose up shortly afterwards, would, however, have proved the observer wrong.

Her husband opened the door and stumbled downstairs to the ground floor. Through the cracks in the shutters, the timid yellow morning light crept in from outside. When the shutters were open, Monsieur Ciboire was outlined against the black background of the room, lit by the oily stain of a lamp, like a character in a badly-reproduced etching. The street-lights, awaiting the heavy tread of the extinguisher who was bringing their night-caps, gave a flash of joy at the sight of him on the shop's doorstep, which was for them a regular presage of pleasant slumber.

But Monsieur Ciboire did not look at the street-lights or the rare early morning pedestrians. He did not go, as he usually did, to stand momentarily on the sidewalk on the other side of the narrow street, with his flat hands hooked on to the front of his belt, to contemplate the familiar façade proudly. Above the iron bars surrounding the low bay of the shop swayed the sheet of canvas on which Brancowich had painted a Crowned Ox in colors whose crudity would have brought a smile to the faces of anyone who had ever set out to cook such an animal, in any kind of oven.

Glumly, the proprietor of the Crowned Ox started collecting the glasses and bottles left on the counter the previous evening. His eyes no longer paid any attention to the things that surrounded him. The philosophical poison was beginning to take effect. When Brancowich arrived, he expressed the desire to have a serious conversation with him. They were visible in the rear of the shop, to either side of a bottle of old wine, tracing geometric figures on the account slate. Their silhouettes were profiled as gesticulating black shadows on the frosted glass of the partition.

New theories were put forth in the following days, and the innkeeper felt the sane and calm ideas that had previously inhabited the narrow dwelling of his brain without any complaint become unsteadier with every passing minute. Now, he too debated in the pipe-smoke, under the puerile pretext of keeping his clients company, as a good host should. In the society of painters that frequented his establishment, his behavior was gradually transformed. His nascent skepticism gave him a pretext for irregularity. He went out in the evenings with

141

Brancowich—and the disturbance imported into his conduct and the calmness of his employment was manifest when he returned from his nocturnal expeditions, in evidences of which the good Madame Ciboire, although astonished by the rejuvenation, did not complain.

It was, in fact, natural for him to discuss tastes as well as colors. His initial negations on the latter subject were gradually developed into timid conjectures, soon to be transformed into ferocious affirmations. As often happens, the placid ox, derided for his amiability, became a spirited bull.

He was seen strolling in the street, shaking his head at the signs whose illumination gave the neighboring houses the air of Medieval stalls. The merchant of colors and varnishes, whose shop was situated at the corner of the Rue Saint-Jacques and the Faubourg, a personal friend of M. Ciboire's, was obliged to listen to him. The innkeeper profited from these moments of liberty to come and tell him about his theories. Since color did not exist, the sale of varied tubes, brushes and varnishes was an insult to common sense. The passers-by witnessed strange conflicts in which M. Ciboire hurled energetic abuse at his neighbor.

If he had ruined that commerce, his own was not worth much more. The painters, happy to have succeeded in their humorous enterprise, better than they could have hoped, took their paradoxes elsewhere. His habitual clients made the gesture of shaking their heads while raising a forefinger to the forehead sadly, whenever M. Ciboire turned his back. His wife, troubled by day with tyrannical explanations and at night by nightmares, thought of seeking refuge with her mother. Her remonstrations were in vain. Her husband's madness only got worse. He bought technical books and dreamed of a great work that he would write, which would render his name immortal.

Anyway, although his wife did not appreciate him, and little children ran after him in the street, there were compensations. An avant-garde review, seduced by the theories that he explained to a few editors who had strayed into his establish-ment, entrusted essays in art criticism to his authorized pen.

From then on, he claimed the most rigorous rights from the external world. Only being able to modify, according to his whim, the things that he knew to be no more than a whim of his imagination, he wanted, at least, to see them differently. Evenings were taken up in the fabrication of an ingenious in-strument designed to demonstrate his ideas. It was an enorm-ous pair of spectacles in the form of a spherical skullcap, ap-plied to both eyes and only allowing light to pass through the window that sealed them in. That mobile window-pane was, for M. Ciboire, the pretext for the wildest orgies of color. He adapted painted lenses—red, yellows, blues—to his spec-tacles, through which external objects seemed to him to be magnificently illuminated. It was a sort of magic lantern in which his eyes enjoyed the focal point. Thus, when he went out in the evening, with his two enormous portholes, one might have taken them for the red and tremulous headlights of an omnibus.

People came from far and wide to see him, driven by cu-riosity. He was cited, with ironic eulogies, in the medical jour-nals. Reporters came to interview him. He talked to them about Nero, to whom he compared himself because of the carved emerald that the Roman emperor had worn in his eye.

He had even better ideas. He made plans, briefly, to in-ject red madder or ultramarine blue into the very globe of the eye. His wife had a great deal of difficulty persuading him to renounce them.

She had stayed with him, in spite of everything, out of devotion. His madness got worse and became dangerous. Now, he bounded through his colorist doctrines like an acro-batic clown, bursting through them in the middle of painted paper hoops.

He had to be locked up. He languished behind the walls of an asylum, and then, after several weeks, died in a fit of frenzy. The exact cause of his death was an abuse of reason. One had to believe, he knew, that colors do not exist, but one nevertheless had to live as if they did. A true philosopher knows full well that there is nothing but appearances, but consents in practice to regard appearances as realities.

Monsieur Ciboire died at the age of forty years, six months and four days. A respectable funeral was held at the church of Saint-Jacques-du-Haut-Pas, and his widow continued his business, having mourned him for a decent interval.

Eulogy to the Moon

For Anatole France[28]

The temple was illuminated with a yellow and placid light, which a wind fresher than the wind of tombs, coming through the high windows, caused to vacillate. The aisle was equal in its red splendor to that of any poem. From the numerous nave where my presence was evidently indecisive, a scene of absolute happiness was revealed to me. The attitude of the witnesses was resigned. All the usual features of churches were gilded by an ideal magic. Even the old women shifting their chairs and rattling the keys in their belts gave evidence in their bearing of a supreme and involuntary dignity. One sensed that the familiar ridicule associated with the person of sacristans and beadles was the indulgent ridicule of something holy. They were far above the most noble among us.

Even the stones of the pillars, by their manner of holding themselves, one above another, very squarely or according to the rounded form of arches, let a discrete and contained joy shine through. Lost in the crowd, a venerable old man with a white beard was pointed out to me, whom I was assured was the good Lord; he seemed intimidated. He might really be the Absolute for the host of exterior entities, but here, in the actuary of the ineffable secret, the good Lord, benevolent and embarrassed, was doubtless glad to be a modest unity. The real God, the one whose anticipated arrival was making all hearts tremble, had not yet come.

---

[28] Anatole France (1844-1924) was the most prestigious writer and critic in France while Lautrec was active; he published several classic collections of fantastic stories, but nothing remotely resembling this one.

I do not know in the midst of what noise of vesperal bells or what formidable silence the doors of carved wood would open, between the vascular marble of the double fonts. Those who were coming were not advancing though the open air and the trees, beneath the blue sky, but along shadowed corridors with liturgical lamps, whose oil was renewed by pious hands at dawn as at dusk. Their procession seemed o have been wandering forever beneath vaults and though closed cloisters. In advance of the royal cortege, as a superb reminder, in sadness, of carnal joys—dead, O dead, one knows how profoundly dead—a choir of naked and disdainful adolescents was dancing a slow dance before the unknown master. An adorable sweat perfumed the secrets of their young flesh like an incense. They were the servants of voluptuousness.

Then, nodding their heads in a manner concentrated by habit, doubtless having come from some presbytery situated in a street with arbors of faded roses, with the maternal care of an old maidservant afflicted with extreme infatuation, and knowing all the bells in the district by their baptismal names, the canons of the Beatitude, in golden capes and violet robes, advanced two by two toward the choir.

There were strange things there, a world in revolt against conventional forms, a desperate appeal to the new. People were standing about the hall, their hands upraised, sustaining old gilded missals in their slanted palms. Devoutly leaning over antiphonary lecterns set in front of them, the red face of cantors were singing the daily psalms.

Then the choir of virgins made its entrance.

Their prayer rose up, at first, in a vague and confused voice, as the mist rises over the wheatfields at dawn. Clearer and sadder notes gushed from their lips in light ramifications. They could not be singing anything other than a eulogy to the Moon. There were alternate and slow verses, as in amoebic poems. Each one found more sumptuous eulogies than the last. I was delighted to hear that sacerdotal homage rendered to the old Moon, the ancient goddess known on Earth for such a long time.

146

"O Moon of Chaldean nights, which shines upon the silence of herdsmen! They have planted their curved staffs in the sandy ground to sustain tents. In the melancholy of thresholds never to be attained, they demand the horizon.

"You are the resigned landscape in which every dream finds a dwelling. You are the repose to which, after death, the light souls of poets go, dead cicadas scattered over the blanched soil of memory. A pale-faced lady, gazing through the importunate clouds at her reflection in the polished mirror of the sea. On the oval frame, a work of genius, mountains and forests are silhouetted.

"But O Moon of the seas! The Moon laughs, the Moon insinuates; the Moon mocks the vain waves; beneath its impassive face, like some silken mantle, the last ripples spread out toward the most distant shore, trickling like a sob. The Moon laughs, the Moon insinuates, the eternal Moon bites the waves.

"Moon of incantations! White basket in which, for centuries, the amorous have poured their roses, tragic and glowing mask. The Moon triumphs over the entire line. She is celebrated by the chair of virgins, like all vain things, like modesty, lilies, and unique love, the ivory and divine scorn of joy.

"Inviolate vestal of preambles and purifications! Are you the mystery and do you know the key? Perhaps, if we had followed you in your errant course with our eyes, we would have found it traced by your passage through the blue ether.

"What charming and fearful face will you reflect this evening, beautiful unparalleled mirror?

"Is the comedy that has held you in distant hands played out? One awaits the scenery eternally. Do the prophets distressed by eternal suffering bear the ebony flute or the golden zither in their bosoms? Is it not true that a sublime drama, of which we are the reflection, was once played out up there? Our words are like the echo of an apocalyptic clarion. The stars, O Moon, are the incompletely darkened ramp of the ancient stage, and you, the grandiose mask that the divine protagonist throws disdainfully aside, once the words are spoken."

147

Thus the virgins spoke to the Moon, that evening. The Hebrews, by the waters of Babylon, spoke of Jerusalem. With the gold of phrases and the pure crystal of music, they built the temple in which regrets come to pray.

When other torches had been lit, the silence was absolute. Except, in the depths of the temple, at the moment when the eulogy ended, a black velvet curtain moved aside, to reveal in the distant blue the two white horns, Diana's bow, the slender cradle of chosen hearts.

An infinite sadness penetrated hearts. The pewter incense-burners placed on the altar consumed themselves at the touch of red embers on which the Levites poured odorous and intoxicating grains.

A violent wind lifted up the curtains, like a despairing hand. Was the master of the strange going to come? The king of the country of the Moon, the counselor of poets, the god whose mouth knew the words to open the door to occult treasures, the choir-master of adolescents who refuse to believe in life, the unique in sadness, and the beloved?

The fear of not knowing the words to salute him made my retreat from the arch toward which my gestures had extended. These people where like those who put a finger to their lips, listening to redoubtable footsteps grow louder on the staircase—but my soul was almost absent already, and I fled, dreading the appearance, after that parade and that game, of the being with the sad and lunar face, the man with the goat's face who leans over the cradle of some among us, scornful of them, ashamed of them, the dear master of human disquiet— the one, in sum, who is well-known to us but whose name we dare not pronounce.

Expiation

For Colette[29]

Considering the causes that led to the death of my friend Désormeaux, and the circumstances of that death, I cannot help experiencing, modest as I am, a very legitimate pride. Never was a wisely-conceived project put into action with more security, or procured a more profound joy to the perpetrator.

To tell the truth, I had wanted to kill Désormeaux for a long time. His existence had become incompatible with mine. I was used to the ingratitude of men, but that of my friend Désormeaux was something so monstrous that it exceeded the extraordinary. For several years I admired that special case, and came to cultivate it curiously, incessantly giving the wretch new opportunities to prove that radiant ingratitude to me. I furnished him with benefits, as a sumptuous king heaps gold upon the artist of genius whose works magnify him, but it was only gradually that I tasted the full savor of his inverted gratitude.

A miserable hack when I met him, he was able, thanks to me, to enter into relations with the serious editors who helped him earn money. The old Duc de B*** , who dabbled in literature, confided the editing of his memoirs to him at my request. Thus extracted gradually from poverty, Désormeaux settled down comfortably, abandoning the Bohemian life he had led

---

[29] Sidonie-Gabrielle Colette (1873-1954), who only used her surname, became notorious after divorcing her first husband, Henri Gauthier-Villars, alias "Willy," who had published her early novels under his name; she became one of the most flamboyant figures in the Parisian literary *monde*.

until then. He was married, too, and had a little daughter about ten years old. I paid little heed to his family, for he alone interested me, by virtue of the delightful manner in which he discharged his debts to me, according to his mores.

When my name was mentioned to him, he sighed—or talked, which was worse. Friends warned me. I laughed at them. In the course of several years, he represented me successively as a German spy, a homosexual, a vampire and a forger. I only exaggerate a little, for he had a fine imagination. He worked hard to blacken my name—to no avail, happily—with all the people to whom I introduced him in his interest. Some of them came to speak to me about it, indignantly, and I was obliged to sacrifice them, to my great regret. The excess of his infamies attenuated their effect, and stung my generosity. When, maliciously—and very rarely, besides—I made allusion to some new dirty trick of his, he blushed lightly, with stammering and voluble protestations of friendship. Until the day when I wearied of it, as one wearies of everything.

A few innocents began looking at me disapprovingly. It appeared to me that my purse had then been open to the impudent fellow's hand for a long time. I was, moreover, tired of him, and took pity on the efforts he made, every time we met, to conceal his hatred, the natural fruit of my benevolence. The strangeness of the case itself gradually ceased to interest me. Finally, I decided that enough was enough, and that it was necessary to get back to normality and punish the wretch as he deserved.

That happened a month ago. Once the resolution was made, I waited patiently for an opportunity, preparing my security by means of the necessary precautions, with no harmful exaggeration. What dooms the majority of criminals is the extravagant care they take to ensure their impunity in advance. I had, meanwhile, avoided meeting Désormeaux. I made arrangements to run into him one evening, late, in a deserted quarter, as he was coming back from dining with friends.

On seeing him, I manifested an extraordinary surprise, in order that he should not think of being astonished himself. I was able to draw him into some waste ground whose layout I knew. Slightly fuddled, it seemed to me, by the fumes of the wine, he followed me unreflectively, recounting things of no interest, in stammering and voluble words. I supported his tottering steps with my left arm. And nothing was easier, after looking around to make sure that we were alone, than suddenly to take a revolver out of my pocket.

One second, and the barrel was pressed against his breast; another second, and I pressed the trigger. I saw my companion's eyes open very wide. He had time, I am sure, to realize and understand. I knew by his expression. He fell without uttering a sound. In the direction of that which, in others, is the heart I discharged the rest of the revolver's bullets. Then I left unhurriedly, lighting a cigarette as I left the waste ground, and went home by an indirect route.

They were able, thanks to his papers, to identify the cadaver. An investigation was opened, which obviously produced no result. The burial is tomorrow. The widow came to see me. A grotesque and ugly creature, living under the brutal dependence of her husband, I had only seen her once or twice before, some years ago. I had, in fact, always avoided Désormeaux's domicile; I knew full well that had I accepted a simple glass of water from him he would immediately have borrowed the money necessary to hire a cab for an hour, in order to go to all the editorial offices to say that I was a shameless sponger and a repulsive parasite—for that was his nature, and some calumnies are more wounding than others. But I could not refuse to see the woman, in the dolorous circumstances.

She was perfect, anyway, without any affectation of exaggerated despair. She talked about her daughter, about whose future she was worried. I enquired politely and was astonished to learn that the child was about to turn eighteen. Then we sighed, with an exquisite naturalnesss on my part, over the unexpected misfortune that had struck the two poor women.

The widow, to assure me of her sympathy, as I gave her the money to pay for the funeral, made a delicate allusion to the services that her husband had incessantly rendered to me. My joy no longer knew any bounds. The man truly had genius. I kissed the widow's hand respectfully, and promised to arrive early at the following day's ceremony.

Oh, the wretch! How well he has been able to continue his work of hatred, and to avenge the death that I childishly thought to inflict upon him! We have taken him to the cemetery. Insane! Should I not rather have fled? What demon made me pursue my vengeance beyond the permissible bounds?

In my blindness, I exulted, with that interior joy that is all the more powerful by virtue of the fact that one cannot manifest it. The weather was radiant. I had seen two women come out of the house and take up positions behind the hearse, wearing the mourning-dress that makes it impossible to perceive the features. I knew that one as the widow, though, and in the other I divined the gracious silhouette behind the black veils of my enemy's already-grown-up daughter. In addition to them and me, there were only five or six unknown people, vague relatives or tradesmen. I was the only friend he had been able to retain.

We went through the outlying districts. We arrived at the burial-ground. The ceremony was brief. When we found ourselves back at the cemetery gates, the few witnesses took their leave. I remained alone with the two women. The widow thanked me in emotional terms, and I heard a tremulous voice beside her. The young woman that I had only glimpsed as a child lifted her crêpe veil in order to smile at me sadly. And then…then! The miracle, in all its astounding rarity, occurred. Love entered my soul, imperious, all-conquering, immediate and definitive. I knew, from that moment on, that it would be futile to struggle, and that I will adore, for as long as I live, the daughter of the man I execrated. Oh, the frightful vengeance— and how small I feel by comparison with my vanished enemy!

Transformed into its most redoubtable avatar, his hatred has bequeathed me love.

Polar Terror

For Pierre Louÿs[30]

Now, the ship had set sail for the unknown lands of the South. The men had always had the desire for new stars, although still finding them indifferent to the miseries, as to the joys, of humankind. There was hope of discovering a passage, and verifying certain laws. Is the temperature at the two poles the same? Does the magnetic axis extend, like the central timber of a gigantic vessel, from one extreme to the other? And does the monstrous Earth, of whose form we are ignorant, as Homer and Ptolemy were ignorant in respect of other images, follow a regular movement of propulsion through space? Perhaps there was also some thought of filling with unexpected riches, for a sumptuous return, the supple cedar-wood hold solidly braced by shiny ribs with polished nails. Over the glaciers, at a timid pace, blue foxes with expensive fur and sadly pointed muzzles are running. And the ivories that the long night has rendered blacker than Erebus are buried in the depths of caverns immured by the ice, and the lugubrious wind no longer agitates even a single dead branch.

But who can describe the familiar nostalgia of embarkation, and the afternoon on the indolent beautiful blue sea? Faces were leaning out of the old windows of the harbor. They have seen so many hopes perch there, white hair beneath worn headwear or pink cheeks and fluttering hearts. Sailors on shore leave were hastening out of the hospitable side-streets on to the steeped cobbled roadway. Yard-arms and rigging were

---

[30] Pierre Louÿs (1870-1925) became one of the central figures of the Decadent Movement, famous for the lavish eroticism of his novels; this story bears no resemblance to his work.

silhouetted against the sky. As on the flanks for ancient hulls, the vessel had borne away regrets, garlands of roses and, in its masts, the echo of romances. It had, however, wandered over oceans as polished as breastplates. Every passing brush of a sail by the wing of a marine bird dispersed a memory into oblivion. Shorelines had appeared in the distance, like clouds, green with wheat, with trees and joyous cries. And so far had they voyaged that they arrived in the latitudes that extinguish all smiles. It is there that the Ocean mingles its waters with those of the river Lethe. The paler Sun rises more slowly. It wanders over the summits of the waves like a gaze; its yellow light brightens faces and the play of expressions more troubling than in other climes. The legendary geographers made these shores the domain of obscure terror.

But that Sun with the lunar gleam, that dead Sun, will soon be lacking itself. The women who have followed the crew hide their eyes in their hands, their elbows prostrate on their seated knees. We were approaching the frightful pole of the Earth, which human beings had perhaps never known, but only the stars and the supreme intelligence, like all absolute things. It is there that the genius of the planet, raising its weary head above the gaping pit of the axis, sees whirling around it, in an eternal round growing more rapid with distance, the parallel continents and equators.

And the ship constructed to make the discovery, which bore within its flanks the familiarity of old Europe, was imprisoned in the ice amid the whistling of tempests and the bleak frisson of cold. White ice, then grey, having been seen, there no longer remains any but black ice and monstrous icebergs.

All hands were obliged to grope in the dark, and all gestures to hesitate when we left the vessel—but the snow that, without being seen, was heard falling on the deck in muffled volleys, like mourning kisses, would have buried everything. We searched for higher ground in order to put up the tents, and caves hollowed in the rock. Forms passed in the night, with hair furtively loosed over shoulders, which men followed,

155

consoling them. The waves of the invisible sea were like floods of ink gripped by torpor.

The winter layover lasted a very long time.[31]

As was its habit, the external world slowly reappeared.

The most ordinary things, however, had taken on a solemn hue. And as the open sea never permits them to retrace their steps, they will forget the Sun and the foliage of the Equator. All the things of this world will be what the things of ours are, plus the shadow. Soon, it will be a long time since the memory of the vessel itself was lost; their new existence, which was only an adaptation to real life, made them forget that. They will construct a city and invent laws. People with quotidian preoccupations will be seen wandering through the streets. Those men will become accustomed to the cold, the darkness and the fear. Those who, having gone to hunt bear and walrus in the hollows in the ice-sheet, do not return, will be glorified as warriors who have died for the fatherland are. There had been love, a love to which the cold gave supplicant forms, and hands crossed over the heart. The slow years will run by. Someone found light and was regarded as a god. That light was, however, fainter than the brightness of the constellations and its flame was so feeble that people had to warm it up in their bosoms. But it was a triumph over the intermittent tumult of the polar volcanoes, whose formidable eruptions they heard in the distance without being able to perceive the glow. Proudly, they will erect a beacon on the edge of the city, on the summit of a sheer rock where, during the hours of summer, the black waves of the lugubrious sea tempted the genius of a Theocrates or Anacreon.[32] It was a shroud that the wind, momentarily has caused too undulate. A yellow aurora

---

[31] As the reader will notice, time has an extraordinary elasticity in many of Lautrec's dream-fantasies and farces, but the bizarre alternation of tenses in the following paragraphs is unusual even for him; it may be intended to signal a transitional phase in which the story becomes a posthumous fantasy, and certainly moves its hallucinatory quality into a new phase.

[32] Theocrates and Anacreon were Greek lyric poets.

wandered over the houses and the roofs with confused silhouettes, where the sullen as troubled by calls for help. Faces will appear at windows, blossoming at that great novelty. Other shadows, in the doorways, will chat idly. There were rich people insulting the miserable passers-by at the crossroads with their luxury. People will pass by, will labor, concerned for their daily bread, or the intermittent desire for revolution. And the heavy atmosphere extended its ancient wings over the gleams of shops in the streets or rosy idylls in the black rocks.

They will live thus, as people do, until the moment when the successive generations are exhausted, after years of which no one knows the number, and what furtive apparitions of feminine faces with enchanting eyes and hair the color of ebony or burnished gold? But they will succumb by virtue of the absence of light and joy. The man who had found the light was long dead, massacred by the blind crowd. Afterwards, alters had been erected to him, and the sacred fire of the beacon had been jealously guarded. Soon, only a few families still remained in the city that had become too vast, and which wild animals were gradually reconquering. One day, the last woman will die, having sobbed for a long time. With her the possibility of love disappeared. The ultimate survivors will know that they are condemned henceforth to imminent extinction. Perhaps they will weep together. Perhaps madness will take possession of their vacillating souls, and they will fight desperately, to hasten the advent of the final destruction. But for a moment, all the families having vanished, in an outlying district of the city, in the depths of a room full of silence and puerile memories, there had only been one single man, his forehead in his hands: the sole survivor of the shipwreck, the melancholy Adam of the night.

The man came back from the cemetery on the sea shore. He had hollowed out the hard ice, painfully, in order to deposit therein the last body enveloped in a symbolic shroud. The dead city's walls were arranged in tiers on rocky steps. Up above, the beacon was like a red lantern in the fog. The eternal silence had begun. He dared not trouble it with a final prayer, and slowly returned to his house, darting furtive glances at the street-corners, as if in expectation of some impossible encounter. It was the only one that had not yet fallen in ruins, for the survivors had take refuge there, as in an illusory asylum where death was bound to search them out one after another. When he found himself alone again in the torch-lit room, beside the now-empty bed, a grim despair took possession of him. He thought that it would be better for him to lie down too, in the same place, to await the visitor, the only visitor who could knock on his door henceforth with the handle of a scythe. He no longer had any reason to live. In the solution of the problem, and the normal disappearance of that entire humanity, the permanence of one individual seemed like a refusal, a rebellion against the law. If he were annihilated in his turn, the final consciousness protesting against the night and solitude would be inducted into the silence. The storm winds would carry away the ruin of the houses and the beacon. The black demons would spread out again throughout their unlimited empire. But he experienced something like an impulse of revolt then, like an obscure joy in knowing that he was henceforth alone in fighting against the darkness of the pole. His hand closed the door carefully. He reanimated the fire and the wretched lamps fuelled by seal-oil. Then he prepared the primitive weapons with which he pursued animals over the ice. Their flesh was his nourishment and their furs his garments.

He became accustomed to his new existence, for one adapts or dies. Sometimes, he still felt a pang of regret for his dead companions. But the memory was vague, and the departure of the last man did not leave any determined anguish in his mind. The absence of polar successions, in the middle of that durable day that was only a single night, prevented the return of a date and the depressing anniversary. Besides, words themselves vanish when they are not perpetuated by new speech, and there is little pain in a dolor whose name one has forgotten. Reasonable beings were gradually replaced by commonplace forms. All he things in the house slowly woke up. Inanimate objects have souls. They remain mute in the presence of humans but, by night, they wake up and whisper, and the night here was endless. The presence of an isolated creature, almost motionless and always mute, could no longer frighten them.

The master of the dwelling conversed, via his eyes, with the furniture and the lamps, and that later conversation was the most habitual. All beings go to the light, which is the image of life. It populated his desert. It was, besides, before the weapons his best defense against the attacks of the insolent animals that had invaded the dead city and were enjoying themselves on the ruined walls, covered once again with ice, like the rocks. But the inhabitant of the solitary house had long ago lost any fear of seeing the muzzles of bears leaning over the window-panes.

Except for hunting, he only went out in order to make his way, through the storm winds, with the folds of his back cloak flapping furiously around him, to the citadel overlooking the city and the sea, two rival obscurities. He climbed up the unsteady steps, feeling the tower's walls with his hands. He went rapidly through the walls and terraces. On the highest terrace, the beacon shone, cutting through the darkness with its red light. The man poured the oil that fueled the fire into the enormous lamp. The flame grew immediately, driving the unfathomable clouds back into the sky and the sea, like defeated enemies. And every time, along the shore, the seals and bears with savage gaping maws welcomed that renaissance of light with their clamors, of terror or enthusiasm.

The guardian of the beacon sat down, and turned toward the fire to warm his body and heart again.

He dreamed.

Without being aware of it, he adored the only divine image that his brain was able to suppose. The warmth gave birth within him to unusual flowers. Distant memories revived and addressed gestures to him that he strove to understand. The nave tales that had cradled his infancy reappeared. Nursery stories must be the same everywhere. Doubtless, under other names, Barbe-Bleue and Peau d'Âne passed over the blank wall of his mind, with the adventures of Petit Jour and Aurore,[33] killed by a stepmother clad in mourning. But one more marvelous tale pleased him more than all the rest. Through distant lands, chimerical and amorous encounters, the hero always had a handsome lord in golden vestment. And gradually, in his obscure imagination, the legend of the Sun was born and became more precise, like a red corolla opening.

They were ancestral visions, whose imprint went back several generations. He rediscovered now, in the beliefs of his forefathers, the idea of a lost happiness. There was another world, another existence, from which he felt cut off, but which he might perhaps succeed in reconquering. The vast Earth did not end with the monstrous icebergs. On the edge of the horizon an enormous wall of darkness undoubtedly extended, but the other side of that wall was turned toward an ineffable light and eternal warmth. A believer can evoke, in rare moments of ecstasy, the blue paradise that he has never seen. The dreamer had, in the flight of his dream, the confused impression of azure lands, trees, mild Mediterranean seas with ships and birds.

Suddenly leaving behind the tower and the dream, he went through the streets of black snow, accompanied along the facades by the awkward flight of bats, to the threshold of his house. Everything seemed old to him, in the face of a young decision. It was a desperate march toward light, toward warmth, toward other human beings. As the ancient Adam, risen with the dawn, had known, suddenly that he was naked, the new Adam, the nocturnal Adam, had just perceived that he was alone.

---

[33] All these names derive from Charles Perrault's classic collection of *Contes*, the first two [Bluebeard and Donkey-Skin] serving there as titles, while the last two are the names of the children born to the heroine of "La Belle au bois dormant" [The Sleeping Beauty in the Wood]. There is no wicked stepmother in Perrault's version, however, and the reference might be to Lautrec's own sequel, *Le Mariage de la Belle au bois dormant* (1912).

The fear was born within him of having made the decision too late. His entire past life appeared to him to be a nightmare from which one wakes up. The sight of familiar objects, on the walls of his house, suddenly made his heart capsize in fabulous melancholy. He was afraid of days elapsed far from the promised land, not even on the frontier of lands where shadow smiled, like a charming demigod born of the marriage of Erebus and Apollo.

Toward what goal would he direct his course? He only knew that he had to go. He wrapped himself up in his cloak, like a second darkness, and closed the door of his dwelling. Perhaps he wanted to protect the shelter where the residue of a human population had taken refuge against the invasion of the polar bears for a little while longer. It was a successive tomb. Every thought and every dead soul, as the people had diminished in numbers, had left its light and it sensations in the souls of the survivors, like a testament. And thus, the last of them had been the ultimate heirs. The whole existence of the ancestors was summarized in that house.

He went through the deserted streets, and came to the gates of the city. Once, they had been made of heavy wood, held together by solid bronze bars, but their hinges had been broken, and the ice and squalls had separated the stones of the walls. The storm wind had brought them crashing down one day upon its shoulders, like Samson.

The vast Earth extended. It was a living form graspable beneath its mourning-dress. The man drew away from the city and was submerged in the darkness like a swimmer in the sea. In the distance was the shore, where his bewildered arms might find purchase. He marched, doubtless guided by a vague gleam that he imagined, without seeing it, on the horizon. He went through the solitudes and turned round furtively, with the apprehension of being pursued by the black demons of the pole, which were gripping his shoulders with their hooked fingers. How long did he wander, perhaps turning round his point of departure, stopping at long intervals, exhausted, to lie down and sleep in some cave sheltered from the wind? A mo-

161

ment came when his eyes, hallucinated by virtue of looking out for the future light, believed that they saw it in the distance.

That melancholy gaze wandered over the edge of the world for a few seconds, then disappeared. The man thought that he had been the dupe of an illusion. It had returned to the beautiful land, having brushed the depths of obscurity with a timid wing. But he suddenly suspected that one ought to march toward illusions. And his surprise, finally, was great, on seeing it renewed. As he got under way again after the habitual halt, still barely awake, his eyes saw the same mirage surge forth, and from then on, it showed itself regularly. The traveler could, at intervals, readjust the axis of his course; the arrow of his desire flew henceforth straight toward the unknown goal of which he had the presentiment.

His soul, however, was troubled by the unexpected phenomenon. Why did the horizon brighten at the same place at the same time? Was the hidden god afraid of the cold and darkness of the pole, and was he fleeing before them like an ancient hunter frightened by the monsters of caverns? Did an unsuspected law preside over those returns? But already, without having the name, he imitated in the alternation of fatigue and sleep the apparition of what he did not yet know to be day and night. Hours passed. Suddenly, the temperature was milder. A warm breath caressed the ice and the rocks. It was warmth, almost light. But the next day, the rainbow of dubious whiteness appeared to have grown. It grew without interruption. The man discovered days and nights. The surface of the ground was grey. And every dusk, he lay down to sleep and wait, on the darkened route. The ancient anguish gripped him, of feeling the lugubrious mantle of antiquity extending once again over his weary head.

But the returns were divine. It was a kiss on his forehead, less timid. His heart opened to thoughts of childhood, the possible hearth and flowers. His eyes smiled at every commencement. Little by little, by means of its peaceful struggle, the Sun invaded the entire territory, coming anew to the azure battlefield every time, with new force and new splendor, like a knight exchanging silver armor for gold.

Already the heralds were sounding. Cries were attempting joy. The glaciers opened slightly for a pale corolla. A few birds were flying in the sky.

One morning, it arrived. The day before, the curved horizon had retained its color for longer. Belated clouds resembled hot coals beneath a delicate blue ash.

The nocturnal delay was brief. Invisible trumpets saluted the awakening. The man was in the middle of a great plan of almost-melted snow. Vapors quit the firmament, gliding in vaults over the rounded surface. A paradise developed. The glaciers sparkled. Their surfaces, like a variously decomposed mirror, send back red, violet and yellow. The man was only able to appreciate that unusual sensation by evoking, in the anterior existence, the touch of jewels. The prism expanded the flag of daylight. The man thought, for the softness of his eyes, of the last young woman to die. The polar foxes that had accompanied him until then, cleaving the darkness with their muzzles, hesitated, then suddenly took flight toward their sad native land, howling with fright, pursued by penetrating arrows. In the distance, the night in revolt, dragged by the movement of the Equator, was like a rolled-up shroud that was being carried away. The spectator remained standing, his hands raised, his eyes dilated, like a fanatic before a god abut to appear.

The blaze was still rising. Birds fluttered their wings. Breezes passed through the tender blue. And suddenly, red and vivid, the eternal head of the god appeared on the horizon.

It was Apollo, driving the last monsters back into oblivion. The entire Earth quivered. The man uttered one last cry, of distress and enthusiasm. Then, like a prophet in the presence of the face in the burning bush, he fell dead, arms extended, like a black cross upon the ground, while, behind the wall of darkness, the great volcanoes of the pole that he would never see again continued to hurl monstrous icebergs and blocks of frozen lava into the lugubrious atmosphere.

The Lover of Death

It seems to me that the moment has come to write this confession. If I delayed any longer, I would risk being taken by surprise by time. If I can judge by the progress of my moods and my decline, the hour is nigh. I may doubtless set out to destroy, without any risk, certain false ideas that people have in my regard. All interpretation is error. For ten years I have been, so far as public opinion is concerned, a man trying to kill himself by virtue of disenchantment with life.

People able to comprehend noble sentiments are so few in number. One admits right away, without reflection, as an explanation of some action or other, stupid cowardice. When people learn that their neighbor has jumped from his sixth-floor window into the street, they pity him for his lack of energy.

Certainly, it might have seemed rather difficult to give a definition of my existence and state of mind during the ten years since that bizarre mania made me famous.

Public attention was attracted by my first suicide attempt. By virtue of a touch of snobbery—I was young then, and did not yet understand the naked beauty—I wanted, for my gesture, the most sumptuous surroundings. The story of that fête can be found in all the newspapers of the time. It was classic, with its Platonic banquet and dancing-girls. Roses shed their petals all night. The poison that I drank at dawn, from an authentic gold cup, a mixture cleverly calculated to give me the death of all apprehension, without death, which has become the fashionable remedy for common people in despair. Almost everyone, less fortunate than me, dies of it. They are negligible in quantity.

At the second attempt, the administrative powers got excited. In the circumstances, however, there was nothing revolutionary about it. Still somewhat romantically-inclined, I had my veins opened in the bath by an expert surgeon, who carefully resealed them at the moment when the languorous ecstasy and admirable faintness were about to make me expire with joy. That was, perhaps, the occasion when I truly felt closest to death, and was happiest.

Since that time, moreover, I have taken all measures to ensure the relays of my life, from the viewpoint of comfort and tranquility. Ingenious schemes, payments redeemable on particular dates, under such and such terms and conditions—everything was arranged so that my relatives had a strong interest in not passing me off as a lunatic. Even when its exercise does no harm to anyone, one has so much difficulty, in our barbaric society, in using one's liberty!

The police, however, opened an investigation, which yielded no result. I was summoned before the commissaire. It amused me to go, arbitrary as the summons as. He was a charming and learned man. We had a courteous discussion about the relationship between metaphysics and common law, and I left him promising that my next suicide would take place outside his jurisdiction. It was, in truth, the least I could do for him.

I shall pass over the comical consequences of these repeated gestures. Prospectuses and offers of the services of funeral directors became more numerous at every new attempt. Journalists came to ask me my opinion of the death penalty. An automobile manufacturer offered me a hundred thousand francs—what would I have done with it?—to kill myself in a car bearing his trademark. At the same time, I became a sort of hero in fiction. I had my caricature or portrait in all the papers, of modern youthful despair. The causes of my despair were sought. That desire to die, always frustrated, was attributed successively to an unhappy love-affair and the remorse of an unconfessable crime. For everyone, however, I was an Oedipus pursued by an inexorable fatality.

No one suspected the truth. No one accompanied me in my wanderings through the lofty halls of the mysterious palace. The tall, profound mirrors sent back my pale image. How many times I had dreamed of passing into that phantasmal world, the double and reflection of ours, which exists on the other side of mirrors, repeating our gestures. Perhaps that's what we call death. I drew aside heavy curtains. Vases of iridescent crystal, flowers covered in frost, on the side-tables, symbolizing the frail grace of life. I opened the doors of dream, one after the other, and in every room, successively, I felt the anguish of divine oppression more forcefully, and the approach of the ineffable secret. But I stopped every time at the last funereal door, behind which, surely, was the winged horse of Oriental legend, which would carry me away who knows where. I would open that door when I wanted. Why hurry? I wanted to live for a long time yet, to taste, at every reprise, all the joys of death. I was like a diner who takes in hand the cup of absolute intoxication, but only sips therefrom, just enough to savor the profound and divine taste. My explorations were soon so numerous that I acquired a perfect experience and the surest touch.

A clockwork mechanism opened the window of my room to let air in, and close the tap of deleterious gap, at a precise moment. I knew when to deflect the barrel of a gun, to the hundredth of a second. Various poisons and their doses no longer had any secrets from me. It was by mean of poison, especially, that I truly loved death. They intoxicate before killing, and we plunge a diamond dagger into the heart. We enter into the black domain through the gates of dream and gold. One knows nothing, if one has not crossed the threshold of forbidden paradises. Those who have attempted it, at the risk of passing over the other funereal threshold, will never forget the landscapes of a melancholy and supernatural blue....

It is, however, a higher voluptuousness that I have sought in death. I have approached the sphinx, which has revealed to me all of its secret that it could tell me without devouring me. My eyes have leaned over the river, and I have seen my obscure reflection, a new Narcissus whom an elegant gesture incessantly throws back toward the bank and the flowers.

But the face that I see in the mirror of flat water is modified insensibly every day. Its expression is gradually reverting to anxious expectation and anticipation. Every day, it inspires me with a more gripping and more profound love. I have realized that my delay is a kind of infidelity. I foresee, with increasing imminence, the moment when I will not longer be able to resist the attraction of the dark lips extended toward mine. And I encourage myself with the idea that I have earned my reward, since the day that I began, with wild desire and apprehension of the supreme kiss, to pay court to Death.

The Old Demon of Leprosy

For Georges Aubault de la Haulte-Chambre[34]

After the theater, friends invited me to supper, and I got home late at night. I was drowsy, and yet, quite exhausted, I sensed that I would not sleep. The best thing to do was to seek in opium the wakeful calm that would suffice to restore my strength, magically.

I've just smoked the tenth pipe. The tenth, or the twentieth? A mystery. It's impossible to count the pipes one has smoked. The greatest mathematician in the world, if he took opium, would not succeed, even with the aid of logarithms and the integral calculus. Come on! Another one, and that will be all. Ah! How hard this one is! I've just broken my needle. It would be best to give up. Besides, I have a head full of dreams. Let's put the pipe on the tray, in front of my eyes.

My eyes have fixed themselves on the stove. Its surface is smooth and rounded. In the middle, a minuscule funnel-shaped hole resembles the crater of an extinct volcano.

It might have been an illusion, but a few light swirls of smoke were escaping from it. I gazed at it for a long time. Gradually, the smoke condensed and took form. The form grew and became more precise, and I perceived a bizarre little being, a gnome or demon. I love dreams that enable us to see the inhabitants of the invisible. This one abruptly leapt down into the room and went to sit on a stool, facing me.

---

[34] Comte Georges Aubault de la Haulte-Chambre (?-1935) was one of the most flamboyant figures of the Decadent Movement, far more renowned for his exotic costumes than anything he wrote, although his memoir of his friendship with Joris-Karl Huysmans is fascinating.

The individual was as tall as a five-year-old child, but well-proportioned. His feet were shod in espadrilles. He was wearing trousers with turn-ups, too short to be full-length but too long to be culottes, which left the mind undecided. His excessively tight ancient chestnut-colored frock-coat, had stains on the back that seemed to me to be rust. It was closed all the way to the waist by buttons of different colors and sizes. No collar or cravat, but a sulfur-colored neckerchief wound several times around, forming a complicated ruff. All that I could see of him made him seem quite wretched, and yet an innate elegance guided all his movements. In his left hand he carried the fingers of a glove, separate and different, like those one puts on to hide cuts. Sticking out from the pocket of his frock-coat was the end of a telescope, on which, once seated, having extended its compartments, he leaned as if on a walking-stick. From time to time the telescope folded up and he fell forwards. These repeated falls punctuated our conversation.

He greeted to me very correctly, in well-chosen terms, which smacked of old French politeness. I had just finished my examination of his costume, and I set about considering my visitor's face.

I could not suppress a fearful gesture.

His face was strewn with white patches. The nose, the mouth and the ears were shriveled vestiges. The left eye no longer existed; it had been replaced by a minuscule lamp sheltered beneath the brow—but the right eye had a gaze stamped with nobility and generosity. The voluminous cranium was bald, except at the rear, where a host of little figures had been inscribed in black ink, which, at a distance, gave the illusion of curly hair.

"You find me vulgar," he moaned.

"Not at all," I said, hurriedly. "On the contrary. Your lively physiognomy is out of the ordinary and pleases me a great deal. But I'd like to know…let go of that tranquil cane…it's ridiculous…I'd be glad to know to whom I have the honor of talking."

"Why should I remain incognito any longer? I'm the old petty demon of leprosy."

I started at these words, pronounced with a childish insouciance, and I recoiled slightly.

He reassured me immediately. "Oh, don't worry there's no longer any danger now."

"What business do you have with me, though? Why are you here? What reason do you have for paying me a visit, rather than the tenant of the floor above, or the one below?" My voice was rude and imperative.

The little gentleman began to weep timidly. "It's because I saw you smoking opium like a sage, and conceived in consequence a high opinion of your faculties. I hoped that you might overlook my somewhat unattractive physiognomy and appreciate my true value. The true beauty is that of the soul. What do the vain charms of the flesh matter? My own beauty is entirely moral. And I'm not even talking about the qualities of my heart and mind. By virtue of nothing but my influence, I have the right to the greatest eulogies. Think of all the devotion to which leprosy has given rise. Those who have leaned over their sick brethren, who have cared for them and consoled them, who have become saints and the heroes of charity in so doing—to whom do they owe their sanctity? To me, Monsieur. Without me, they would not have had the opportunity for devotion. All that moral beauty belongs to me."

He raised his head proudly. The abrupt gesture caused the tiny candle in his left eye to go out. He asked me for a match. Obligingly, I held one out to him.

"I admit that," I replied, then. "I'm even very flattered by your visit. But what is its purpose, and what can I do for you?"

The old petty demon of leprosy seemed a trifle embarrassed. Finally, he admitted to me that he had come to ask me for a favor, being aware of my numerous connections and influential situation.

"I'm getting old. Life is becoming difficult. It's no longer what it once was. Antiseptic methods have done us a great deal of harm. It's necessary to eat, though. I've taken my courage in both hands and I've come to ask you to find me an administrative position of some sort. The most modest employment would suffice. I have simple tastes and don't spend very much. It would be an honorable retirement. You could do that for me."

"I don't know of anything free at the moment," I replied. "The minister seems very solid, and the Academy has just replaced its deceased fortieth member. There's only a job as night-watchman in the administrative division where I work, but I can't decently offer you that."

"I'll accept it," he sighed. "There's no dishonor in earning one's living, even when one has been what I was. If you only knew! Hold on, here's a souvenir of long ago that I've kept. It was in the eighteenth century. Look."

He handed me a heavy object wrapped in silk paper. I unfolded the wrapping, for I was beginning to feel a genuine sympathy for my visitor. For a moment, I regretted remaining a bachelor, and not having a daughter to give him in marriage.

It was a rather large bronze medallion. It bore an inscription in unknown characters, which he translated for me.

"Presented by the Rajah of Samakura to the little god"—here a name escaped me—"for good and loyal service rendered in the war against the English."

I handed the medallion back to him, congratulating him warmly.

"I would so much like to make a favorable impression on you!" he exclaimed. "I sense that I've found a friend in you, even a companion, dare I say, and that our amity will last. Don't you have a few documents concerning me among your books and papers?"

I rummaged momentarily in the bottom of an old cupboard, from which a rat fled. My research was successful. I brought out a wad of yellowed newspapers, half eaten away. I sat the little demon down on a high chair and set the pile in front of him. His minuscule legs hung down from the chair like those of a child. I felt compassionate.

"There you are," I said. "Here's the *Courrier du Chili* and the *Gazette de Montréal*. These papers surely mention you."

"Indeed, and in what eulogistic terms! Read them for yourself. What descriptions! Those were good times. How poor the present epoch is, compared with those heroic ages! What, I pray you, is appendicitis compared with leprosy or the Black Death? My glory is past, alas, and I didn't know how happy I was!"

"Ingrate!" I said, in order to appear to be following the conversation. And I got up to go in search of other documents on the top shelf of the bookcase. I was on the ladder for a few seconds, rummaging around the shelves. When I came down, the old demon of leprosy had disappeared.

I went to bed, very tired. It had been a bad night. And I saw the bizarre little man again in my slumber. Eventually, my dreams gave way to a profound unconsciousness.

I've woken up. It's broad daylight. I must be pale his morning. Let's take a look in the mirror. No, my face isn't too bad. I have a rosy tint. Except, there, on the left cheek...I must have slept on that cheek.

A sort of white patch, elongated in form. When I put my finger on it, it becomes livid.

It's nothing at all.

The Talisman

For René Chaillié[35]

At the hour when the twelve nocturnal crows fly away from bell-towers, I was dreaming among unknown faces.

People were standing in the middle of a room. They had the sadness of immemorial regret in their gaze; their enigmatic faces, although I had never seen them before, were frighteningly familiar to me.

We were looking at an object that one of them had bought and set down in front of us, with gestures of profound veneration. It was a rectangular tablet, longer than it was broad, with the approximate dimensions of a quarto sheet. Its shiny surface appeared to be made of ivory, or perhaps the bark of a tree with a very narrow grain, polished extensively. It obviously came from a distant and fabulous civilization, and who knew how many hands had held it respectfully before ours? On drawing nearer, I distinguished lines traced on the ivory. Everyone was admiring the delicacy of the design. But it seemed to me that the details were fluctuating before my eyes, as sometimes happens in dreams, without presenting any precise significance. I felt annoyance in consequence, and a sort of humiliation.

It seemed to me, moreover, on seeing their faces, that it was the same for most of the observers. Only two or three individuals, with wonderstruck expressions, remained plunged in an attention that allowed me to deduce that nothing of the scene represented had escaped them.

---

[35] René Chaillié was a sociologist associated with the school that formed around Émile Durkheim, and a notorious Freemason.

I took hold of the tablet respectfully, in order to associate myself with the sentiments of my companions; I held it up to the light that was coming from a high-set window, and which was lending everything an unreal yellow tint. I maneuvered it in all directions, trying to obtain some clear vision.

After my fruitless researches, one member of the company, drawing nearer to me with a sad smile, said: "That's not it. You could have turned the tablet in every direction and it wouldn't have become any more intelligible. I'll tell you the secret, for you have in your hands the summation and votive offering of long dead souls. It's appropriate to have a profound respect for that survival of the immemorial past. It's a talisman clothed with all the successive adorations of the scene it represents."

And I evoked visions of yesteryear on the black wall of my thought, imagining the hands raised in temples whose very dust no longer exists, the lips chanting supplications for the dead in a language forgotten for hundreds of centuries. There were gods. The most ancient known to us did not even suggest their names to us. Prayers were addressed to them. They were invoked in their anger, or, at other times, taken as witnesses to trembling desires of love. Who can name, in disappeared religions, all the ancestors of Eros?

The man who had read the tablet leaned towards it again, and by looking at it with me, enabled me to see it. The lines gradually became more precise. It was as if a picture were slowly emerging from the depths of the past. Born of vague undulations, a majestic river flowed between widely-spaced banks. On the banks stood trees resembling our palm-trees. And at intervals, between the trees, the ruins of temples could be distinguished, in various architectural styles, which moss and ivy had invaded. I glimpsed mutilated white statues beneath the sacred arbors, like those which we still venerate today in our museums. The gods are quitting the temples for the museums—but those marble fragments respired all the beauty and the dream created by the effort of generations.

There was no living creature in the landscape, but the river carried boats that seemed to be coming toward us. In their prows were idols, which did not have human figures like he gods of today. They did not resemble those of Egypt, whose features represent forms that we call animals, and which preceded us. Thus, when we have disappeared, the image of our gods will doubtless survive us for some time, perpetuating the memory of our present appearance, and future humankinds will retain idols after us. But those forms of strange and terrible aspect told of a fabulous epoch. They must have been contemporary with the earliest ages of creation. Sad muzzles leaned over the water of the river. Membranous wings flapped like veils. They still seemed damp with all the mud of the Deluge. And passing over their hideous faces, first sketches of humankind, like smoke dispersed by the wind, I saw the love, hate and anguish of the eternal becoming. I held out my hands, in supplication, toward the frightful apparitions. I knew that after the vision, it would not be possible for me to talk about them in terms capable of evoking them again.

And beneath the boats with the divine cargoes, sailing toward some unknown shore of nocturnal adorations, the river slowly rose and respired like a loving wave.

As one changes individuality in revelatory slumber, I had been one of the ignorant at first, then one of those who knew. I was now part of the scene that I had been contemplating a little while before, as if my fabulous ancestors had beckoned me to follow them in their headlong flight toward the future. The river overflowed its banks and I found myself borne away by the current. A limpid joy invaded me, along with the pride of reliving my most distant past. The anxious words of the people standing nearby still reached my distracted and disdainful ears, muffled by the water—but I finally faded away into an unconsciousness laden with sentiments and memories.

SELECTIONS FROM *POEMS IN PROSE*

Glorious Action

It was a happy city; in the streets bordered by low houses with polished walls, air and sunlight circulated freely. The rare strollers who ventured out during the hottest hour paused on the thresholds of doorways, overtaken by a sudden nonchalance, to listen to the monotonous song that some idle poet was singing beneath a pale-leaved fig-tree; and through their vibrant souls passed, everlastingly, the thrill of musical harmony that takes flight but never dies, being the very respiration of the gods. Through the wide open porticoes, horizons like those painted by Leonardo da Vinci could be glimpsed, where blond adolescents struck artistic poses beneath foliage and beside marble states, while others caused grave music in the Dorian style to resonate on their musical instruments—and all the streets, paved with lava, descended in gentle slopes toward the market place on the edge of the sea.

The glorious sea, younger sister of eternity, breathed in silken waves beneath the subtle caress of the air. Slow ships could be seen gliding smoothly over its surface to the sway of lateen sails. From a green transparency at the foot of the coast, the sapphire infinity of the waves became bluer with distance, in successive water-color shades, and far away, on the distant shore formed by the crease of the gulf, the waves extended immutably in a sheet of profound indigo.

Sometimes, in the sultry afternoons, the young ephebes descending rhythmically to the beach, as far as the eye could see, took off their clothes with calm and beautiful gestures, worthy of causing the desire of a troubled soul to die; naked, arrogantly proud of the cadenced movements of their subtle movements, they impregnated the lukewarm air with their perfumed youth. Philosophers, lovers of souls, expatiated on the good and the beautiful, while courtesans with firm breasts and algal gazes let their purple garments fall about their ankles with gestures like the flutter of wings, in order to prove the divinity of the gods, and stood up straight beneath the Sun, haloed by their russet hair.

These people adored only one god, leisure, and one goddess, beauty. They knew, thanks to fabulous travelers' tales, that other peoples lived beyond the hills, and other gods than their luminous and gilded demons, but their souls had been open since their dawn to the intelligence of all supplicant attitudes to the ideal, and in their temples they had dedicated, albeit while smiling, temples to the unknown gods. At the very least, they did not want a religion that was not a joy. Sometimes, at solemn festivals, they gathered in vast enclosures, where skilful performers made representations of an even more intense and harmonious life quiver before their eyes. The chimerical imagination sang in beautiful lines, before their eyes and lips, of the misfortunes and gigantic works of demigods, and the legends of which their ancestors had formed the brazen pages of their golden book. Passionate for the sober and living crease that a movement of the soul imprints on the floating peplum of the performer, they did not permit clownish gestures and grotesque spectacles, and sent rope-dancers and bear-handlers back to the barbarian lands. They lived thus, searching with solicitude for beauty in all things, and profoundly ignorant of everything that was not the inutility of life—but all the porticoes were painted with frescoes, and white marble statues stood in the streets, launching marble arrows toward the sky!

One day, in the public plaza, a bizarre individual presented himself, dressed in a somber garment that made a sinister stain on the gilded brightness of the surroundings. They thought at first that he had come from the fabulous land of legend where darkness reigns uninterruptedly; it is there that the larvae of indeterminate form roam, which come to suck the blood of children by night and drag themselves over their shadowy soil as they return, blinking their eyes at the yellow light of the Moon. On the head of the unknown was a strange hat, black in color and extraordinarily tall, like an Asiatic tiara with a broad brim. His black peplum, like the dresses of female mourners at a funeral, extended from his shoulders to his waist and then, bizarrely cut short in front, was elongated at the back as far as his knees in the form of a bird's wings. A narrow and rigid double tunic was wrapped around his legs, his feet disappearing into two supple and shiny black animal-skin caskets. And his beard, far from imitating those of the majestic philosophers, was separated on the two sides of his shaven skin, like the acroteria on the fronton on the temple. An old fig-merchant who was sleeping on the hot pavement rose nonchalantly to his feet and came toward him, while the children playing knucklebones on the threshold of a theater fled in fear.

But the people flocked from all directions, amused by the craziness of his appearance, and by the hoarse and muffled intonations with which he pronounced their language. A passing courtesan took off her saffron cloak and threw it over the unknown's shoulders to veil that ugliness, more obscene than nudity. He told them that he had come from a distant country, different from theirs, whose more advanced civilization had realized prodigies that they could scarcely imagine. There were immense cities there, with tall houses sheltering thousands of citizens; all the industries and all the sciences were ruthlessly and desperately cultivated, having given new forms and new words to life. By night, gigantic light-sources insolently replaced the light of day. Powerful machines multiplied labor and human strength tenfold. It was a grandiose civilization, disdainful of ideas and dreams, hostile to philosophers, poets and jugglers of words—and the unknown man found inspired tones to paint for that naïve and credulous people the beauty of the gospel that he was preaching to them.

The people listened; some of them, leaning of columns, put their heads in their hands pensively. Others extended their words and gestures toward him, interrogatively. He told them that their idle existence was unworthy of free human beings, and that their facile happiness was not the only dream in a world of avid competition and hostile efforts. They were frightened by these ideas; the unknown man appeared less grotesque in his appearance and the ugliness of his clothing, and they understood confusedly that they had, until that day, forgotten to live, while gigantic forms and mirages of feverish activity appeared to them on a misty dream-horizon, in the midst of a forest of chimneys, ships' masts and tall houses, beneath a fuliginous sky that the divine light of the Sun no longer penetrated.

Months went by. The unknown had not left the city, but a gradual and inexorable metamorphosis had transformed everything, and nothing remained of the smiling and calm life of earlier days but a memory. There was a new décor and new mores.

After having laughed, in their esthetic arrogance, at the stranger's bizarre garments, the people had adopted them. They had discarded the long, brightly-colored tunics, the gilded sandals so well-adapted to treading on shifting sand or the large flagstones of streets and the loose peplums adapted to the majestic gestures of orators. One might have thought that the obscurity that extended over the Sun was composed to the wing-beats of their old chimeras, flying away from their eternally dreamy eyes. Tall houses of desolate appearance, with dark windows, had emerged from the ground as if by the power of magical evocation. The polished ground had been covered with a layer of mud, as black as the preoccupations that haunted their hearts. New crimes had become manifest. Hands armed with daggers were seen emerging from obscure coverts, and men were learning to take human life by means of iron, fire, poison and vibrations of the ether. A devouring activity having replaced the former nonchalance, labor now extended from one dawn to the next, even for those tormented by no anxieties. The odors of coal, oil and filth had stifled the delicate aromas of oleanders and the mysterious warmth of female bodies that had once brushed the soul. And the city offered an aspect of unspeakable horror, even though gigantic sewers had been constructed with the marmoreal ruins of the temple of beauty, feverish veins through which the corrupt blood of the city ran.

From then on, instead of ancient leisure pursuits, it was practical action that ruled. In the violet hour of evening, tradesmen, bankers and travelers came together in the marketplace and formed a circle, gesticulating with barbaric and unknown words.. There were people who lived and grew old behind grilles, sitting in exactly the same place, eternally covering sheets of paper with complicated and incomprehensible symbols, without anyone thinking they were mad. Networks of metal wire criss-crossed the city at an extraordinary height, in order to transmit thought, for which slow and harmonious language fallen from the lips of gods was no longer sufficient. By night, heavy vehicles of massive form, deprived of harness, ran noisily through the streets, sowing sparks and fear as they went. And one day, after a terrible riot in which all the people took part, a company of actors, the last remaining priests of the mysterious religion of art remaining in the city, were shamefully expelled. They went along the lugubrious boulevards, insouciantly sad, with their tambourines and charming masks, on to highways fringed with gorse, heading for the rosy horizon of the ideal.

The beautiful blond ephebes who had spent their lives in the sunlight, and in the shade of plane-trees, put their supple limbs at the service of useful tasks. Forgetful of the dawns of olden times, they no longer went along pathways at the belated hour of confessions, humming tremulous songs of love with brightly-laughing girls who drank fresh spring-water between two kisses. Their joy was extinguished in nights of fabrication, and their bodies took on the rigid and complicated forms of the machines in the midst of which they lived. Slowly, their blue eyes became dull. The buzz of their trades made them forget the refrains that they had once circulated in their sonorous cups when drunkenness in bacchanal dress, the folly of divine nights, had knocked at the door of feasting. Fever made their teeth chatter and their skin crawl.

Even those who died—and how numerous they were!—did not escape the triumph of practical action. Their calcined bones were reduced into chemical substances; their tanned skin was exposed to the Sun like that of animals; ropes were made from their viscera for the rigging of vessels that set forth to search for unknown treasures, and small works of art from their teeth, displayed in the showcases of the noisy city under the wan glow of artificial light.

But when that vigorous and esthetic race was dead, and the sparse semen of men no longer gave rise in the wombs of sterilized women to any but paltry and sickly children, prepared by their birth for that new life, the work of civilization was complete—and the Sun, which was still shining, went out. The divine demon that is naked humankind disappeared forever beneath the grotesque burden of clothing. In their narrow breasts, no longer lifted by the sob of lost things, the blood, beating in isochronic movements, imitated the monotonous coming-and-going of crank-shafts and pistons, and a powerful and terrible voice was heard in the dismal night, proclaiming the eternal death of ideas, dreams and beauty, while the triumph of modern horror—and unlimited action—extended like a shroud over the filthy streets, the black houses and the lividly-gleaming sea, mocked by the Moon.

Ambush

That there is a secret in every life is certain. But the secret is not what it is imagined to be. Love's belief that it is something unique is vain. Mysteries do not usually bear the names under which they are adored.

An unknown face haunts dreams, generating apprehension. During the nights of youth, at the same hour, a circle of shadows is seen, which one is afraid to distinguish. People with unknown or familiar faces converse, but we cannot hear what they are saying; there is a secret in the room. With every passing moment, the faces threaten to become more revealing—and the secret brushes their mouths like a black butterfly in flight.

Were the sinister password—which is perhaps that to life—to be revealed, it would, we know, sow mortal terror. The sphinx has intimated as much to us. We would see the convulsed face and the upraised hands bring forth the image of things that we ought never to see.

A shadowy hand rises up, slowly, beside the bed. The nightlight is on watch, fortunately. But will not the visitor's first concern be an obscure breath toward the whispering furniture? The spare clothing of one of them takes on a precise appearance. Lines stand out from their hazardous folds. One gets up, hands fluttering madly, to disturb the fortuitous harmony, but along with the new creases, another face appears.

On the window, now pale, the wooden frame stands out, making the sign of the cross. It is the blessed dawn. Happy are we to have avoided the crepuscular landscape, even more frightening than the livid afternoon sunlight. In the morning, cold and shivering, beneath the pallor of the great definitive sky, an unreal fifth-floor balcony in the distance displays a frozen plant—to the north.

The children of the apartment, who are asleep, brought their wooden horses on to the balcony a little while ago in order to watch our vain cavalcade, an enchantment of the forest and ourselves, passing by in the street, on a chariot pulled by two large birds, with a little page astride the neck of one, at hazard, in ambush, skirmishing, toward the light.

Nocturne

The low-set door opened to me on the edge of the city, near the vineyards. Dry stone walls commenced there. From the open country, on the evening breeze, came the green aroma of olives.

A voice called: "Are you coming in?" and I found myself in front of an old woman. In her hand, in order that she might recognize me, was a bronze lamp in the form of a cup; beneath the other hand, forming a shade, black and blinking eyes interrogated me.

Then, having passed through corridors and bolted doors, I was seated next to a timid and pretty woman, whose loquacity amused me.

The woman I met there shook her head bitterly and said: "What do you want me to talk about? Tell me whether I recognize you. I don't know anything. Sometimes I go down into the courtyard, in the dark, and I sew. Sometimes a wicked fairy breaks the needle. But I sew. It's my great afternoon celebration. You did well to come this evening."

She had a charming laugh and her thin hands stroked my face. Then she said: "The chimney's smoky. It doesn't require anything else to make one cry. Yesterday, it poured down. That's the cause. Don't you think so?"

I absorbed myself momentarily, with benevolent emotion, in the logs that were burning poorly. My companion had lain down on the divan and spoke to me sparsely, her head raised at the chin by her oblique palms.

"I frighten you, I know. Did you see, when you came in, the tall Egyptian woman watching out for you? But you didn't notice anything. Men are so stupid. She would have told you her story. It's a terrible story. I've heard it."

She stopped, putting a finger on her mouth, holding her breath.

"Listen," she said.

Voices were coming from the staircase.

The entrance being closed henceforth to transient visitors, they said goodnight two by two. It was an ancient refrain, for everything remains the same, and sad priestesses invoke love in the same phrases. Their rhythmic steps announced that their hands were baring lamps.

"You," I said to her, "are not in love. Which of your sisters reflects your solitude? Are you too new? Isn't there anyone left to love?"

"Oh, if I wanted to—if I wanted to—I would have to confide my secrets to the Egyptian. She's the latest arrival. She's fretful, I think, but I can't console her. She sings the songs of her homeland, in a cracked voice. Then again, she has no heart. I know. Don't ask. It's a secret."

The old woman had appeared. She shook a bunch of keys, impatiently. When I raised my head, she was obliging and hastened toward us.

It was a decrepit and dilapidated house. The doors we had passed through in the corridor had groaned when they were opened. Everything seemed far from the sunlight and the other life.

The narrow, hot room was suggestive of the exoticism of a lost land. There was an armchair next to the bed. On the mantelpiece, two candelabras lent a hint of luxury. When everything was closed, I dreams visions so distant, beyond the olive-groves, that I suddenly started. But I recovered the infamy, the nocturnal course, and the woman gravely sitting beside the fire. "Do you want cigarettes, adored monster?" I offered her one. We lit up, and I praised the interior.

"It lacks many things," she sighed. "I have a nice armchair. They're jealous, would you believe? Then again, the curtains need changing. The wallpaper's ancient. On rainy days, one would think one were in a tomb. I sit here for hours, listening to the drops fall. With the window open, I breathe in the odor of dust moistened by round patches. It's the perfume I like best of all. In the evening, I lean out over the dark street

186

and I'm scared, so much liberty comes in through the window."

She supported herself on her elbow and fell silent. The air was empty. The plaint of a belated traveler came from the corridor.

"How wicked they are," she said. "That one's been here some time. He was told to wait and that someone would fetch him. Now, she's got distracted with someone else, and the two of them are laughing. He might well cry out. When he goes home, she'll demand that the lamp be put out and turn toward the wall. The poor thing is sure to have a good night."

We laughed together at that thought, and I bestowed a few distracted caresses on the girl who amused me. She let me do it, her eyes continuing to speak in a hesitant fashion. When she appeared naked, in the red shadow of the fire, young as she was, she realized, in spite of everything, a white statue, stripped of anxiety and clothing.

Of her own accord, for my eyes, she adopted docile poses. The illusion of goddesses appeared in her poor pupils. Unconsciously and without understanding, her body painted the definitive images of desire in response to my gestures. Even crouching, her hand like a veil, she deified modesty; lying down subsequently, with her head on her shoulder, she gave the impression of drinking from springs that her simple eyes had never seen. One might have thought her one of those long and supple branches that the wind causes to bend in all directions. Leaning over to flee or listen, the harmony of leaves imitates fear, sadness, or an undulation toward a kiss.

When she was tired, in the room now free of invocations, she shivered. I took her in my arms, and on the vulgar bed, I gave her the amicable poses of sleep. By caressing her like a child, I gave birth to a puerile soul in her. She thanked me with her lips.

In the morning, she let her head hang back and breathed with a light rhythm. The twilight of dawn brushed the windows. The raw light made the shadows in the corners sharper. Primitive objects appeared. Everything stood forth in the horror of that light that is not yet daylight, with its ardent magic, which is no longer the blurry night and merely nudity. From outside, the song of a drunken man rose up, joyful at seeing the black boundary-markers on the road turn grey.

I slipped toward the staircase. The windows in the corridor were livid. The horrible old woman came in response to my knock, her eyes misted with heavy dreams. She made the lock creak with one hand. The other reached out to me, in the form of a cradle. I was outside in the dizziness of the fresh air. Trees of every shade of green were stirring on the horizon. The Sun was born. And I fled into the neighboring countryside, breathing in my hollow palms, produced by the night or the dawn, a light odor of voluptuousness.

Empedocles' Sandal[36]

Since early youth, he had been seduced by the mystery of fire. One encountered him on the threshold of forges where hammers struck large red sparks. Elsewhere, for the curiosity of puerile strollers, travelers from Libya or Asia Minor showed off brazen jewels twisted by flame on the steps of Agrigentum. No one knew whether they had acquired their bizarre forms in the caves of Etna, where an evil god had taken refuge. But the Sicilian winter, not being very harsh, only shuts up the children and herds for a few days. In the great dark room he spent hours sitting and staring under the mantelpiece of the fire. On the brick wall irregularly blackened by the smoke, he saw confused visions sketched out that he would recover later. A moment comes when one knows henceforth that the light cares of youth are only passing the time while waiting real life, but also form a prelude and a bass-line to what comes after.

He remembered these things when he shut himself away, at the approach of old age, in the catacombs of old Egypt, from which one emerged with trembling knees and a grey beard. For he was one of those, marked by an occult influence, who describe mysterious forms with a rattle in the cradle. They see veiled figures speaking in low voices in the dreams

---

[36] Empedocles of Agrigentum was a philosopher/poet active in the mid-5th century B. C. Exiled from Sicily for his political activities, he traveled extensively in Greece and Italy. He acquired a posthumous reputation as a magician and miracle-worker, and was said to have committed suicide by throwing himself into Mount Etna, which was then alleged to have coughed up one of his sandals by way of evidence. He was the first person to popularize the notion of the four elements. I shall not annotate the names of all the earlier philosophers with whose ideas Lautrec alleges that he must have been acquainted, lest the notes threaten to exceed the text in volume.

of the twelfth hour. And for such men, forever children, and yet old men from their very first hour, the astonishment of life increases incessantly. The human herd, turning their heads mechanically toward the stars or he dawn, is used to seeing life as a natural thing. The Sun rises and sets, one breathes, the trees are green, we see hatching in our souls, at every moment, the vision of the external world. How familiar all these things are, and is it not necessary that they should be? Those who think that an incomprehensible mystery, which renews itself with every heartbeat of life, but nevertheless remains a mystery, are eternally taken for madmen.

In the meantime, they have lived, and their life and their disquiet is one. Isis is the only goddess. Make all instruments resonate and drink the wine of forgetfulness from cups of every form. Press against your scarlet-clad bosom slaves with trembling hands and beautiful hair. Can you hope—vain desire—to impose silence on the wild dog that bays at the Moon in your heart from dawn to dusk?

Has the unknown goddess a face and can one take it in one's hands? If we knew the unique substance we would be gods ourselves. Is it necessary to adore with Thales the formless water that coats all forms? Is it necessary to believe, with Heraclitus, in the divine principle, fire? We shall return one day to the bosom of the eternal flame, of which our illusory life is a temporary death. He who called himself Empedocles meditated on the decade and the luminous center of the universe. Pythagoras informed him that the Earth is endowed with a double movement. Heraclitus revealed to him that the ground devolved to humans is a plane surface. For Democritus, its hollow form resembled the edges of a cup. God is one, says Xenophanes, and the Earth is motionless on a base that plunges into the inferior abyss. When Zeno wanted to believe, all truth disappeared. It was necessary to doubt everything, even doubt, in order to be a philosopher.

So he knew science and the principles of reasoning, and he knew that the elements are water, earth, subtle air, and the most powerful of all, fire. That was the one he worshipped,

190

although well aware that terrestrial fire is only the image of the real fire. That which burned in his soul gave him the desire for immortal things. His name, from then on, wandered over the lips and through the thoughts of men. He was famous. People walked the monotonous roads to come and consult him. He travelled in Greece, and the walls of cities opened breaches, strewn with cloaks. Prodigies were attributed to him. One day, aided by the ardent faith of a numerous crowd around him, he resuscitated a dead man. Then he went on his way, sheltering the divine torch against the night wind in the folds of his robe.

Sicily, fallen into the sea like an Egyptian pyramid, was one of the cradles of humankind. It was there that Empedocles, after his initiation, driven by a slightly vain desire to contemplate, as a mature and clear-seeing man, the scenes by which the child of the same name—who was no longer the same in anything but name—had been excited in some fashion. He came preceded by his renown, like a robust runner. The isle consecrated to Demeter gave an enthusiastic welcome to them man who might perhaps have encountered the goddess during his subterranean excursions. The people of Agrigentum wanted to make him king. But gold and silver, jasper and emerald, and other ornaments of the Sicilian soil found him disdainful. A more powerful wine than that of Syracuse intoxicates some hearts. He was one of those who prefer a temple for their future shade to palaces populated with beautiful slaves for their mortal body. In the sacred ground of the ones named the funereal Venus he was obliged to take refuge. The horses harnessed to the chariot on which Hades ravished his spouse, impatient, were whinnying still. Orphnaeus, Aethon, Nycteus, Alastor![37] Their hooves hollow out the ground. Their hindquarters wrinkle at intervals, toward the flank, in regular

---

[37] These four names are given to the horses pulling the chariot of the god of the Underworld in the unfinished epic *De Raptu Proserpinae* by the Roman poet Claudian (where the god in question is called Pluto rather than Hades).

191

pleats. You can take in hand the fawn-colored gold-embossed leather reins. The coiled serpents of the wheels roll over the road, toward the land of shadow watered by the rivers with the slow black waves. Throughout the nocturnal day, the strange accursed amours of human beings wander there, which alone pursue, vainly and sadly, hearts besotted with divine nothingness.

From then on he informed those who surrounded him of the mysteries of old Egypt, such as he had understood them—for all truth is reflected in a soul, and everyone sees the face of pale Isis beneath a different shadow. Adolescents formed a crown of young hearts around him. Sometimes, by night, they came in the silent countryside to the familiar wheat-fields of Henna, where the goddess disappeared in the obscure hands of the rapist. No landscape was more apt for the unrolling of the scrolls of the occult tradition. The Earth does not float on the clouds, nor on the ocean wave, but springs forth like a spark from the ancient fire. Too distant, the voice of the stars cannot reach us. Each one is an animate sun. And the Earth in its turn is a body, having the genius of the planet for a soul. The sea, fecund in shipwrecks, is its sweat. The living beings on its surface are the molecules composing that great body. Beyond our Sun are other stars and other earths and other humankinds. A thousand immense torches are hidden behind the light finger that a traveler raises in front of his eyes by night. It is an abyss—but the other is more terrifying. The idea of the infinity that Anaxagoras set in everything makes everything into an infinity. In one of the supple hairs of a beloved woman other worlds and other suns orbit, and thus forever. A man hesitates between two follies when his eyes reach toward either of the two directions. He marches toward science along a passage narrower than the blade of a pointed sword, between two unfathomable gulfs. Each extremity of the passage is guarded by a black angel with blue eyes.

And thus all our troubled thoughts are like the stems of flowers that the wind disperses. To reassemble our sadnesses and reconcile our soul to that infinity in which it wanders, lost, requires a red cord that reunites the flowers in a tight bunch. A single child, in his small hands, carries the red ribbon; he is Eros, the greatest of the gods. He reigns over the stars as over the invisible. The human being who raises his hands toward the mystery forms an angle whose branches extend to infinity, and of which, inversely, the obscure reflection descends into the depths. We are, by virtue of desire and love, incessantly at the very heart of the universe. Our soul is the crepuscular crossroads where two roads of pilgrimage intersect. Every human being is at the center of the cross, his gesture extended toward both of the immensities. It is the sign of the unknown and the problem, which is that of love. For a cry of love goes further than the stars, making its way toward eternity. It is the golden arrow that a messenger fires toward the universe. It is the terrestrial or divine fire. All things, at their origin, repose in the bosom and the unity, and if today's stars are constellations, and if hearts suffer from being separated, every sigh and every amorous sadness restores the desirable marriage, as a child clad in black will guide the hands of pale fiancés toward the altar. It is not true that adieux exist. The tomb does not bury those who have once loved. We know that the gestures that separate us will one day reunite us, and that funerary crowns will be roses in the future. The beloved being always lives alongside the one who loved, by virtue of imperishable hope or divine regret, even when borne away to the shade of unknown trees on the most obscure of planets orbiting the most distant of suns.

The one he loved was a shepherd in the Sicilian mountains. All descriptions of love are vain compared with the image of Eros. He came down, red-lipped, from the hills to the city, along paths where stones rolled, bordered by citrus trees. He chewed an insouciant flower, born of his breath, and his supple gestures, beneath the folds of his tunic, revealed his young body. Such a soul resembles empty urns that water-bearers take to springs. Whoever wanted to would cause the blue water of dreams and the red wine of love to tremble there. And his magnificent role was to provide a living image of the

193

symbol, a statue resembling the god that one worships, toward whom incense rises. We only know images, and the immortals only appear to us in mortal veils. In order that the messenger from afar should be worthy of evoking future forms, Empedocles set out to make him a soul equal in beauty to his body. And, as the skillful potter always has his eyes fixed on a model with light handles made of the supple bodies of two bacchantes, the man who desires to imitate him with respect to souls also keeps his interior eyes on a model. He contemplates the divine forms that are elsewhere, of which humans are merely the shadow.

One encountered them on the road, at the hour when the other shepherd, nightfall, brings the white flock of the clouds toward the fold of the horizon. Empedocles spoke of triple Hecate, and the mystery of sanctuaries hidden in the depths of silent forests. By night, they slept in the shade of squat oak trees with twisted branches. But dawn, especially, caused them to marvel. Dawn is the image of life. The child knew the beautiful legends that hide the truth like a cloak embroidered with gems. Their stroll was through the sacred wood of symbols. Empedocles was clad in a red robe and wore a red headband over his forehead. On his feet were brazen sandals. Over the bronze, the work of an unknown artist, ran carvings depicting the glorious stories of the heroes. The Trojan War could be seen there, a wine-growers' dance, and the labors of Heracles. All around, in waves simulated by metal studs, rolled the ocean. They trampled the grey dust of all the roads. They rested on the sea shore, and the sea breeze was a caress. The entire Sicilian landscape comprises a shelter on the rocks in the shadow of dark green pines, in front of the disconcerting blue of the limitless sea. An odorous bed of twigs has fallen on the ground from the treetops. In the melancholy of the evening, by virtue of translucency, the foliage of the pines becomes violet. It is the hour when words rise like prayers toward the nocturnal vault.

In the beginning was the uniform world, the spheros, the circular god. Everything was at the center of things and the center as everywhere. The demon with the curved wings, Anteros, dispersed everything.[38] Stars and hearts, weaving crowns, attempt in vain to renew the ancient and perfect form. The eternal serpent bites its tail. The world of appearances and the world of love are submissive to the same laws of attraction. When time is complete, Anteros will be defeated in his conflict with white-winged Eros—and, in truth, the choir sings the strophe and then the antistrophe around the altar, as a symbol of universal desire.

It is necessary to love. That is the great secret. The heart swells toward the horizon—and our lives march to the rhythm of the heart, as a child clad in a red robe dances along. The sole verity is that of working to construct the temple of the future Unity. Let the poet, for his praise, write a poem, and let others offer to all the beggars wandering along the road the royal gift of a kiss. Every poem that one realizes by means of the pen, marble or the lips—and the last-named are the most beautiful—steals something permanently from the grim grip of nothingness, and unveils a few features of the visage of the Unknown.

Fortunate is the man who, when he dies, leaves after him in his wake a beautiful form that did not exist before him. We are like the virtuous bee who collects her honey untiringly for a tomorrow she will not know but that she knows will come. For all humans weave their shrouds of dreams and weave down here their immortal crowns, and the future heaven will be for each of us absolutely what we would have wanted it to be.

As if to play on the lightest of flutes, at other times, he said, softly:

"Some want an empire and triumphal chariots. Their faces joyfully reflect a crowd with a thousand faces. Cries and gestures come toward them.

---

[38] This identification of Anteros as a "demon" and a sort of "anti-Eros" is unorthodox; in Greek myth Anteros was Eros' brother, identical in form, and the god of requited love.

"Others imprison gold and jewels in rare caskets.

"Some are able to pass their entire lives without suspecting any other intoxication than that of tables laden with wine.

"For myself, let no one salute me as the servant of mystery; I would like, when my funeral comes, to have been, of all men, the one who knew most of love. My ashes, if all falls to ashes, would be the most perfumed."

Meanwhile, the child listened, and his face became pale, and his eyes more beautiful. But with the passing days, it was soon no longer the mystery of narrated mysteries that was the strangest, but that of his own life. It seemed that the breath of his young heart became as profound as a sigh. Like adolescents who run, in their supple ardor, toward the Temple, he overtook the hierophant at some cypress-bordered crossroads. And thus, as the words took on the solemnity of holy things, the roses of Paestum mutated into black roses and the wheatfields of Henna beneath the warm Sun became the nocturnal wheat-fields to which the goddess sends down young people matured too soon. One sees Hermes, the guide of the dead, bearing a fearful little soul in his arms, caressing it in order to console it. Is not the sadness of dead youth the only image that poets never wear out, that is always new? Momentarily, he lay down on the moss of dreams, and died.

"You will no longer run along the edges of springs, your light feet colliding rhythmically with the soil.

"You will no longer go into the divine sea, where your naked body shivered with joy.

"Gone, you will take account of the message that has been confided to you. Can you say to the one who is all beauty and all mystery that our inn was the most regal and our gestures the most supplicant?

"Child of legends, every evening, demand hospitality.

"My pride is crowned with asphodels; your hair is now like the foliage of the willow, the sound of your heart like the murmur of a spring descending into the depths.

"But we shall find one another again on the threshold of magical cities.

"Farewell, messenger!"

With the flute-players, the divine night commenced. The Sun had fallen into the sea, after a heavy gaze of glory. Gloom is favorable to mysteries. There are words to be heard to the sound of funereal instruments, and loving faces that only acquire all their reflections of profound beauty beneath veils of mourning. Thus the child, like a basket full of violet petals, had sown immortal regret along his route.

What a regal pyre on the shore of the sea! The cedar wood sends up its perfumed pride toward the clouds, and bowed forms shed tears over the eyes forever closed. It was in the cool evening, with the gestures with which one places an infant in its cradle, when one crosses his arms over his heart to ensure a beautiful sleep. For hours, the sea sobbed, with stifled waves, in an incessant silken undulation toward the shore. A shroud enveloped the limbs, henceforth of marble and later of dreams. The adolescent departed for the eternal game upon the deceptive search for his body, scattered in smoke.

O messenger!

The chimera that hides in the depths of our souls is awake. We shall depart, since we have wished it. We shall march without fatigue, devoured by the fire than burns within us, as the terrestrial fire caresses your flesh, and makes no more ash of it than a bouquet of burned roses. Having wished to know the folly of living, instead of being seated at the foot of the Temple, it is better to have knocked at the door and that no one has answered. Does eternal life desire anything but to be tempted by all roads? The disciple who rests with the serving-women by the winter hearth until cockcrow is less pure than he who tempts the Master in the depths of nocturnal gardens, and whispers in his ear, for the sake of folly, love or treason—it hardly matters which. Whatever the incense of the Temple may be, the flame is always pure. The worship of images glorifies the one whom all symbols reveal. And we can bring to you in votive urns, O Master, on the thresholds of future houses, all poems, bouquets and kisses. You will recognize the kisses, and you will count the bouquets. We shall return to the natal hearth, like prodigal children, but exiled by your will.

We have known that love which alone gives life to the phantoms of our unreal life, by putting into their faces one of your reflections of beauty. Without seeking the phantoms' names, you will be able to smile and forgive us, knowing what we have wanted, and that even if we erred, it was perhaps for love of you.

In vain, the slaves erected a sanctuary consecrated to Empedocles, and young women came, with crowns, to forbid him to die. He gathered his friends together for an evening banquet. When the ritual wine had been poured on the table for the gods, someone pronounced a eulogy to love, which enders humans similar to gods—and immediately, it was perceived that Empedocles had disappeared. They searched for a long time in the city, in the forests and on the sea shore. Had he gone to travel the roads of Sicily, bearing a heavy burden in his heart? Some said that he had gone to pay a visit, in an inspired fury, to the god of flame in the depths of Etna. Thrown on the lava, on the summit of the mountain, a brazen sandal was found, as at the door of sanctuaries that one enters barefoot. But of the ashes and the urn beloved by the hierophant, nothing remained on the edge of the gulf. He had taken his dream with him.

Latin Symbolism

For Edgar Poe

It is not necessary to have read many occult books to know that mystery is purely nominal. The same tenebrous meaning is hidden beneath various forms, and in all the temples, from Egypt the mother of shadows to the sects of present-day initiates, the same luminous triangles are inscribed on the ceilings. The language of books and that of lips are merely a procession of worn-out images. All forms are symbols and symbols of other symbols. We only live by virtue of metaphors, our eyes fixed on the cavern wall where the shadows of realities passing outside are gesticulating. One can only obtain one formula clearer than an unknown forever unknown. What gives value to signs is their variable simplicity. The simplest are, in language as in magic, the most redoubtable, being closer to unity. And in the nobility of thought, as in that of the Middle Ages, the most illustrious blazons are those with the most sober designs. For everything that draws away from its origin becomes complicated—and depraved, being less pure.

It is not necessary to regard philosophies and religions as a collection of beliefs of which a single sign is the summary; on the contrary, they only develop a single sign or word. The formula is the origin and not the consequence. After Pythagoras, the law of number that he proposed was verified. The number or the word is the most intimate essence that we can ever attain. All religion rests on a word, expressed or not; and the word is represented by a figure.

The trinity and the triangle are equivalents. At the very least, since human concepts, in spite of our craze for the absolute, are only the exteriorization of forms in the human brain, the representation of a triple god, and the triangular symbol expressing the same law, are born in the same obscure fold of the grey matter. The altars of every religion are based on a geometrical figure. The Egyptians set up the figure of the triangle; the pyramid represents the union of the ternary number with the square. It has four faces, each limited by three lines. Three of them face the sky. The fourth is the obscure face turned toward the ground and humankind. Other religions have enclosed themselves within the eternal serpent, the circle, the form of the horizon, the formless form appropriate to receive everything. The mages placed on the threshold of their dwelling the five-pointed star, the pentagram, which is man, and the double triangle, and many other things if one desires. The letter with which the name of Zeus begins describes the lightning. The Christians have made the right-angled secant divine.

If one wants to press to the end, exasperating it, the paradox that they are all merely the enunciation of an obscure verity, one may say that there is a meaning hidden not only in words but in the form of words. Words, like images, have an esoteric meaning. The marvelous genius of Edgar Poe has seen this verity. No one could have developed the idea we have broached better than he did, and, while exaggerating the methodical rigor of the explanation, simultaneously giving it a discursive and flexible aspect. He is the king whose rich imagination, better than of De Quincey, would evoke the sumptuous scenes and dazzling visions of opium merely at the summons of the sonorous word: the Roman consul. Since he has departed for the land of dreams—to the paradise, whatever it may be, that he has created—it is at least appropriate that these notes be submitted to him, as a poor monkish illuminator, before bending over his folio, addresses a fervent prayer to Doctor Angelicus.[39]

Let us suppose that a curious philosopher, one of those who searches in all things for the homunculus and the sum-

---

[39] Thomas Aquinas

mary, imagined that he had found a word that completely satisfied his love of symmetry, a word whose form and complex meaning might lend itself to amusing variations. It is, in sum, a matter of a vocable appropriate to illustrate the vague theories already emitted. Like Edgar Poe when he invented the word Nevermore in "The Raven," one will ensure that the word is possessed of all the necessary virtues. As it is a matter of speculations on symbolism, the language that imposes itself is Latin, so muscular, sober and compact. It is, in any case, appropriate that it should be thus, for what honest excuse would these discursive fantasies have is we were not speaking Latin?

Every formula that is easy to remember must be brief. What is required here is a summary, and easily-citable exemplar of the symbolism of words. We cannot, in consequence, think of some Abracadabra. Two or three letters will suffice. They can be more easily engraved on the fronton of the mysterious temple. As it is a matter of occult things, we shall be led to choose the number three, the most perfect of all. If one cares to remember what was said at the beginning about geometry, one will not be astonished if we demand that the essence of this vocable should be the essence of known lines. As they are three in number—straight, broken and curved—if we care to recover them, the word will, it seems, emerge from the shadows, as an unknown planet emerges from the depths to the summons of a calculator. It can be no other than the Latin word VIS—force—the most significant of all.

Geometry being the principle according to which all forces develop, as one can see by looking at the images of elementary physics, it is natural to expect that the word designating force would also have a geometrical form. A drop of water abandoned to itself adopts the form of a sphere. Falling snow crystallizes in designs of an admirable regularity. The line is everywhere.

And so is number. We have chosen the number three as being the most perfect. Not only that but, additionally, we can make from these three signs all the others that we may please.

201

The second letter is that which, for the Latins, represented unity. The first is the number five. Two Vs united at the extremity will give us the number ten. The last letter of the word offers us, it is necessary to say, no satisfactory interpretation. It is too undulating to designate any definite number. But is it not necessary that in any theory, no matter how precise it may be, that there should be an indeterminate part? In addition to the limited numbers, does there not exist an unlimited one? The series of numbers is infinite. It can always go beyond. It would be inappropriate for this word, the summary of the theory, to be closed in too definite a fashion. The S, with its imprecise form, allows the supposition of the infinity that numbers do not exhaust. Praised be the god of Pythagoras, who has furnished us, in our embarrassment, with this legitimate explanation. It is thus that the sage Epictetus was able to get out of anything.[40]

It is not enough that the form of the vocable should satisfy natural logic. What is the meaning of the word? If we accept the idea that modern philosophers have of the world, matter disappears; there is nothing beneath appearances but forces in action. Every movement, one of them has said, reveals a force expressing itself, every form a force expressed. In consequence, the term that we have had the good fortune to choose, appears to be the summary of all theories of the universe. From the viewpoint of form, as from the viewpoint of meaning, this benevolent vocable leaves nothing to be desired.

It would, in consequence, be unfortunate if it did not present to us a summary of philosophy—but let us be reassured; philosophy comprises the study of three faculties: Voluntarism,[41] Intelligence and Sensibility. Let us combine the

---

[40] The Stoic philosopher Epictetus was reputed to be a very persuasive orator, highly skilled in the art of rhetoric.

[41] In English, of course, this faculty would normally be called "Will," but that would spoil the symbolism. What Lautrec does not mention, however, is that the Latin alphabet originally had 23 letters, lacking the English j, v and w; V was originally the capital form of u, but was subsequently adapted as the consonantal form of that letter and is

initial letters and we shall rediscover our word. Intelligence is placed between the two other faculties, which serve as its intermediaries, one active and one passive, with the external world. And each of the three is expressed by an appropriate gesture.

Intelligence, which pierces and goes straight to its goal, is the straight line. It is the arrow. It is the magic wand opening the treasures of thought. It is the eternal parallel to the progress of reality. It is the thyrsis around which the spirals of sensibility rotate to form the image of the caduceus, the entire anagram of Isis.

For Voluntarism, however, a more powerful form is necessary. And what is more expressive than V, the corner that penetrates and separates, whose action is unlimited, since the two branches extend to infinity. As accrued voluntarism is, in sum, the whole of magic, it is only just that the triangle and the pentagram are made up of Vs. The flight of doves, generation, and all things that go far are imaged there.

The curved-back S, fleeting and perverse, as if undulated by a spasm, represents sensibility. Under every appearance was revealed, to the gaze of the first man, the ancient serpent: the two halves of the circle each turned the other way; aptly representing impotence to satisfy eternal desire, they do not meet.

In what order is the synthesis of the three signs presented to us? Voluntarism comes first, as per the meaning of the word. Power is voluntarism. Intelligence is on the second level; intellectuals are not men of action. As for poor sensibility, it is understood that she only lags behind, timidly. What fairy will come to punish her two ugly sisters, and put the glass slipper on her so that she might marry the king's son?

---

used in that way in modern versions of Latin texts. Some scholars think that the consonantal form is question was pronounced as we usually pronounce the letter w and still pronounce u in such words as "suave"—a situation further confused by the fact that German speakers pronounce w as we pronounce v.

One can demonstrate the truth of what has been said by reversing the proof. Let us change the order of the three signs. Let us put Intelligence ahead of her sister Voluntarism. We would have less wild ideas, in which wisdom is dominant. In that new disposition, one obtains the Latin word IVS: law.[42] What is justice, other than intelligence mastering blind voluntarism?

Let us also observe that in both cases, sensibility is sacrificed with a praiseworthy emulation. Justice, like force, carried a sword in her hand.

So many things can be found in a word that it is true to say that everything is in everything. One might extend these comparisons infinitely. The universe is like a sumptuous cloth; as soon as one grips it edge it unfolds completely. There is an immanent logic and things, like words, are captives of the golden chain. The principle escapes us, but if we believe, with the ancient metaphysicians, that the cause of life is the heat that force and movement produce, we can, before closing this fantastic explanation, recover in the word taken as a symbol the proof of this new meaning: the first sign is the vase in which one places hot coals, the second the flame that rises up, the third the smoke that coils around. The symbol of fire brings all symbols together in the future unity, as its image, terrestrial fire, melts rare metals together.

---

[42] Normally, the Latin word in question would be rendered *ius*, but, for the reason explained in the previous note, *ius* rendered in capital letters in a Latin inscription would indeed be IVS.

The Shadow

Behind the doors the musicians rubbed the catgut strings and the concert began.

It was an almost-invisible harmony, which the heavy wall-hangings seemed to hear as it pass through; and the conversationalists lying on supple divans modulated their words to the slow violins.

The oval flame of candelabras, amid the mirrors, was reminiscent of distant blue landscapes.

A flute-player: Stella.

She was sitting in the room, a delicate courtesan, with fine black wings on her forehead.

The poet bore exile in his eyes; the metaphysician with heavy eyelids evoked it in gestures with his hands; the third was one of those who go, in the evening, via the streets or gates of the city, toward the violet sunset, pausing before everything with keen senses, as before a painting.

For all three, and for her, the chimera of gold, the fragile ornament on her young bosom, had been placed around her neck in the solemn hours of infancy by an unknown god. It woke up from its metal sleep, the following day, on hearing a heartbeat.

A little while ago, the velvet portals having been lifted, the poet had welcomed Stella, when her laughter drew near, and had greeted her, without the irony quivering on the lips of other talkers, in his own language. Stella's light soul, rising to her mouth in astonishment, had rendered them happy.

The window was closed on the profound blue.

Then the divans drew together, the doors were sealed and the third, thoughtfully, said to the others: "If I were not fearful of a ridiculous game, I would be saddened, as you are, by the absence of ivory skeletons in the hands of the king of the feast—you cannot, as he does, between those who remove the petals of violet thoughts, play distractedly with death. But since smiling life is born on Stella's lips, let us evoke the lugubrious frame in which that rose flower will be wearing black.

"The *danse macabre* of frescoes cannot equal of the one that dances in our skulls. We shall lean over our souls, as over a well, with a sad gaze, and each one of us will describe the landscape that he has seen.

"Here come the young women of allegory, bearing urns in their hands.

"A king of oriental Sadness, standing on the threshold of his palace, makes an idle gesture, which the guards obey; the prisoners are set on their knees, their heads and faces upraised. Their grotesque fingers are agitated, for the executioners have come, and with their flexible phalanges, in response to the king's whim, they have removed the sufferers' eyelids. The eyelids have been removed in order to flutter no longer with any dear emotion, and the eyes, playfully, have been slowly turned around in their orbits. Now, what can be seen is two bloody circles in a pale face, and the nerves, exposed to the light, quiver, while he pupils are permanently directed into the obscure hollow—and these men, who no longer caress the magical décor of the external world, gaze immutably into themselves.

"The king approaches all the sensualists, laughing, and asks them: 'What do you see?'

"The first says: ' I am leaning on a windowsill; the window opens on to a high wall; it is night; the wall extends above me to dizzying heights; beneath me it plunges into an abyss, and seems to occupy infinite space. The lamps in my room have gone out; only the window is open, and I gaze in bewilderment. Large fiery birds streak the obscurity, and I hear moaning, and I am sure than on the other side of the wall of exile are bright forms, and a blue park—but all the other windows are closed.'

"After that one, very slowly: 'Similar, I remember, were the nocturnal halts I once made on the highway. I arrived at dusk, delightfully repenting having marched for twelve hours through perfumed hemp-fields. The hostelry was open and the joyful landlord in his white bonnet bowed to me on the threshold. I knew the same of the serving-women, and the puzzle of the sign was my friend. At the thought that the heavy treasure was buried in the cave beneath us, the evening's delay seemed light to me. We went down with the landlord, the candles red and the keys forged; though the two open doors, which are eyes, through the webs where agile back spiders perch, I saw the immense and somber cellar, with its steps. But the cellar was empty, and the treasure gone. Someone, digging a tunnel through the ground, had fled toward the city in the fraternal night, knocking on doors to give evidence of his joy.'

"When they had both spoken, the last, an old blind man, spoke. 'I have directed my eyes toward myself, and looked at myself. Let the executioner put his hand in mine that I should kiss it thankfully. In spite of the pain, a cry of ecstasy would have taken flight from my lips if my lips were not closed disdainfully—for what I see is the dream toward which my fleshy arm reached out in the luminous life of yesterday. You have partly lifted the veil or me, and I am now, O king, like a grim king, sitting alone with his wives and his beautiful silence, in the hall of his palace.'"

"What a gloomy story," said Stella.

The storyteller turned to her and kissed her eyelids, then said:

"A frisson travels through space and pauses in our hearts, like a bird on a wall. When it sings, we think we are alone, not knowing from what horizon it came, and that other birds have a voice, but every soul is a landscape, and we bear the universe within us. Infinity leans its pale face over our mirror, and eternity weeps or is delighted by every moment of our life. What light can breach the ether of our extinct eyes, what speech that of our closed mouths? Everything is naught but shadow, and the shadow of ourselves. With the vestments of mages and the gestures of enchanters, we extend the glass eye of observation toward our brains and the stones of the highway—but the life that pursues us through the meanders of the grey matter refuses, and flees toward some willows, torch in hand, and leaves us nothing but formulae, amulets in the mouths of a mask, with which scientists are content. And the stones on the highway, beneath the magnifying eye, separate out an infinite number of atoms in a vertiginous explosion. Everything escapes us, and that is nothingness.

"A damned thing that gnaws the heart eternally, that is consciousness. No one should seek to know, and forms are what they are. Let us play the game of humanity, with roses and fine sobs, without desiring the true name of roses or whether the sobs emanate from a true heart. The great fall into the divine night, after the sad passage of life, only frightens us by virtue of the enchantments of that Circe, our soul. She creates appearances and pours the liquid marble of her soul into them. But we ought to be light forms, which are unaware, whose delicate vestment is never creased by the brush of any care, and go forth like shades, a hand holding before us a golden rod. Beneath the marble gaze of the sphinx, we would arrive at the shore of the vast sea, without interrogating the oscillatory night, nor touching the blue vault on the edge of out cloak. The words of the philosophers, from the very beginning, in their unfolding, are vainer than the delicate rosy spirals of a sea-shell that a walker on the sand crushes heavily underfoot."

"Now," said Stella, "the poet ought to reply and knock on the door of the Temple. If the guardian of the threshold is a female shade, she would take him to breathe the incense, and perhaps it would be appropriate to pray for her."

The poet said: "I shall, therefore, say my prayer to the shadow, as I do every evening, asking her to bestow the invisible caress upon us and forgetfulness of the black cup. If nothing exists, everything is to be created, and we shall describe the profile of our dreams, as a child draws with charcoal on a wall.

"It is necessary not to use formulae, but to speak to you as to those ancient women whose disciples named them the muses, for you are the sister of the night. And you only come at nightfall after having wandered close by us all day, without our sparing you a glance. Once, I even thought I had lost you during a stroll on the sand on a motionless summer's day. The Sun was so high overhead that you had vanished, doubtless having descended into the depths of the Earth to continue, among your sisters the shades, the obscure dream of my life. But in the evening, you climb the darkening stairways with me that vacillate in my torchlight. You march obliquely along the walls, like a thought, and you knock at the door at the same time, Shadow.

"The worship to be rendered to you is discreet, and without smoke, shadow and incense, perhaps you are already good to us, a companion for eternity. Supple and fleeting, you love walks in the dusk, where the street-lights make decreasing and dying circles for you. And you will remain until the hour when we become phantoms in our turn, to go on alone, somewhat emotional, through magical cities, O obscure face of the real, whose shadow we are, and who looks upon us with pity.

"Thus I speak to my companion, not really knowing which of us is the shadow and which the real individual. I always find her there, in the solemn lamplit hours; I'm sure that she doesn't sleep at night, for I often wake up, with the light turned down, to spy on her, and I've seen her moving faintly on the wall. I move about, moaning, and make signs to her, to which she always replies. I am, therefore, not far from believing, which would please a Platonist, that she is my familiar demon."

Everyone laughed, most amused by this bleak game in which their thoughts were undulating like fingers on black ivory piano-keys, and the philosopher, nodding his head gravely, explained:

"I don't think that a shadow has the consciousness of being alive. We are sitting on the edge of the river, and our shadow is a reflection. While very young, Stella, you must, in the vast dark grounds of your inexplicable sadness, which you dare not explain, have leaned anxiously over clear pools in which the trees, colonnades and clouds appear to you, inverted. You were afraid of that chimerical world, into which vertigo threatened to tip you, but you knew that it was a chimera, and that made you love your fear. So you leaned over toward our shadow and toward the river of life—the fear that it inspires in us is a game we like; we know that it is our shadow, but it is surely unaware that we are its reality. Its thoughts, if it thinks, are those that the slightest sunlight causes to vanish. It is, therefore, in its true role, and must set its footsteps in ours, knowing nothing of the route, unable to guide itself to the starlight or the sunlight. And the shadow, and ourselves, and that of which we are the shadow, only have the reality of vague forms dancing on the wall of the room, which will disappear when the fire has gone."

"Personally," said Stella, in a sad voice, "I believe that the world is comparable to the explosion of a beautiful furnace—the suns are red sparks, the earths on which we live grains of ash; the servitude of worlds bows down before fire. Life is hot. The legends of the inferno are the proof of the terrible respect that only the absolute inspires in us. Light, mobile water, forms captive in earth, yellow amber, are the masks of Monos,[43] whose face is fire. Sparks are luminous, and then die, and that is true everywhere. The passage of ardent life to the oblivion of ash is the same. On cold earths appear the monuments of human thought, the temples, the triumphant arches, the palaces, with their silky and emotional life, and crystallizations are produced on the surface of infinitesimal molecules in the dust of an apartment; they are the same phenomenon at different levels of infinity."

---

[43] Monos is usually identified as the Greek god of pain and sarcasm, but that does not seem to be the meaning intended here, which might be more closely related to the notion of the phenomenal world as a monad.

"If the world is infinite," said the poet, "and if every form encloses every other form to infinity, on what horizon of the voyage will we encounter the gods?"

The philosopher ventured:

"All the gods and all the demons in which humans have believed, traverse the magical château of or thoughts every night. There is a god named Pan, in an obscure pathway, with patches of sunlight filtered through the braches overhead on his viny hands. And in the forest stands Isis, standing on a marble slab, in a gesture of silence. They are the greatest. Mystery is the supple veil of Life. After them, Buddha, Zeus and all the gods of light, and the gods of darkness, the god Lucifer seen in the form of a handsome child, and Beelzebub, with a fiery headscarf."

"The gods of darkness," said the poet, are the only ones that are able to love; they are good. We see them in their obscure faces, and hardly know them."

"A necessary comparison," continued the philosopher, "born of familiar images. Suppose, O Stella, a people of inferior form, too small for our gaze, one of those which live below us, and for whom we are gods. A race of mandrakes, black and sad, would be an example that would make you smile. But to remove the possibility of an objection from your eyes, and safeguard the poor unexpected device, I shall take as a symbol a population of scarabs, brothers of Isis, inhabiting a shivering corner of the mute forest.

"A stray voyager passes by. He crushes two or three scarabs underfoot. They for amusement, he takes one of them between his delicate fingers, whose color pleases him. He caresses it, lifts it up, and makes it fly into the air, toward the sunlit leaves. The scarab-people would fear that mysterious being, drawn away without showing his face, because of the dead, and would implore his anger liturgically, while dressing in praise the one that he raised toward him. That one would be regarded as a prophet, who rose up into the superior world.

"Via the lips of the elect, they name the being that passed by, and call him a god. Those whom he wounded speak of him with anger, and make use of the term demon—and that is how gods are created.

"Other scarabs, in their march through the great forest, encounter other stray humans, and worship them under various names. They have, in the eternal course, encountered different gods. But all the gods are true in whom someone believes. They are furtive apparitions of misunderstood and feared beings. Thus, in the sphere superior to ours, lives a population of gods who are only gods to us, who are enveloped by another sphere, haunted by others, who serve them as gods in their turn.

"An emerald is enclosed in a perfumed bag, and that bag in an exceptional casket, and the casket in the great hall of a palace, and the walls of the palace retreat to the horizon, which other horizons complete and delimit eternally."

The poet, who was playing with Stella's hair, got up then and said to her:

"Another day, we shall speak of real things, and perhaps find the secret. Alternative ideas are vain; only the form is to be implored; you are, by one of your gestures, the most divine recantation. Renewing the evenings with torches, in a fine fever, you will come...."

"I consent," she said, "but"—and her hand made a slow gesture of rejection—"we shall not welcome to the feast either the lord of the flies or the king of diamonds."

"The satans left on the threshold, I shall not speak as a poet to shadows, but to you."

"All is but shadow," said Stella.

The Mourners

They were living on a solitary island on the far side of the great Sea. And they lived there, separated from other men by fear. They were called the Mourners, and whenever they chanced to descend toward a town, with their long beards and their heads partly shaven, as if in mourning, as they passed by, the people traced the cabalistic signs that were used to chase away evil spirits.

The people of that distant epoch lived on Death. When one of them was about to expire, the body, placed on a deep raft, was sent to the isle of the Mourners, to the accompaniment of violas, violins and drums, and yellow candles burned with pale flames beneath the Sun and on the ea.

For it was the Mourners to whom the lugubrious care of the dead had been consigned. They were the priests of a melancholy and definitive Cythera, save for the fact that, unlike that other embarkation by Watteau,[44] the passengers bound for the happy isle were not heading for Love but for Death. In great sumptuous palaces with profound mirrors, the bodies were laid out and subjected from then on, to the ceremonial ritual. Before transforming the human remains, the priests wanted to ensure the absolute freedom therefrom of the delicate soul, still anxious at the gates of the body, and their religion was primarily composed of powerful chanted formulae that disengaged the immaterial. Then there were aromatic pyres on which the bodies were burned—and the ashes were reserved for the communion of the living.

---

[44] Lautrec makes frequent reference to Jean-Antoine Watteau (1684-1721), whose *Embarquement pour Cythère* was the inspiration for a famous poem by Baudelaire, in which the embarkation for the island in question, famous for the worship of Aphrodite, became symbolic of the initiation of an erotic adventure.

They actually ate the ashes of the dead, and their lives was perpetuated thus, in a sad and lofty symbolism, by which the souls of their ancestors found a definitive transformation in them. They were ignorant of any other nourishment, and their souls of any other poetry. Love did not exist yet, and humans reproduced without joy. Their only mystery, perhaps of a grandeur that they did not suspect, was that of a human race living on the problem of its own death. And their soul, haunted by the fear of, and also the desire for, the Mourners, was like a lunar landscape in which there would have been no forms, no music and no perfumes.

One day, among the bodies transported on a daily basis to the island, that of a little child was found, so melancholy and so delicate that the Mourners wept, in an emotion never felt before. His white wings, soiled by every kind of mud, were those of a vagabond, but his dead eyes had a gaze whose malicious and arrogant pride was that of a god.

The body was dispersed according to custom, and soon the fragile lines from which that subtle flower of beauty were born were broken and lost forever. And the people ate the bitter and unsuspected ashes that were to give them an endless regret for the Beauty that was real for a single moment of the past. Oh, what white-clad seraphim would recover the lost lines of the Form too dolorously beloved!

For, as soon as the unknown child as dead and his ashes dispersed, I believe that Fear in its most charming and palest form descended into that universe. A terrible sickness fell upon the cities. Those who ate the divine ashes were poisoned forever. Their eyes lit up. Prey to an intense fever, they ran into the country, the daylight dying on the fragile stems of flowers and the night mingling the mystery of alcoves with the voluptuousness of blue stars. They conceived mysterious affections for the trees, the clouds and motionless nature; then, like the Chaldean shepherds of ancient times, they saw rising in the eyes of women the midnight sun of Love.

And for the first time, they knew that eternal thing, love, and that painful and nostalgically personal thing, the frisson of beloved flesh.

Their dull eyes, their burning lips and their halting respiration permitted them to recognize themselves in one another; with love, too, came forms, music and perfumes.

Now, those who ate the eyes of the Child would have love in their eyes for all eternity; those who ate his lips would have it in their lips; those who drank his blood would have the blood of a god eternally in their veins. And they were beloved for their lips, their blood or their eyes.

Others would have his harmonious voice, and knew the secret of making people weep by means of music and words.

They were seen going along the streets, isolated from everyone else, fearful of their strange appearance and seemingly-immeasurable dolor. Disdained and disdainful, they lived in one of those worlds parallel to the real one, which are the worlds of dreams, mirrors or madness. They invented measure and rhythm, according to the new intonations that their words had taken since the coming of the Child. With the vague memory of the divine reality that had once existed, they knew their role as mysterious reflections. Sometimes, on contemplating the dolorous face of beloved individuals who loved them for the tender frisson of their eyes, they saw a line appear there, a smile, a gaze, a lost fragment of the Form, and fixed in their poems, like a streak of luminous gold, that sparse laughter of the Absolute. They were men of genius, those who made manifest by means of the pen, the word or the brush.

And the remembrance of the strange event slowly disappeared from memories. And the lovesick lived on, forever incurable; to console them, they had the delicate caresses of the stars, of wings, of pupils, and in one supreme moment, in every life, the suffering and advent of the Kiss. For the kiss was born after Love, a thing more amorous than Amour. The children descended from them, sadder and more beautiful than humans, sang beneath balconies for their daughters. And more mournful than the Mourners themselves, they bore on the forehead from then the mysterious sign that drives women mad, and also makes them afraid of love. And it is since then that the incurable suffering of immortal poems has been born.

This happened on a very distant epoch. The funeral organs of eternity had scarcely fallen silent to listen to the tremulous prayer of the first new-born world.

Thus was born the race that suffers from lovesickness.

SELECTIONS FROM *STORIES OF TOM JOE*

The Haunted Château or, The Adulterous Virgin
A Great Passionate and Meteorological Romance[45]

I. The Bloody Pipe

Five to midnight chimed in the belfry.

The lugubrious wind was blowing through the trees so strongly that it would have uprooted all Maurice Barrès' heroes in a trice.[46]

Large clouds were racing across the sky, succeeding one another without interruption. The rain was furious. The weather was as grey as a Pole.[47]

By the side of the road was an ancient oak, from the low branches of which a hanged man was swaying ominously.

An automobile stopped at the top of the slope. A man dressed in a cloak the color of a wall and a hooded lantern

---

[45] The inclusion of the term "météorologique" [metereological] in the subtitle pays homage to the way that weather is used in melodramas to reflect the emotions of the characters, by means of an artistic inversion of the celebrated "pathetic fallacy."

[46] Maurice Barrès (1862-1923) became famous for a trilogy of novels devoted to "the cult of the self," which recommended urgently that people should strive to discover their "roots" in the personal and collective unconscious.

[47] The French *gris* [grey] can also mean "drunk." I shall not annotate the other untranslatable puns in this piece, because it would become rather tedious.

came down; with a distracted hand he caressed the fuming rump of the steam-horses and gave them a few sugar-lumps. Then he took a massive gold watch from his fob-pocket and checked the time.

"Five to midnight," he murmured. "I have time. The train doesn't leave for three days."

He was an old man. He might have been forty-six or forty-seven years old. A few white threads were beginning to silver his beautiful black hair. Precocious wrinkles creased his forehead, which was furrowed in a bitter rictus. A profound suffering, stoically borne, was legible in his thin face. Beneath his rather frail appearance, however, Baron Jehan des Entournures[48]—our readers will already have recognized him—concealed a will of iron combined with an indomitable courage. One sensed that the man was made to combat destiny.

A flash of lightning streaked the sky and cut out of the darkness, in jagged ridges, the profile of the high mountains of Estremadura. The Baron made a despairing gesture and got back into the automobile. He pronounced a few words into the acoustic tube. The black chauffeur in the driving-seat started trembling in every limb, but not one of his facial muscles stirred. Following the orders he had received, he launched the automobile forward in eleventh gear.

The road was on the edge of a ravine devoid of any parapet. The rock-face fell steeply away. Three or four hundred meters lower down, sordid huts were perceptible inhabited by wreck-looters. The car bounded toward death. Just as it was about to cross the fatal breach, the Baron leapt out of the door and landed on the road, safe and sound.

He had time to attach a long green beard, evidently false, to his naturally beardless chin, and to put on rose-colored glasses. Thus disguised, the Baron could go anywhere unno-

---

[48] The literal meaning of *entournures* is "armholes," but the word is more familiar in an idiomatic phrase vaguely echoed in the Baron's full name, *gêné dans les entournures*, which means "in an awkward situation."

ticed. He stood pensively for a moment on the edge of the ravine, listening to the noise of the car bouncing off the projection of the rock as it plunged into the valley. The chauffeur's cadaver must have been little more than a salty pulp.

The satanic rictus reappeared on the Baron's face. "Another one," he sneered. "Number seventy-four tomorrow morning."

Wrapping himself in his cloak, he headed for the village visible a few hundred meters away. After a few steps, however, he paused. His feverish hand rummaged in his clothes. Soon, he drew out of an interior pocket of his doublet an object carefully wrapped in a blue headscarf, which he unfolded with devout gestures. It was a pipe made of Boulogne wood, admirably carved. There were bloodstains on the bowl. The Baron kissed it piously and felt stronger. He folded it up in his handkerchief, set it next to his heart again, and then, now sure of triumph, he strode off rapidly on the road that was leading him into the unknown.

II. A Love Story

The life of the Baron des Entournures was a veritable romance.

Born in the Spanish mountains, he had grown up with his father, an old fanatic and Huguenot. At the age of twenty, however, he felt the blood of his audacious ancestors, the conquistadors, seething in his veins. The calm life of the château became odious to him. His father was obliged to consent to his departure.

An old friend of the family took responsibility for him. The Captain of a long-haul vessel, he was going to Tierra de Fuego carrying a cargo of ice, intended to combat the effects of that country's torrid temperature.

Young Jehan quickly revealed himself to be a courageous and enterprising fellow. Scarcely had the cargo been unloaded, still streaming with melted ice, than he went in search of a means of utilizing his activity. A friend of the captain, who had settled in the region some years earlier, offered him employment in his sugar-cane plantations. It was there that he met the woman who was to become his wife. Her name was Flora.

She was a young woman of Brazilian origin, whose beauty was perfect. Very well-educated, she had passed all her examinations.

Unfortunately, as the adoptive daughter of a black man brutalized by alcohol, she had allowed herself to be carried away by that deadly passion. A day rarely passed when she did not get drunk two or three times.

The Baron's love saved her.

On the eve of the marriage, just as she was about to retire to the nuptial chamber with her happy spouse, before the assembled relatives and friends, she demanded a cup of monstrous dimensions, poured into it the contents of four bottles of rum, and emptied the cup without hesitation in a single draught.

Then, turning to her husband with an angelic smile, she said: "From now on, I shall no longer drink anything but water."

Incredible as the fact appears, for a woman, she kept her word.

Every month, a ship charted for that exclusive purpose brought a barrel full of Seine water to Tierra de Fuego. The beautiful Flora knew no other beverage.

So, life went on happily. But grim destiny was lying in wait.

The arrival of Baron Jehan had, in fact, stirred up terrible jealousies in that cosmopolitan society. Young women were scarce, especially those whose beauty was as perfect as Flora's.

There was a black man who worked in the house of her adoptive father, who was madly in love with her. He was about thirty and had already been married. His name was Ripolin.[49] His first wife, Dolores, was a white woman of very pure race. He had therefore become a mulatto by marriage.

She died, unfortunately, after three years of a cloudless union.

As a widower, Ripolin had become black again. Perhaps blacker, because of his mourning-dress.

With the courage that draws its energy from profound conviction, he used every possible means to whiten himself again. Every day he took a number of Pink Pills for Pale People[50]—but the result was insignificant. He continued, however, partly out of vague hope but much more for reasons of snobbery.

In seeing the young Flora grow up alongside him, a mad desire gnawed at his heart. He dreamed of being loved by her. As soon as she reached her twelfth birthday, he asked for her hand in marriage—but she adored Jehan and rejected the black suitor disdainfully.

From then on, Ripolin only lived for vengeance.

One day, the Baron left the plantation early. He went to the nearby town to have his grandmother's portrait framed. It was the only souvenir he had of his distant childhood.

When he came back, the beautiful Flora was dead. The wretch, taking advantage of a momentary inattention, had murdered her in a cowardly fashion.

The Baron found his wife lying on a bed of sugar-cane that had been laid down to ease her last moments. He hurled himself on the cadaver and covered it with kisses.

"Oh Flora!" he cried, "I was unable to protect the treasure that heaven entrusted to me! My imprudence has doomed you. But henceforth, I will devote my entire life to seeking the means to avenge you. I swear not to marry again before pu-

---

[49] Ripolin was, and still is, a well-known brand of paint originated in France.

[50] "Dr. Williams' Pink Pills for Pale People" were one of the most popular patent medicines of the late nineteenth century, marketed by the Canadian G. T. Fulford & Co. as a cure for St. Vitus's Dance and practically every other disease under the sun.

nishing the infamous murderer. Sleep peacefully, my dear Flora! I swear it on the ash of your blonde hair!"

There was not a moment to lose. It was discovered that the treacherous Ripolin, after his cowardly sin, had fled southwards. He hastened he funeral, and departed two days later in search of the criminal.

The weather was splendid. The birds were singing in the trees. The Sun inundated the macaroni fields with its hectic rays.

As he got nearer to the pole, the heat began to diminish.

That was the only notable incident of the voyage.

The Baron crossed the strait in a frail skiff. Soon he perceived the ice-sheet and the glacial solitudes.

He interrogated the natives he found on disembarking. None of them could give him the slightest information about the fugitive.

The Baron was not discouraged. In any case, scientific curiosity was allied in him with the desire to avenge his wife. He was too close not to take advantage of the opportunity. The south pole attracted him. Armed with a sextant and an astrolabe, he set off courageously. When he arrived, it was dark. He was obliged to wait for the next day to contemplate the polar landscape.

In the morning he woke up, refreshed and in good heart. He emerged from his tent.

O stupor! In front of him, solidly erected on two posts, was a gigantic poster, on which he read the words: *Closed for repairs. While work is in progress, please apply to the north pole.*

So that was where his efforts had led! He uttered a howl of fury and headed northwards again. A few days later, he reached the shore again. Without hesitating for moment, he started swimming, resolutely.

Twenty years later he came ashore in Morocco.

III. The Haunted Château

It was a little town, such as one sees in old pictures.

There was a gate at the end of the road with stone benches for old people and an arch from which a broken lantern was suspended.

On the other side, a long street began, which went all the way through the town, with shorter streets to either side.

Every street corner was marked by a boundary-post. One could not go wrong.

The street was full of people. The noise of saucepans being moved around kitchens was audible through the windows. Bald men were smoking their pipes on doorsteps. There were children playing with dogs in the gutters.

The Baron considered the spectacle affectionately. As he did so he noticed that it as dinner time. He looked for an inn-sign. Prudence instructed him not to arrive unexpectedly, when it was time to sit down at table, at a château abandoned for fifty years.

There was no indication on the horizon. Neither a Pewter Pot not a Crowned Ox. Feverishly, he passed a cosmetic stick over his moustache and interrogated a young man who was coming toward him, carrying a fat child in her arms, whom she was breast-feeding.

"A hostelry? Lord! Why? No travelers ever stop here. There's only the villagers, and when they travel, they go elsewhere."

Idlers were gathering. Shaking his head like a cracked bell, an old man said: "There's only the château, with at least thirty beds—but one can't think of staying there."

The old man bore all the stigmata of debauchery on his face.

At the word *château*, the women present made the sign of the cross devoutly, as if they had seen the Devil.

"It's precisely at the château," the Baron said, "that I want to stay."

"Unfortunately," the odious old man continued, "it's an ancient haunted château. The noble lord, whose soul is with God, died a long time ago. His son went to the Turkish lands and never came back. Every night, a phantom walks the terraces. Once, a traveler wanted to spend the night in that accursed dwelling. He was never seen again."

"That's probably," said Jehan, "because he left by another door."

And he insisted on being given a few provisions and the key. They decided to go fetch it. It was the sacristan who kept it, with those of the church. For fear of spirits, every time he went past it, he sprinkled it with holy water. It was, in consequence, very rusty.

A few hours later, the Baron was installed in front of a good peat fire in a ground-floor room of the château. He gazed affectionately at the old furniture, which had been the playmates of his childhood. He heard the wind moaning in the trees, as before. On the table in front of him the villagers had laid out a very comforting supper. A large jar of red fish added a picturesque note to the severity of the décor. And in the next room, a bed awaited the traveler.

But Jehan des Entournures scarcely thought of sleep. Haunted by his desire for vengeance, he had not slept for fifty years.

The snow fell uninterruptedly, burying the dahlias and sunflowers under its white cloak. Through the arched window came the faint echo of bells ringing for Candlemas.

A noise rose up from the cellar. The steps of the staircase creaked. The Baron took from his wallet one of the latest love-letters from his numerous mistresses, rolled the piece of paper into a trumpet and put the trumpet in his left ear, in which he was slightly deaf since his campaigns in the Himalayas.

Footsteps became audible, drawing nearer. Soon, no doubt about it, there was someone behind the door.

"Come in!" Jehan shouted, in a voice weakened by emotion.

The door opened and the phantom appeared.

A vast white sheet covered it from head to foot, and from foot to head, rising up again. It advanced into the middle of the room.

"Who has permitted you, audacious immortal, to come and trouble my repose?" it said, in a severe tone.

Its voice was cavernous, so low in pitch that the Baron had to lie flat on the ground to hear it.

With a noble gesture, the phantom signaled for him to get up again.

An oppressive silence followed. A profound silence. One could have heard a watch being stolen.

In the end, the hero gathered his courage and spoke to the pale visitor: "Are you not," he said, "the spirit of my dead father? If you are, you know why I have come to this dwelling—and you would be very kind to tell me, for I have no idea."

The phantom reached out toward its interlocutor and handed him an object, which the Baron accepted mechanically. It was a piece of cigarette paper. While he contemplated it stupidly, he saw the phantom's hand rose slowly toward the ceiling. Jehan's eyes followed the movement—and what he saw was so frightful that his hair instantly turned black.

There were footprints on the ceiling!

The Baron uttered a cry of impotent rage. The phantom had just thrown back the flap of the white sheet covering its face—and his visage, with a sinister rictus, was none other than that of Ripolin. Doors opened noisily. Before Flora's unfortunate husband was able to put himself on the defensive, the Brothers of High C[51] had invaded the room and gripped him tightly. Few minutes later, he was lying in a dungeon with a piece of stale black bread and a wicker jug.

---

[51] *Frères de l'Ut de Poitrine* in French "*L'ut de poitrine*" was a high C that only a few tenors could hit, and which became something of a challenge for that reason; the quest was the theme of an eponymous 1853 vaudeville by Eugène Labiche, echoed in several subsequent dramatic works.

IV. An Evening in High Society

The Comtesse's reception-rooms were brightly illuminated.

Never had the historic town house, whose imposing mass stood at the junction of the Boulevard Poissonnière and the Rue Mouffetard, seen such affluence.

That evening, all that Paris possessed of elegance in the world of politics had come together there.

The Comtesse de La Tourprengarde was one of those enigmatic individuals whose star suddenly appears in the Parisian sky, and who owe a great deal of their harm to the mystery surrounding their origin.

Many stories of a scabrous sort were whispered on that subject. But she was rich, young, very beautiful and her hair was naturally curly. That was sufficient. The most difficult socialites solicited her invitations.

The best-informed said that she was the widow of an unsociable Brazilian, to whom she owed her fortune. She never talked about it. Perhaps she still thought about it.

A few years after her arrival in Paris, she had married her second husband, a famous surgeon, already old, who had since died, prematurely. Some *femmes fatales* are marked on the forehead with a stigma handed down from numerous avatars, and strike in the heart, successively, with a sure hand, all those who chance to love them.

The Comtesse, whether out of hypocrisy or calculation, wept sincerely for her spouse.

Soon, however, the weakness of her creole nature was stronger than regret.

She was a woman. She succumbed.

Among the numerous guests crowded, at the present moment, into the vast reception-rooms of the house, there were very few who could not boast of having obtained her favors.

The music had stopped, though. The orchestra had taken advantage of that circumstance to have a drink. Lackeys in fine costumes were pouring champagne in the parlor. The distant echo of drinking songs was faintly audible.

In the middle of an attentive circle, Captain Pamphile was telling tales of his voyages overseas.

The Comtesse gave the signal for applause herself.

She was a woman of small dimensions. She was scarcely a meter twelve in height—but the majesty of her bearing made her resemble a giant.

Her dress was green muslin, decorated with large ruche roses. A blue girdle fell from her waist.

Thus clad, the Comtesse was irresistible.

Around her neck she wore the famous necklace that her last husband, the famous specialist surgeon, had given her. That necklace, a veritable masterpiece of modern jewelry, was entirely made of kidney-stones.

"So I left Paraguay," Captain Pamphile continued, "Not wanting to remain under that infamous accusation a minute longer. Certainly, I had played for high stakes. My entire fortune had been swallowed up in agricultural exploitation. I began to obtain brilliant results. The first crop of snails exceeded my expectations. The production of cows' milk had quintupled since my application of rhythmic traction to the development of the udders. But what did that matter! I was in a hurry to remake my fortune. It was therefore indispensable to unmake it first. Then again, I admit, from another point of view, I wasn't displeased to disappear for a while. The love of the *camerera-mayor*[52] was beginning to weigh upon me.

"In passing through the Bermudas, our ship had to endure a dangerous storm. We only just had time to take in a reef and tack toward the coast. We were only a few cables from Tierra del Fuego, whose high volcanoes…."

A shrill screech interrupted the orator. The Comtesse had just fainted.

While people pressed around her, one of the guests who had been in the outermost rank of Pamphile's audience slipped

---

[52] The *camerera-mayor* was the chief attendant of the Spanish queen.

away to the left and headed for the door of the next room. The man was wearing a glass mask over his face, which permitted him to see clearly everything that was happening around him without revealing his own features. He spoke Spanish and answered to the name of José, but an attentive observer might have noticed, every time, an involuntary quiver of the cutaneous and zygomatic muscles. The man had to be a great criminal or a hero.

Meanwhile, the Captain, used to making light of the most critical situations, had summoned the servants. On his orders, someone went in search of an old horseshoe and a red hot shovel.

While the devoted guests held the Comtesse, her head and upper body slumped forward, he passed the shovel, on which he had placed the horseshoe, under her nose.

A pestilential odor filled the room.

The Comtesse woke up, passed her hand over her forehead with a distracted gesture, and then sneezed three times.

"Where am I?" she asked. "What a delightful scent of roses!"

And she dissolved in tears.

She was saved.

"...Whose high volcanoes," the Captain continued, without letting go of the shovel in his hand, as a precaution, "projected a greenish fuliginous light on the horizon. We landed. Immediately, however, we were forced to flee from a danger greater than the one we had just escaped. Monstrous Lepidoptera rushed upon us, uttering savage cries. Fortunately, the mountain offered us inaccessible retreats. A few hours later, we where sheltering n the depths of an immense natural cave, doubtless hollowed out by prehistoric humans. In that cave we were, it is true, at risk of dying of hunger and thirst. The wild Lepidoptera were crouching outside the entrance and licking the ground to extract salt, of which they are very fond..."

The Captain paused momentarily to moisten his lips with the grog that a scarlet-clad lackey had just brought him. There were a few minutes of silence.

At that moment, a Compagnie Richer[53] carriage passed along the street at a gallop.

V. The Righter of Wrongs

For seven years, the Baron des Entournures lived in the dungeon in the château.

The seasons succeeded one another. After autumn, summer; after spring, winter. He was still a prisoner.

Well-treated, however. Two meals a day. Three dishes by selection. Two desserts. Cheese. Bread optional. A half-bottle of red or white wine.

The Brothers of High C took turns to serve him. Each of them came in turn, dressed in the great green cloak of the order, wearing on a chain around the neck the Salted Herring first class, enriched with diamonds.

A rigorous discipline, however, prevented them from saying a single word. In the midst of these mute servitors, the Baron was more alone than in the most frightful desert. He had absolutely no knowledge of what was happening outside. The only echo of external life that reached him through the somber vaults was the sinister laughter of his enemy.

When the initial surprise had passed, therefore, after five or six years, he had begun to search for a means of escape with a sudden grim energy.

The floor of his cell was simply compacted earth. By means of an old crust of bread that he had the patience to harden, he dug in the ground, devouring the soil little by little as he went, to conceal his work.

At a depth of fifty meters, he found impenetrable rock. He also had a stomach ache. His health was in jeopardy. He had haggard eyes and an earthy complexion.

---

[53] The Compagnie Richer was the largest and most famous of the companies contracted to empty the cesspools of Paris.

This time, the unfortunate was about to abandon himself to despair, when one day, by chance, his gaze fell upon the cell door.

Absorbed for such a long time in his escape plans, he had not had time to look in that direction.

The door was wide open, without his ever having noticed it.

An automobile arriving at top speed stopped in front of the perron of the house.

A man got out and came up the steps.

He threw his fur cloak negligently into the hands of the impassive servants. His lace ruff, spangled with fabulously valuable black pearls, fell in cascades over his waistcoat. Pinned to the button-hole of his jacket was a hard-boiled egg.

Only the sewer-worker's boots rising above the knees lent a picturesque note to that correct ensemble.

That was because he had two missions to carry out. The first was the concern of the man of the world, the second, symbolized by the boots, of the righter of wrongs.

Deep down, Jehan des Entournures believed in his wife's fidelity.

She had died too young to have been able to deceive him very often.

The heavy curtain was raised. The Baron appeared in the doorway. He darted a circular glance around the square room. His eyes alighted on the Comtesse. Master of himself as he was, he could hardly stifle a cry of joyous amazement.

But the moment had not come. Without paying any heed to the acclamations that greeted his entrance, he bounded toward the door through which Don José had disappeared. It was the gaming room.

Seated at a baccarat table, the Spaniard was delivering himself body and soul to his fatal passion.

He had set his transparent mask down on the baize in order that, when chance went against him, he could swear more easily.

His feverish hands were dealing the cards with sardonic gestures. His features were contracted. One might have thought that he was searching, in that unhealthy emotion, to forget some remorse.

Someone tapped him on the shoulder. He turned round, shivering. Half an hour later he was standing up, stiffening himself against drunkenness, face to face with Jehan.

VI. Conclusion

"Wretch!" cried the Baron. "The hour has come to expiate your crime! Commend your soul to God, if he wants a dog like you!"

Then, bringing a carefully-wrapped object out of his pocket, he brandished it in Don José's direction.

"Do you recognize this pipe?" he asked, in a dull vice. "It's the one that the old black man was smoking on the day of Flora's death. But Flora isn't dead, since she's alive…and it was the black man who succumbed, a victim of his devotion. Distracted by dolor, I've been the dupe of your subterfuge for sixty years. Since then, my eyes have been opened. Prepare yourself. You're about to die…."

Lightning might have struck Don José and he would not have been more thunderstruck. His face paled frightfully. By virtue of a singular phenomenon, that pallor caused the white make-up with which his face was covered to disappear. In all its primitive blackness, the terrible face of Ripolin became clearly visible.

Already, though, Baron Jehan had run to the door. An instant later, he had the Comtesse in his arms. The Comtesse was none other than Flora.

After numerous vicissitudes, destiny had reunited the victims of an abominable plot.

The guests pressed around the happy couple. The Comtesse—or, rather, Flora, for it is under that name that she will figure henceforth in this story—was sobbing with joy, like a child.

Suddenly, a gunshot made everyone start. They ran into the gaming room. Collapsed on an armchair, his eyes glabrous, Ripolin was still holding the fatal dagger in his menacing hand.

The old black man was avenged.

Monsieur House

The individual lived on the ground floor of a five-story house with attics. His lodgings consisted of narrow passages and one room that he had made into his library, in which he lived.

That library was vast and the shelves high, laden with books; their number might have been estimated, by means of the most moderate calculations, at twelve thousand five hundred.

To reach the most difficult shelves and explore the in the midst of folio volumes, sextants, marine charts and dictionaries, the old man had been obliged to install a whole system of apparatus: ladders of different lengths and forms, straight or curved; smooth ropes swaying within arm's reach. There were many trapezes in spiral stairways; beams at various heights facilitated access and respiration.

As the old man rarely went out, confined to his lair, where he received his friends, the interior disposition of his lodgings permitted him to make up for the absence of movement. He had been able to reconcile his intellectual advantage and his need for activity. His muscles and his mind developed along two strictly parallel lines. It was the harmony of body and soul preached so ardently by the Pythagoreans.

The charm of the library was, moreover, its variety. Its possessor was no more a stranger to poets than philosophy. With a vigorous readjustment on the rings he could reach Aristotle's *Metaphysics* in five stout volumes, with marginal notes in Hebrew. Or, departing from the uppermost shelves on the flying trapeze, he could describe the arc of a majestic circle through the air to end up, down below, at the magical works of Éliphas Lévi. To get as far as Lamartine, a gentle swing was sufficient.

Reading a great deal, he made notes in the same way, and his volumes were full of pieces of paper inscribed by his hands, in which he summarized. Sometimes, in the course of reading something else, the need to consult one of these notes arose. Poorly endowed with memory, he devoted himself, in order to retrieve it, to exercises of which the most picturesque description could give no idea. He took all the volumes successively in hand—about twenty thousand—and riffled through them. He shook them, threw them into the air, juggled with them. An intense dust blackened the atmosphere of the room. The old man continued. Sometimes, he shook his head, with a discouraged expression, to make large suspended tears fall. He swung on the apparatus holding a book, which he pulled apart, like a monkey with a coconut. The volumes flew across the room. Finally, the recalcitrant piece of paper would escape from the pages of one of them. Taking possession of it was then, for him, child's play. He had adapted to this purpose and old butterfly-net in which the palpitating page would soon be captured.

One day, however, a long time after the first, he sat sadly on a pile of old books on a shadowed shelf set beneath a large high-placed window. Reaching down to the floor, with his legs bent, he manipulated a few works beneath his blue-lensed spectacles. When he picked each one up by both edges of the binding, turned backwards like the wings of a captive insect, the body hung down lamentably. Moving the volumes through the air in this way, brushing others and the floor, the corners broke, the gold-leaf was eroded and the boards lost their freshness. Even treatises of philosophy could not resist the proofs of such an agitated life.

He re-covered them with sheets of cloth; he put large copper nails in the corners and iron rods in the spine on which he heaviest folios slid like light skates.

After that the volumes were sturdier, but another inconvenience presented itself.

Previously the house had eroded the books; now, the book eroded the house.

The iron roads and nails caught on the curtains, scratched the parquet, broke the chandeliers and the Japanese curious. By night, on the various floors, people developed the unnecessary habit of waking up for every volume consulted. Muffled noises were heard coming from the dark corridors, of creaking floorboards and windows opening to the street, and uncertain forms, shielding a candle from the wind, calling the watchman. The interrogation of three voluminous works, killers of sleep, having coincided with childish teething in the vicinity, Monsieur House was threatened with eviction.

He took the thirty-one thousand volumes down from his shelves and suspended them throughout the room by mean of ropes or chains, as solidly as he could. At head height, one could easily consult them. The old books dangled from the ceiling: for the thinnest, simple threads; for the others, the necessary apparatus. Kant had imperiously required the employment of a solid cable. For Larousse, incessantly consulted, a system of pulleys was installed. The light works and frivolous tales of the eighteenth century and other eras, unlike the other volumes, rose from the ground, retained by subtle silks like captive balloons.

From then on, there was a magical spectacle for visitors. They marched through a profound forest, and by night, the noise of chains terrified burglars.

But the man fell victim to these vain precautions.

One evening, next to his lamp, the old man was absorbed in reading his favorite book, Blumenbach's *Decades octo craniorum diversarum genium*.[54] He was gazing at the old black letters on the yellow paper when a sudden sinister crack caused him to shudder. His spectacles rose up on to his forehead, then fell back, and his anxious eyes peered over them. But he did not have time either to get to his feet or call for

---

[54] Johann Friedrich Blumenbach (1752-1850) was the anthropologist who pioneered craniometry as a method of racial classification, popularizing his work in a series of publications individually entitled *Decas craniorum*, of which the volume cited here is evidently an improvised omnibus.

help. Beneath the weight of thirty-nine thousand eight hundred and fifty volumes, copper plates, nails and chains, the entire ceiling collapsed, and with it the upper floors.

Monsieur House's body was found under the rubble, his back broken by the iron-reinforced quartos. Thus he died, a victim of the good order that he had established in his home.

The Submarine Airplane

The first person I saw when I opened the door was my friend Tom Joe. Although I hasn't seen him for two days, I didn't find him much changed. He still had his benevolent ruddy face, and a little hat on his head of the most cheerful appearance. Besides, give the late hour. I was not unduly astonished to see him sitting at the counter on top of a high chair, or rather a stool, with a large glass of whisky to either side in front of him. It seemed to me that he was having some trouble maintaining his equilibrium. He was oscillating in a disquieting fashion, but he contrived ingeniously to recover his aplomb every time by drinking a mouthful of whisky from the other side.

His greeting was excessively cordial. He complained of not having heard my news for such a long time. I expressed the same regret. Tom offered me a drink and sighed:

"Life isn't always easy. The last time I saw you, I was finishing eating and drinking an inheritance from my old aunt in Greenland. It didn't take long to burn through it, with the liquids; I was soon reduced to the worst expedients. The modern era isn't favorable to men of genius. That's been known that since the remotest antiquity. I've tried to launch a number of products, among others a shaving cream for politicians and my famous capillary water, the Nevermore. Nothing has succeeded. My last attempt was the construction of a factory for the manufacture of meter rules made of rubber.

"Rubber, Tom Joe?"

"Rubber. All great discoveries are due to commonplace observation. Newton, for example. I was suddenly struck by the idea that objects come in different sizes and that a meter rule, by definition, is never anything but a meter long. Hence its absolute uselessness for longer or shorter objects, which are much more numerous. With a meter rule made of an elastic substance, on the other hand, if you have to measure a room, for example, you attach one end of the meter firmly to one of the walls, and pull on the other end, until you reach the opposite wall.... It's infantile, and genius. The factory burned down. I don't even have enough left to measure the extent of my own misfortune."

"Poor Tom Joe!"

"I'm not discouraged. Now I'm taking an interest in aviation. I have everything necessary to succeed. You know that I was the first to anticipate, fifteen years ago, the creation of watertight bulkheads inside balloons, to attenuate the danger of falls. Imagine my surprise and emotion when I found out that, not only had my idea been realized, but that gradually, people are dispensing with the envelopes of balloons, only keeping the partitions! These marvelous kites have been made, which are called airplanes. From there to realizing the submarine airplane is only a short step."

Admiration rendered me mute. Tom drank a glass of whisky and continued:

"There's one certain fact, established by all scientists. That's that reverse logic is always the best. Let's consider, for example, not airplanes but present-day dirigibles. Haven't you noticed how they all affect the form of enormous fish? From that, a conclusion imposes itself. If, in order to move through the air, that form has proved to be the best, it naturally follows that submarine apparatus ought to resemble birds.

"I see, in fact, airplanes as being much more in their element in the water than in the air. Their employment would get rid of all the dangers of submarine navigation. Naturally, it's necessary not to think of constructing them in canvas, even tarred. But let's imagine one or two inclined planes, in aluminum, with a simple seat for the pilot in the middle, with the propeller at the rear, or in front, or at the side. The airplane, by virtue of its inclination, would dive as soon as it was started up. The man would be dressed in a diving-suit and would carry a sufficient provision of air. There wouldn't be any difficulty. Thank God, air is the only thing whose price hasn't yet gone up. One can have as much as one wants for a minimum price. There's no comparison with whisky."

"But don't you think, Tom Joe," I observed, timidly, "that there might be some danger in plunging into the depths like that?"

"Danger? What danger? That of falling to the sea-bed? Child! What is there to prevent you from fitting your machine with large empty spaces, full of air, or covering your aluminum with sheets of cork, in such a way that the whole thing is lighter than water? Then, the worst that can happen to you would be an engine failure—but instead of falling, as in the air, you'd rise calmly to the surface. I know that you're going to raise a serious objection..."

"Yes, Tom Joe? What's that?"

"You're going to tell me that it would doubtless be difficult to maintain, amid the waves, any sort of incandescent engine. I've foreseen the difficulty. I'll use a whisky-soda engine."

"Hurrah, old man!" I cried, positively enthused this time.

"Hurrah!" replied Tom Joe, waving his arms weakly, as if to take flight in the bosom of the waves.

This final attempt compromised his equilibrium irredeemably, and the unfortunate fellow, having tried in vain to cling on to the bars of the stool, fell heavily to the ground. Aided by a few courageous citizens, I carried him to a bench, where we laid him down, and where, a few minutes later, doubtless pursuing his brilliant idea in his dream, he imitated the sound of an engine in a surprising fashion, with his nose.

Voyage to the Moon

When Cyrano de Bergerac decided to go to the Moon, it was only after mature and serious reflection. There is no reproach more unjust than that addressed to poets of dissolving into levity. Poets are, on the contrary, essentially practical men. They seek in all things their advantage and their pleasure. The truth is that they do not find it in the same place as more vulgar minds. But should one reproach them for preferring sunbathing, or a pretty woman, to a joint of meat, especially when they have eaten?

Thus, our hero had his idea well worked-out when he departed, to the extent that one can depart with a fixed idea. Very precocious, he had anticipated the verses of Alfred de Musset, and was dying to write his own ballad on that planet. Voyages shape youth, and poets are forever young. That is how one recognizes them, even when they are very old.

The bottles full of subtle air that he had attached to his belt did their job marvelously. He did not have the misfortune of seeing his waxen wings melt over the Aegean Sea, like Icarus. On the contrary, having no wings, it all went like wax for him. He rapidly surpassed the crystalline or primary sphere, which is, as everyone knows, the last terrestrial region.

Immediately, lunar attraction being less powerful than terrestrial attraction, because of the difference in volume, but predominant, because of proximity, the resistance the bottles offered to that attraction decreased in proportion, and the voyager's descent to the lunar surface increased rapidly—to the extent that Cyrano scarcely had time to perceive the lunar volcanoes that loomed up in front of him like monstrous funnels. Before he knew it, he fell on the lunar soil, with an impact so violent that all his bottles were broken and he lost consciousness, remaining insensible, lying full length with his nose in the air.

When he awoke, it was broad daylight. He spent a few moments rubbing his sides, which were aching somewhat, then looked around. He saw trees that bore a singular resemblance to the trees of France, except that they were smaller. And when he tried to get up, even though he was rather tired, he observed that his inconsiderate thrust launched him ten meters into the air. But he was suddenly reassured on remembering that the volume of the Moon is five times less than that of the Earth, and that its mass can be estimated as an eightieth of that of our globe, because of the difference in density, according to the most reliable authorities.

Meanwhile, he was in a hurry to make contact with the inhabitants of that fabulous land. He had read in Plato that the Moon is the abode of the souls of dead poets, and he was very impatient to enter into conversation with Homer, Vigil, Villon and a few other excellent men of ancient times. Mechanically, he searched around him with his eyes for the flowers of the lotus and the asphodel.

But all he saw was a dusty road, devoid of interest, except that three silhouettes were perceptible in the distance that were approaching rapidly. When they were closer, he found that they were human, or something analogous. One of the lunar men was dressed as a gendarme. He had a crescent of flesh for a head, with tapering bony points, one eye in the middle and a quarter of a mouth underneath. The second had a whole sphere for a head, redolent with health, and a peasant's costume. He seemed to be middle-aged. The third looked like a policeman. He had no mouth, and only a quarter of an eye.

The gendarme began speaking in English. He asked in a surly manner for Cyrano's papers—who rummaged in his pockets distractedly and found nothing but the verse manuscript of a tragedy. He gave it to the gendarme for want of anything better. The latter had scarcely given it a glance when he began making broad gestures and his face welled up, almost completely, with indignation. Then all three of them fell on Cyrano, tied him up and carried him off at a run, with so much brutality that he fainted again.

On recovering consciousness, he found himself between four walls, in some sort of cell sealed by an iron door, whose narrow window was furnished with bars. The floor was simply compacted Moon.

He deduced that he was in prison.

A lugubrious daylight descended in an oblique beam from the window. The prisoner's eyes went to something white that was lying on the ground, crumpled. He got to his feet and picked it up. It was a fragment of a newspaper abandoned there.

He looked for the feuilleton, in order to read it while awaiting events, but there was no feuilleton. The only page still intact carried an account of a session of the lunar Academy awarding prizes for virtue, with the list of murderers to whom the Prix Montyon had been awarded.[55] There were also details of the arrest of a vagabond, recognized as a non-functionary and immediately taken into custody, plus the story of the execution of three poets, one of whom had taken cynicism so far as to recite a sonnet on the scaffold.

Then Cyrano understood that the old Moon was more civilized than the Earth, and that it was our planet, the true Moon, that was the abode of lunatics. He thought that it was necessary to hasten to live there, while waiting for age and the progress of civilization to render it similar to our satellite. His energetic resolve gave him strength enough to loosen the bars of the window and to run away into the country. An ardent Sun was shining there. The problem of departure was less difficult to solve, because of the weak gravity. Cyrano dived into river that ran alongside the road, then exposed himself to the rays of the day-star. As the heat caused the water with which his clothes were soaked to evaporate, the voyager felt himself gently lifted up, as if breathed in by the Sun. He found his way back easily when he was at a certain height, and steered un-

---

[55] The Baron de Montyon endowed four annual prizes, one of which was the celebrated "prix de vertu," awarded for the most conspicuous act of generosity by a Frenchman.

hurriedly toward the Earth, where he arrived just in time for the première of *Chantecler*.[56]

---

[56] *Chantecler* is a verse play by Edmond Rostand, which was written with a view to the lead role being played by Benoît Coquelin, who had played Cyrano de Bergerac in Rostand's previous and most successful play. Unfortunately, Coquelin suffered a fatal heart-attack in 1909, allegedly clutching a copy of *Chantecler*, and the première had to be postponed until 1910.

The Lost Reflection

Jean Loiseleur came home in a state of high excitement. Absent-mindedly, he took his key off the hook in the vestibule of the house and climbed the stairs. Once he was in his room and the door was locked again he turned the door handle two or three times to put on the electric light. Nothing happened.

"Strange!" he murmured. "Am I drunk? That's not possible—I haven't drunk anything except whisky for three days."

Finally, he put his hand on the correct switch. The room lit up. He released a sigh of satisfaction.

A distracted glance in the mirror over the mantelpiece enabled him to see that he was pale. It was an old mirror. Someone had stuck strips of paper similar to the wallpaper, which continued its design, on to the worn and discolored frame.

There was a black marble clock in the middle of the mantelpiece, condemned to remain there in perpetuity, because it had never worked. To either side of the clock were two horrible vases, in white porcelain with a flower pattern, flared at the top and full of artificial green moss, like chaste ears plugged in order not to hear nocturnal chatter.

Jean Loiseleur had spent the evening with occultists and had heard things said that had disturbed him. Jacobus Duboisius had talked about formulae that rendered people invisible. What mysterious power would someone possessed of that gift have! A priest of Pythagoras would spend the night in the cave of Trophonius. Before he went to sleep he would put a small gold plate under his tongue, on which mysterious sins were engraved. Before putting it under his tongue he purified it in the altar fire. In the morning, he woke up invisible for the whole day, and undertook a very interesting excursion through the shops of goldsmiths, money-changers and bankers.

I want to be invisible, Jean Loiseleur said to himself. *I want that.*

He searched the room for a gold plate, or, by default, a gold coin. A fruitless search. He rummaged in his pockets. No money. He remembered, dolorously, that he must have given his last fifty-centime piece as a tip to a waiter who also had no money. All he found in his waistcoat was a five franc bill, payable in gold on presentation at the Banque de France.

After all, he said to himself, very aptly, it's only faith that saves. A banknote is a fiduciary coin. I have only to imagine, sincerely, that it's gold.

So he took the banknote, purified it according to the rites by holding it, for want of sacred fire, in a candle-flame, then went to bed with the talisman under his tongue, pronounced the magic formula, and, after a little while, went to sleep.

His slumber was peaceful and dreamless. He woke up early and was suddenly on his feet. The banknote had melted in his mouth during the night. That was five francs down the drain—or, rather, the gullet. But that was unimportant. He raced to the mirror. Alas, he could see himself distinctly in the mirror. The banknote did not have the same value as gold!

All day long he was peevish, sulking in the office and the restaurant, and consigned all occultists to their patron, the Devil. That evening he got home early, disgusted with life, took his key from the rack and went into his room. To make the situation even more charming, there happened to be a power cut. He did not even light his candle. He undressed in the dark and, after having commended his soul to God, went to bed and went to sleep.

Rosy-fingered dawn had just reopened the gates of the Orient once more, after having carefully closed the gates of the Occident in order to avoid draughts. Jean Loiseleur got up nonchalantly. His life had once again become as banal as that of a fish. He dressed unhurriedly, having nothing urgent to do except go to the office.

Suddenly, in the course of his peregrinations through the room, he passed in front of the mirror. Amazement! He put his hand to his heart, weak at the knees. "And I still asleep?" he exclaimed. "Or am I awake?" He was directly in front of the mirror, but he could see nothing therein but the image of the opposite wall, and the wallpaper whose vertical lines were parallel to those on both sides of the glass. There was no other image in the mirror but that of the facing wall. His reflection was no longer there!

He was looking at himself in the mirror, and could not see himself. Thus are destinies accomplished. Certainly, on looking down at his own person, he did not observe anything abnormal. Al his limbs were directly visible. But that was all. Like the man in the German folktale who had lost his shadow,[57] he had lost his reflection.

And surely, without a doubt, if the mirror could not see him, other people would not be able to see him. The success was complete. What glory, when renown publicized the event! He sat down at his table to write, with a feverish hand, to all the newspapers—and to the Academy of Sciences, to solicit the first available seat.

As he leaned over the table, with his head in his hands, reflecting, and gradually feeling overwhelmed by an immense pride, he heard heavy footsteps on the staircase. Someone knocked at the door of the rom. He got to his feet, enjoying in advance the amazement of the visitor who would hear him without seeing him. He opened the door. It was the house attendant. He was carrying, with some difficulty, a large mirror with a superb gilded frame.

"It was the landlady who said that the mirror in your room was a souvenir of her husband, who had been a *zouave* on the Pont de l'Alma.[58] So, yesterday afternoon, we came to take it, to put it in her room, and she told me to bring you the

---

[57] Adelbert von Chamisso's *Peter Schlemihl*.

[58] The Pont de l'Alma is a bridge over the Seine, named after the battle of Alma, fought in the Crimea in 1854. Its four corners are decorated with generic military statues, one of which represents a *zouave*.

best one she had in the house as a replacement. You won't lose by the swap. Look how handsome you are in it!"

A Cubist Tale

At the exit from the stable the horse whinnied slowly and darted a distracted glance over things. Then it headed at a brisk pace toward the road, which led between two rows of poplars to the administrative center of the arrondissement.

It was a superb horse, the last representative of a long-vanished species. It had a green belly, a curly tail like that of a billiard ball, and eyes shaped like little sausages. As soon as the majordomos besotted with the ideal had introduced it into the vast hall draped with funerary candles where the plenipotentiaries playing *bouchon*[59] were awaiting the opening of hostilities, there was nothing but a cry of admiration— admiration tempered, nevertheless, with a slight bitterness, at the heartbreaking observation that, if one needs eggs to make an omelet, to open a tin of sardines one must at least have, all other things being equal, a winding mechanism But the eyes of the young woman were of a beauty more than human. Her gaze evoked that of the frail heroines of Edgar Poe: Ligeia, Morella, Lady Rowena Trevanion of Tremaine, who died, jealously taking their secrets to the grave. And her flowery abdomen resembled, and might have been mistaken for, the hanging gardens of Babylon built by Semiramis.

As soon as the marine trumpets had announced the opening of the Olympic games, the gladiators, holding sticks of sealing-wax—the emblems of legislative power—in their hands, went into the arena two by two.

Nero, meanwhile, was getting impatient. The lampreys that he had eaten voraciously at midday lunch were beginning to stir in his stomach in a disquieting fashion. A little while ago, to appease them, he had thrown them a Thracian salve

---

[59] A French game played on a billiard table with three balls and three corks—the ancestor of the "bar billiards" played in English pubs.

and a Christian to eat, but in vain. With a feverish gesture, he made sure that his emerald left eye, the color of a *fleur de pêcher*,[60] the ancestor of future monocles, was in place, but in vain. Further away than the circus strewn with cadavers, where the Numidian lions were bounding, he perceived, in a fabulous and monotonous future, the ironic face of Renan, the simoniac exegete and prevaricator.[61]

Meanwhile, the crocodiles were advancing in silence, holding puce silk umbrellas over their heads with firm hands in order not to moisten their crushed velvet stocking-tops and Russian leather boots with their hypocritical tears.

It was at that precise moment that the publican's door suddenly opened. A man came out, his face illuminated by all the fumes of drunkenness. His glabrous rictus could not conceal the mark of infamy inflicted by a red-hot iron that he bore on his left shoulder and which, from time to time, wearied by the weight, he shifted to the other shoulder with a familiar movement. All the stigmata of debauchery were legible in his thin face. In one hand he was holding a woman's leg, admirably beautiful, severed at the knee with a razor; in the other, a deaf-mute lantern, whose light was hidden under a bushel of black wheat. He walked with the haste of a man hastening toward destiny—but when he arrived at the crossroads of the Thirteen Myopic Foxes he stopped and, placing the leg he had in his hand on a milestone, he rummaged in his fob-pocket, from which emerged, successively, a pitch-pine rope-ladder, a *bois de justice* pipe,[62] the complete works of Henri Ner[63] bound in calfskin, an admirably-sculpted Renaissance sideboard and a massive gold watch, which the man, in the midst

---

[60] i.e., pink.

[61] Ernest Renan (1823-1892)

[62] *Le bois de justice* [wood of justice] was the official name of the device that became popularly—and, indeed, universally—known as the guillotine.

[63] The author who eventually became better known as Han Ryner; a sampler of his work is available in translation in the Black Coat Press collection *The Superhumans*, ISBN 9781935558774.

of profound obscurity, sniffed interrogatively. "Quarter to midnight," he murmured. "I have time. The train doesn't leave for six months."

But he suddenly paused, immobilized by the frightful spectacle that unfolded before his eyes.

Cutting through the canvas background, even though it represented a delightful Watteau landscape, an obscene triangle appeared at the biconvex window of the giant anteater. The pilot of the fly-boat suddenly found himself transported into a landscape of that fabulous India where the camels, either by virtue of insouciance or calculation, have three green knees and a fourth in the form of a truncated cone. At sunset the Moon rose, bewildered and in despair at the death of Endymion. Old Theodosius got up. He was bereft of his illusions, since the day when, taking advantage of the Comte's absence, the perfidious steward had taken possession of the cardinal's papers. Theodosius, a stillborn child, had known all the bitterness that life reserves for those who live in the margins of laws. But that evening, to the perfume of Aristolochias, the weight of days gone by seemed heavier than usual on his shoulders. He remained pensive momentarily, listening to the hairs of his beard grow. Then, with the energy of despair, he headed for the beach where, every evening, for countless moons, he took his flock of jabirus[64] to graze the marine algae...

---

[64] Storks (although the term is sometimes applied to smaller wading birds).

SF & FANTASY

Guy d'Armen. *Doc Ardan: The City of Gold and Lepers*
G.-J. Arnaud. *The Ice Company*
Cyprien Bérard. *The Vampire Lord Ruthwen*
Aloysius Bertrand. *Gaspard de la Nuit*
Richard Bessière. *The Gardens of the Apocalypse*
Félix Bodin. *The Novel of the Future*
André Caroff. *The Terror of Madame Atomos*
Didier de Chousy. *Ignis*
Captain Danrit. *Undersea Odyssey*
C. I. Defontenay. *Star (Psi Cassiopeia)*
Charles Derennes. *The People of the Pole*
Georges Dodds (anthologist). *The Missing Link*
Harry Dickson. *The Heir of Dracula*
Jules Dornay. *Lord Ruthven Begins*
Sâr Dubnotal *vs. Jack the Ripper*
Alexandre Dumas. *The Return of Lord Ruthven*
J.-C. Dunyach. *The Night Orchid; The Thieves of Silence*
Henri Duvernois. *The Man Who Found Himself*
Achille Eyraud. *Voyage to Venus*
Henri Falk. *The Age of Lead*
Paul Féval. *Anne of the Isles; Knightshade; Revenants; Vampire City; The Vampire Countess; The Wandering Jew's Daughter*
Paul Féval, *fils. Felifax, the Tiger-Man*
Charles de Fieux. *Lamékis*
Arnould Galopin. *Doctor Omega*
G.L. Gick. *Harry Dickson and the Werewolf of Rutherford Grange*
Nathalie Henneberg. *The Green Gods*
V. Hugo, P. Foucher & P. Meurice. *The Hunchback of Notre-Dame*
Michel Jeury. *Chronolysis*
Octave Joncquel & Theo Varlet. *The Martian Epic*
Gérard Klein. *The Mote in Time's Eye*

Jean de La Hire. *Enter the Nyctalope; The Nyctalope on Mars; The Nyctalope vs. Lucifer*
André Laurie. *Spiridon*
Gabriel de Lautrec. *The Vengeance of the Oval Portrait*
Georges Le Faure & Henri de Graffigny. *The Extraordinary Adventures of a Russian Scientist Across the Solar System* (2 vols.)
Gustave Le Rouge. *The Vampires of Mars*
Jules Lermina. *Mysteryville; Panic in Paris; To-Ho and the Gold Destroyers; The Secret of Zippelius*
Jean-Marc & Randy Lofficier. *Edgar Allan Poe on Mars; The Katrina Protocol; Pacifica; Robonocchio; Tales of the Shadowmen 1-7*
Xavier Mauméjean. *The League of Heroes*
John-Antoine Nau. *Enemy Force*
Marie Nizet. *Captain Vampire*
C. Nodier, A. Beraud & Toussaint-Merle. *Frankenstein*
Henri de Parville. *An Inhabitant of the Planet Mars*
J. Polidori, C. Nodier, E. Scribe. *Lord Ruthven the Vampire*
P.-A. Ponson du Terrail. *The Vampire and the Devil's Son*
Maurice Renard. *The Blue Peril; Doctor Lerne; The Doctored Man; A Man Among the Microbes; The Master of Light*
Albert Robida. *The Adventures of Saturnin Farandoul; The Clock of the Centuries; Chalet in the Sky*
J.-H. Rosny Aîné. *Helgvor of the Blue River; The Givreuse Enigma; The Mysterious Force; The Navigators of Space; Vamireh; The World of the Variants; The Young Vampire*
Han Ryner. *The Superhumans*
Brian Stableford. *The New Faust at the Tragicomique; The Empire of the Necromancers (The Shadow of Frankenstein; Frankenstein and the Vampire Countess; Frankenstein in London); Sherlock Holmes & The Vampires of Eternity; The Stones of Camelot; The Wayward Muse.* (anthologist) *The Germans on Venus; News from the Moon; The Supreme Progress; The World Above the World*
Jacques Spitz. *The Eye of Purgatory*
Kurt Steiner. *Ortog*

Eugène Thébault. *Radio-Terror*
Villiers de l'Isle-Adam. *The Scaffold; The Vampire Soul*
Philippe Ward. *Artahe*
Philippe Ward & Sylvie Miller. *The Song of Montségur*

MYSTERIES & THRILLERS

M. Allain & P. Souvestre. *The Daughter of Fantômas*
A. Anicet-Bourgeois, Lucien Dabril. *Rocambole*
A. Bisson & G. Livet. *Nick Carter vs. Fantômas*
V. Darlay & H. de Gorsse. *Lupin vs. Holmes: The Stage Play*
Paul Féval. *Gentlemen of the Night; John Devil; The Black Coats ('Salem Street; The Invisible Weapon; The Parisian Jungle; The Companions of the Treasure; Heart of Steel; The Cadet Gang)*
Emile Gaboriau. *Monsieur Lecoq*
Steve Leadley. *Sherlock Holmes: The Circle of Blood*
Maurice Leblanc. *Arsène Lupin vs. Countess Cagliostro; Lupin vs. Holmes (The Blonde Phantom; The Hollow Needle)*
Gaston Leroux. *Chéri-Bibi; The Phantom of the Opera; Rouletabille & the Mystery of the Yellow Room*
William Patrick Maynard. *The Terror of Fu Manchu*
Frank J. Morlock. *Sherlock Holmes: The Grand Horizontals*
P. de Wattyne & Y. Walter. *Sherlock Holmes vs. Fantômas*
David White. *Fantômas in America*

SCREENPLAYS

Mike Baron. *The Iron Triangle*
Emma Bull & Will Shetterly. *Nightspeeder; War for the Oaks*
Gerry Conway & Roy Thomas. *Doc Dynamo*
Steve Englehart. *Majorca*
James Hudnall. *The Devastator*
Jean-Marc & Randy Lofficier. *Royal Flush*
J.-M. & R. Lofficier & Marc Agapit. *Despair*
Andrew Paquette. *Peripheral Vision*
R. Thomas, J. Hendler & L. Sprague de Camp. *Rivers of Time*

NON-FICTION

Stephen R. Bissette. *Blur 1-5; Green Mountain Cinema 1; Teen Angels & New Mutants*
Win Scott Eckert. *Crossovers* (2 vols.)
Jean-Marc & Randy Lofficier. *Shadowmen* (2 vols.)
Randy Lofficier. *Over Here*

ART BOOKS

Jean-Pierre Normand. *Science Fiction Illustrations*
Raven Okeefe. *Raven's L'il Critters*
Randy Lofficier & Raven OKeefe. *If Your Possum Go Daylight...*
Daniele Serra. *Illusions*

HEXAGON COMICS

Franco Frescura & Luciano Bernasconi. *Wampus*
Franco Frescura & Giorgio Trevisan. *CLASH*
L. Bernasconi, J.-M. Lofficier & Juan Roncagliolo Berger. *Phenix*
Claude Legrand, J.-M. Lofficier & L. Bernasconi. *Kabur*
Franco Oneta. *Zembla*
L. Buffolente, Lofficier & J.-J. Dzialowski. *Strangers: Homicron*
Danilo Grossi. *Strangers: Jaydee*
Claude Legrand & Luciano Bernasconi. *Strangers: Starlock*